DEATH SCENE

Also by Carol J. Perry

Haunted Haven Mysteries

Be My Ghost
High Spirits
Haunting License

Witch City Mysteries

Caught Dead Handed
Tails, You Lose
Look Both Ways
Murder Go Round
Grave Errors
It Takes a Coven
Bells, Spells, and Murders
Final Exam
Late Checkout
Murder, Take Two
See Something
'Til Death
Now You See It
Death Scene

Anthologies

Halloween Cupcake Murder

DEATH SCENE

CAROL J. PERRY

Kensington Publishing Corp.
www.kensingtonbooks.com

KENSINGTON BOOKS are published by

Kensington Publishing Corp.
900 Third Avenue
New York, NY 10022

All Kensington titles, imprints, and distributed lines are available at special quantity discounts for bulk purchases for sales promotion, premiums, fund-raising, educational, or institutional use.

Special book excerpts or customized printings can also be created to fit specific needs. For details, write or phone the office of the Kensington Sales Manager: Attn.: Sales Department. Kensington Publishing Corp., 900 Third Avenue, New York, NY 10022. Phone: 1-800-221-2647.

KENSINGTON and the KENSINGTON COZIES teapot logo Reg US Pat. & TM Off.

First Printing: September 2024
ISBN: 978-1-4967-4366-4

ISBN: 978-1-4967-4367-1 (ebook)

10 9 8 7 6 5 4 3 2 1

Printed in the United States of America

For Dan, my husband and best friend

All the world's a stage, and all the men and women merely players. They have their exits and entrances, and one man in his time plays many parts . . .

—William Shakespeare, *As You Like It*—
Act. 2; Scene 7

CHAPTER 1

I cranked up the radio in the Jeep, hummed along with a Taylor Swift tune, and glanced at the clock as I rounded the corner of Winter Street, pleased that I'd be checking in early for my job at WICH-TV. I'm Lee Barrett Mondello, née Maralee Kowalski. The Mondello part of my name is almost as new as my sweet, fully tricked-out Jeep Wrangler. My husband, Detective Sergeant Pete Mondello, and I were married less than a year ago. I'm red-haired, thirty-five, Salem born, and orphaned early. I was married once before to NASCAR driver Johnny Barrett—and, sadly, widowed much too young. Pete and I now live on Winter Street, just a couple of blocks away from the home where I was raised by my Aunt Isobel, "Ibby," Russell.

I'd almost reached the corner of Williams Street, just ahead of the looming towers of Salem's top tourist attraction—the Witch Museum—when the orange Toyota in front of me slammed on its brakes. I uttered an unladylike word, stopping the Jeep just in time to prevent damage to either vehicle. I stuck my head out the window, straining to see what was going on ahead. I recognized the Salem traffic cop who approached the Jeep, giving me a smile and a brief salute. Being married to a cop has its perks. I rolled down the window and turned Taylor Swift off mid-"Forever & Always."

"Hi, Mrs. Mondello," he said. "Looks like you might be delayed for a few minutes. The movie company is doing a shoot at the museum and they've got the whole darned street jammed up with a tractor full of equipment, a fancy trailer, and even a food truck. We're trying to get them into some parking spaces." He leaned closer to my window, putting his finger to his lips. "I just got word that they're going to be shooting later today down at the Witch House, so you might want to stay away from that end of Essex Street too."

Of course I knew that Paragon Productions was in town, putting the finishing touches on a film involving witches, called *Night Magic*. Everybody in Salem knew it, and most everybody was pretty excited about it. I thanked the officer for the tip. The Witch House is the only house still standing in Salem that has a direct connection to the witch trials, and according to the station's network film critic, getting shots of the stars in and around the old house was a big part of the reasoning for bringing the cast to Salem to finish the film. Paragon's publicist had sent me a media kit of photographs of the replica room where accused witches were tried, along with some general information about the trials. I'd visited the Witch House on school trips, and my librarian aunt, Ibby, had seen to it that our home library was well-stocked with books about the sad witchcraft delusion that had gripped my city in 1692. The photos looked interesting, though. I put the kit in my top desk drawer for a closer look later.

The movie studio couldn't have picked a worse time to film *Night Magic* in Salem. The entire month of October is one huge Halloween party, and people come from all over the country—maybe from all over the world—to take part in it. Pete had left for work almost an hour before I, so I was pretty sure he hadn't encountered the same delay. Even if he had, his unmarked cruiser was equipped with siren and flashing lights. The Jeep wasn't, so I put it in Park and settled down for a wait. I knew for sure that Bruce Doan, the station manager at WICH-TV, loved the idea of a film about the Salem witches being made—as he put it—*right in our own backyard*. Easy for him to say. It wasn't anywhere close to *his* backyard, but on this particular morning it was only two streets away from mine.

I tuned the radio to the local station, WESX, hoping for a traffic report and hoping too that this would be the only traffic screwup between the Witch Museum and the waterfront TV studio on Derby Street. I had a fairly full schedule laid out for myself for the day. I checked the clock again. If this took more than ten minutes, I'd start my day late.

Mr. Doan likes just about everybody on the WICH-TV staff to—as he quaintly puts it—*wear more than one hat*. I'd already worn several, although, fortunately, not all at once. At the moment my main job was program director, with an occasional stint as a field reporter. He'd recently hinted at awarding me with another title—one I'd held before—executive director of documentaries. It has a fancy sound to it, but it just means that he wants me to find the time to produce a program documenting the making of a movie about witches.

Information about the actual plot of the film had so far been pretty sparse, and I'd heard that the producers weren't granting interviews at all. I did, however, have one possible "foot in the door" of Paragon Productions. My best friend, River North, is the star of WICH-TV's late-night show *Tarot Time with River North*. She hosts the midnight scary movie show and, during breaks, reads the beautiful tarot cards for call-in viewers. For years people who know River have said that if her long, black hair was platinum blond, she'd look like a younger version of glamorous Darla Diamond, the female star of *Night Magic*. River is still in her twenties and Darla is closer to my age, or maybe more.

One of the advance scouts for Paragon had seen River's show, noted the resemblance, and offered her a temporary job as body double and possible stand-in for the star. It would look good on River's résumé for sure, so she accepted the offer. She hadn't done any work for them yet, and I sincerely doubted that they'd welcome a local reporter and camera crew under any circumstances, but hey, River might meet somebody who knew somebody who had access to the right people. Anyway, if the documentary hat fit, I was willing to give it a try.

I kept an eye on the orange Toyota in front of me, willing it to inch forward, giving me hope that this unwelcome parade might be about to break free. My ten-minute window had narrowed to five. Horns began to sound, from ahead of and behind the Jeep. The natives were getting restless. The Toyota began to move cautiously, avoiding jaywalking, costumed revelers. With a thumbs-up signal from the traffic cop, I pulled off onto Hawthorne Boulevard and headed for my Derby Street destination—maybe a couple of miles an hour faster than the posted speed limit.

I've been with WICH-TV long enough so that I have a designated parking space in the waterfront lot beside the station with my name on it. It still says *Lee Barrett*, and to the viewers of WICH-TV, that's still my name. One's own parking space is a handy thing to have, especially when there's a lot going on in Salem and drivers are apt to grab any empty space they can find.

Locking the Jeep and dashing across the lot, I tapped my code into the keypad beside the entrance, and stepped into the cool darkness of the studio. A burst of childish laughter issued from the distant soundstage where *Ranger Rob's Rodeo*, the WICH-TV morning kiddie show, was already in progress.

I headed up the metal staircase to the second floor and pushed open the glass door marked "WICH-TV Executive Offices." Rhonda, the station's receptionist, greeted me with a smile. "Doan wants to see you right away."

"Is that good?" I asked.

"Hard to tell." She spread out her hands in a helpless gesture. "He was on the phone with some old friend of his in Hollywood this morning, if that's any help."

"Hollywood." I nodded. "Okay, then it's got something to do with the movie."

"Yeah. Like everything else in Salem lately. You'd think nobody ever made a movie about Salem before."

"Besides *Hocus Pocus*?"

"Right, and there was that *Bewitched* TV show, where Sam and Darrin come to Salem for a witch's convention," she recalled.

"I loved that one," I said. "Well, I'd better go in and see what's on his mind," I headed for the door marked "Station Manager" and tapped on the partially open door. Mr. Doan prides himself on always having his door open to his employees.

"Come on in, Ms. Barrett. Have you begun work on our documentary yet?" He leaned across the desk, past an arrangement of artificial lilacs—clearly a bit of décor inspired by his wife, Buffy, who has a great fondness for the color purple. "Did you know that Lamont Faraday is a direct descendant of Nathaniel Hawthorne?"

"I don't think so," I said, seriously doubting that such a relationship existed between the male star of Salem's newest movie and the city's most famous author.

Bruce Doan frowned. "What makes you say that?"

"Because I've done a little predocumentary research lately. When Faraday was in the remake of John Wayne's *The Alamo*, his publicity people claimed that Davy Crockett was his great-great-great-grandfather. That wasn't true either."

"So you actually think the publicity department could be putting out false information?" His expression bordered on the incredulous. "How can that possibly be?"

I shrugged, trying to look noncommittal. Nobody wants to disagree with the boss. "From what little I've read about this production so far," I told him, "it's possible that it might be over budget already. They need all the positive pre-release publicity they can get. The TV network movie critics like that kind of *interesting tidbit* stuff. It'll get picked up by the cable networks too."

He frowned again; this time his whole forehead was furrowed. "Like how *much* over budget?"

"I have no personal knowledge of it, of course," I hedged, "but TMZ says several million—so far."

Bruce Doan did not look pleased. I had a horrible thought.

What if he's invested money in this thing? I'd heard some whisperings around the station that maybe he had. It made sense to me. The making of a movie— especially one with well-known stars—could be a huge financial blessing to the city or town involved in the filming. It meant increased business for just about every merchant or service provider in the locale. That, to Bruce Doan, would mean more advertising revenue for sure.

The success or failure of *Night Magic* was going to be a very big deal—for Salem and for WICH-TV.

CHAPTER 2

I left the manager's office with a promise that I'd get going right away on the documentary, with a caveat to *make Salem look good*. Sure I could keep that promise, with the knowledge that everyone I'd talked to—everyone I knew in Salem—was all in for the success of the movie. From the mayor's office to the visitors' bureau to the Chamber of Commerce, along with most of the industries, retailers, and private groups—and except for some good-natured crabbiness about the traffic tie-ups—there was a spirit of cooperation throughout the city.

"How'd it go?" Rhonda wanted to know.

"Not bad," I told her. "He wants me to hurry up with the Salem witches documentary."

"Do you think you can squeeze one more thing in today? It shouldn't take too long." She pointed to the whiteboard where she notes everybody's assignments. I was already scheduled for a meeting with the host of *Shopping Salem* to firm up plans for an antiques show special featuring vintage Salem souvenirs, then a meeting with the billing department about some past-due accounts a couple of my advertisers had run up, along with the usual programming duties for *The Saturday Business Hour,* finding some cute new outfits for Paco the Wonder Dog on *Ranger Rob's Rodeo,* and scheduling an in-person appearance with psychic medium Loralei, who was booked to demonstrate a love spell on *Tarot Time with River North* .

"I'll try," I promised, somewhat reluctantly. "What is it?"

"Scott Palmer phoned in that he's tied up in traffic in North Salem, and he's supposed to do a stand-up at noon over at the intersection of Proctor and Boston Streets. That's where the Great Salem Fire started. The mayor is dedicating a plaque or laying a wreath or something. Not a real big deal. Howie Templeton is out of town for a college reunion. Can you do it?"

"Big deal or not, I can't go on camera looking like this!" I ran my hand through humidity-tangled, needed-washing, curly red hair, then looked down at my faded jeans and short-sleeved gray sweatshirt. My present job doesn't require much of a wardrobe. Rhonda gave me an up-and-down look and didn't disagree with my assessment. Some rapid calculations told me I could keep the appointment with the *Salem Shopping* host, postpone the meeting with the business office, phone Loralei about the love spell, and shop online at home later for doggie costumes. "I can probably rearrange the whiteboard list by eleven," I said.

"I might be able to get you an appointment for a quick blowout with my hairdresser, Jenna," Rhonda offered, "She's very good. She does River's hair, you know. Then you'll need to go home and grab something decent to wear. You could make it in time. Anyway, there's no one else around to do it. Here. I've printed out a few facts about the Great Salem Fire for you."

"Thanks. This will be a big help," I said, accepting the pages. "Who's my ride?" A field report requires a mobile unit with a cameraperson as well as a reporter. WICH-TV has only one fairly new rig and I assumed Scott had that one, along with our top videographer, Francine. "Is Old Jim here today?" Old Jim and I have worked together a number of times and he's truly good at his job. Jim can focus on the small details that the younger photographers often miss. He drives the old VW bus that's been converted into a fair approximation of a minimobile studio. Working with Old Jim was fine with me. Rhonda assured me that Jim was on the premises, working on some editing for a *Wanda the Weather Girl* promo piece.

Scott Palmer is not my favorite person at WICH-TV. He's a pretty good reporter, though, and he'd covered for me once in a while back when I used to be a full-time field reporter. Howie Templeton is Scott's backup. He's also Mrs. Doan's nephew who got handed *my* old job the minute he graduated from broadcasting school and got me *promoted* to program director. I'm not complaining about it. The hours are much better for married me, and it came with a little pay raise.

"It's worth a shot, I guess," I told her. "Want to see if Jenna can take me this morning?" She was already on her phone before I'd finished the sentence.

"Good news." She gave me a thumbs-up. "She has a ten-thirty cancellation. Okay?"

"Okay," I agreed, with no idea how I was going to run through that whiteboard list in half an hour. "I'll be there at ten thirty."

Somehow, with some fancy juggling and a very co-operative Loralei, who knows that River North, the host of *Tarot Time,* is my very best friend, and an always understanding *Shopping Salem* host, along with an annoyed—but accommodating—business office, I was on my way to Chez Jenna by ten twenty.

One of the best things about beauty parlors is the wide-ranging conversation that so often happens when your head is being shampooed, dried, and styled. Okay. Call it what it is. Gossip! (Pete says it doesn't work the same way at barbershops. There it's mostly sports or politics.) A good hairstylist, though, can be a better—and even more reliable—source of what's going on in any given place, at any given time, than any form of news media could possibly hope to be. In fact, River had told me more than once that Jenna was such a source.

It turned out that on that particular day, at that particular time, the woman who'd so conveniently canceled her appointment so Jenna could fit me in, was an assistant to an associate director of costuming on the very movie I'd been tasked with documenting. According to Jenna, she'd had to cancel her hair appointment because leading lady Darla Diamond, in an outburst of rage, had used a pair of scissors to rip open the seams of a custom-made evening dress because it no longer fit her properly, and she'd done what Jenna deemed *a real hatchet job* of it. She'd already appeared wearing the dress in critical scenes that were filmed earlier in Hollywood, so the costume department had to figure out how to somehow repair the costly designer original before they could continue filming.

"You'd think that a woman with such a beautiful face would have a beautiful soul too," Jenna said, "but she doesn't. It's no wonder she doesn't get along with anybody. I've heard that she and Lamont Faraday absolutely hate each other."

"I've heard that too," I said. "I think I read it in a magazine somewhere. It's hard to believe, though, when you see the love scenes they do together in their movies."

"Yeah. There's that. They look so perfect together. Two beautiful people in love." She sighed. "You know how River looks like a much younger version of Darla, but River has a sweet disposition to go with the good looks? The thing is," Jenna went on to explain about the dress, "Darla simply gained a few pounds and the dress doesn't fit anymore. So Darla's tantrum can cost a lot of time. They've built a big temporary studio set up over in Gallows Hill Park—they even built a whole room that looks exactly like the room in the Witch House where they tried the witches in 1692. Most of the story happens in the present, and they shot almost all of that part in California. The part that happens in 1692 is much shorter—just a few flashbacks that sort of parallel the things that are going on in the present. They'll be mostly shooting outdoor locations in Salem, along with a few publicity still photos of the stars in the historic houses around town. They've built a temporary wardrobe department in the park too, and a kitchen and dining room where everybody eats. Most of the working crew have rooms in town, and they use local folks as much as they can, like the hair dressers and the caterers and the florists. There are a couple of fancy dressing room trailers for the stars on-site, and they've even stocked up a supply of the expensive, imported European chocolates Darla insists be on-site everywhere she goes."

"No kidding? Imported chocolates? I've heard of stars that require bowls of green M&Ms or red licorice Twizzlers," I recalled.

"Nothing but the best for Miss Darla," Jenna said. "Maybe the chocolates account for the weight gain. Anyway, Darla has a hissy fit and the whole production gets shut down because the star is bursting the seams of a one-of-a-kind original. What a witch!"

The information about the current slowdown of production that had just been fed into my freshly shampooed and styled head didn't exactly fit in with what I had in mind for the documentary—but hey, a documentary is supposed to tell the truth, isn't it?

I was on my way home to Winter Street by five minutes after eleven. I pulled into the parking space behind our half of the duplex house on the same side of the street as the house where I was raised. Our big, yellow-striped gentleman cat looked up from the spot of sunshine on our back steps where he'd been sleeping. Aunt Ibby and I have a shared custody agreement about O'Ryan. He moves, as he chooses, between the two homes. I was, as always, happy to see him, and as soon as I stepped out of the car, I picked him up and told him so. He favored me with a pink-tongued lick on my nose. I unlocked the back door, and together we entered the cheerful sunporch.

Depositing the cat on his favorite zebra-striped wing chair, I hurried through the kitchen and living room and climbed the stairs to the second-floor bedroom, where I phoned Pete about what was going on. "I'll be doing a stand-up over on Proctor Street," I told him. "The mayor is commemorating the Great Salem Fire."

"Nineteen fourteen," he said. "Burned down most of the town."

"How do you know things like that?" Pete is great at trivia games.

"I had to do a paper on it in my sophomore year at Salem High School," he said.

"I wish you'd saved it," I said. "I'll be totally winging it on this one."

"My mom probably *did* save it." He laughed. "You'll be great. You always are. See you after work."

I pulled together a good enough outfit for a daytime stand-up—tan slacks, white shirt, brown heels, and my WICH-TV green jacket. I checked myself in the oval-framed, full-length mirror. I felt good, wearing grown-up clothes and high heels, and looked pretty good too.

CHAPTER 3

I made it back to Derby Street with minimum traffic foul-ups, pulling into my parking space at eleven forty. Old Jim, bless him, was already in the VW, engine running at the head of the driveway, ready to roll. He waved from the window. "Come on, Lee. Hop in. Let's get this show on the road!"

I did as he said. Sometimes I use a clip mic—one of those little gadgets that most news anchors wear attached to a blouse or jacket—but Jim knows I like the old-fashioned hand mic with the station's call letters on it better for outdoor stand-ups, and he had one ready for me. I fastened my seat belt, began reading the notes about the Salem fire Rhonda had prepared, and we were on our way. Jim knows almost as many shortcuts around Salem as Pete does, so we avoided a lot of the worst traffic messes.

We passed the simple memorial at Proctor's Ledge, the site where engraved stones commemorate several of the accused witches, and approached the Boston

Street intersection. Some people I recognized from other local media had already arrived—the *Salem News* and the *Beverly Citizen* reporters were there, and a guy wearing a WBZ Boston vest with a nice Sony shoulder-mounted camcorder waved hello.

The historical marker, affixed to a large boulder, shows the fire alarm box used to report the start of the fire at the Korn Leather Company. The mayor was already in position to lay the wreath. It wasn't quite noon yet. We'd made it with minutes to spare. I took my position facing Old Jim's camera and waited for his signal. He counted down, "Three, two, one," and pointed to me.

"I'm Lee Barrett, reporting to you from the intersection of Prospect and Boston Streets in Salem. This is the site where the first fire alarm was pulled reporting a fire at the Korn Leather Company back in 1914." Old Jim moved in for a close-up of the plaque on the boulder. "Fast-moving flames, jumping from building to building, soon consumed several more leather factories on Boston Street. The fire continued to spread, burning homes, schools, churches, businesses," I said, depending on Rhonda's notes.

The mayor stepped forward to speak. "Here's Salem's mayor," I said, glad that the city's top official would take over the narrative, because I didn't have much more information to offer. I learned, along with WICH-TV's viewers, that 18,000 people were left homeless when 253 acres and more than 1,000 buildings were destroyed by nightfall. The wreath was laid, the sad story told, and Jim and I were on our way back to the station by twelve fifteen.

We passed the entrance to Gallows Hill Park. I recognized the movie studio's logo on several trucks gathered around some new-looking buildings. "Look, Jim, that's where the movie people have built their own little Hollywood. My hairdresser told me about it. Want to stop and take a look?"

"I think the new chain-link fence and the 'No Trespassing' sign means they aren't welcoming visitors," he said. "They've leased the park from the city for the whole month."

"We can stand across the street and use the zoom lens, can't we?" I pointed to a small crowd of people on somebody's Halloween-decorated Boston Street front lawn, standing between jack-o'-lanterns and make-believe tombstones, most with their phones focused on the posted property. "Don't think we'll get anything from this distance that rates a spot on the nightly news, but it might fit in with my documentary."

"Sure, why not?" Jim often humors me. "But now they've seen the WICH-TV logo on the VW, so those folks will crowd around you, thinking they'll be on TV."

He was right, of course, but I did it anyway—facing the camera with my back to the chain-link-protected assembly of buildings, trucks, cars, limos, and several of those fabulous big trailers you sometimes see on the HGTV Channel.

"Hello. Lee Barrett here, taking a look at the area Paragon Productions has created in Salem's Gallows Hill Park while they're in Salem filming local sites for the nearly completed motion picture *Night Magic*, starring Lamont Faraday and Darla Diamond. It looks as though they've built a bit of Hollywood in this hilly part of the city, where some mistakenly say witches died by hanging back in 1692. Some buildings within this fenced compound are marked with signs telling us what's going on inside. The biggest one says, 'Soundstage.' I've heard that there's a reproduction of the room in the Witch House where the witches were tried inside that one. Another big one says 'Galley,' where actors and workers have their meals. There's one that says 'Costumes.'" I pointed to it. "As most moviegoers know, Paragon is famous for their costumes—often winning both Oscars and Emmys for their designs. Many of our WICH-TV viewers have reported spotting several of the actors visiting some of Salem's many attractions, restaurants, and shops. If you see one of the actors or crew, please remember that they are our guests here and always be courteous and respectful of their private space."

Jim drew a finger across his throat, giving me the familiar cut sign. A large man in uniform was fast approaching us from the park entrance. "Lee Barrett, signing off," I said, realizing that it was time for Jim and me to be courteous and respectful of the production company's private space, even if it was only on a short-term lease from the citizens of Salem. We packed up and beat it out of there, leaving the phone camera folks to deal with movie security.

Back at the station, I checked in with Rhonda. "You looked good on the noon news," she said. "The hair is perfect. Scott called. He said to thank you for doing the gig with the mayor, and that maybe someday he'll be able to return the favor."

I had to smile at the *maybe someday*. My field reports these days are so few and far between that he's quite safe from having to return the favor anytime soon. "Gee, maybe someday he'd like to substitute for me doing clean-up on the days when Ranger Rob brings Prince Valiant, the wonder horse, into the studio." I laughed at the mental picture that idea produced. I told Rhonda about our quick trip past the minimovie studio on Gallows Hill. "They've got quite a fancy setup going over there," I said. "They've only rented the park until the end of the month. I hope they'll get the movie finished by then. I've heard it's already over budget and they've had a costume screw-up that's going to lose time."

"What's wrong with the costumes? They get awards for them all the time," she wanted to know.

"Well, actually . . ." I hesitated. "It's really just kind of gossip. Maybe I shouldn't repeat it."

"Come on, give. Gossip? Let me guess. You heard it from Jenna, right?"

"Right."

"Give."

I told her about the burst seams and the scissors-renting of the designer original. She wasn't surprised by the report of the leading lady's behavior. Her comment was similar to Jenna's *What a witch!* It rhymed anyway.

"Speaking of designer originals, I guess I'll use my lunch break to run home and change back into my program director clothes," I said. "See you in an hour."

"Okay, Cinderella," she said. "Don't lose your glass slippers."

I'd just passed the statue of Nathaniel Hawthorne on

my way home when Rhonda called me back. "Something's going on at Gallows Hill Park," she said. "Cops are surrounding the soundstage area. Can you get back over there and see what's going on? The police scanner says they've called for the medical examiner. Jim has already left. Hitch up with him when you get there."

"On my way," I told her, hitting Pete's number on the display screen on my dash. "What's going on at Gallows Hill?" I asked as soon as he picked up. "I'm heading back over there."

"I'm on the scene right now," he said.

"You've called for the ME," I pointed out. "Is somebody dead?"

"I don't have confirmation from the medical examiner yet," my by-the-book cop husband hedged.

"Is somebody there who doesn't appear to be breathing?" I rephrased my question. "Off the record, of course."

He sighed. "Off the record? Darla Diamond. Gotta go." And he was gone.

CHAPTER 4

I spotted the VW next to the curb about two blocks away from the corner of Boston Street. Old Jim stood in front of the vehicle and waved me down, camcorder on his shoulder and my stick mic under one arm. "If you can park someplace, we'll do better if we go on foot—like running."

I grabbed a laminated press pass from the glove box and hung it from the Jeep's mirror, then took a chance on parking in a customer pickup space in a nearby dollar store lot. With another press card on a lanyard around my neck, and wishing with all my heart for my program director's sneakers instead of my field reporter's high heels, I caught up with Jim and together we ran—he ran, I hobbled—uphill on the uneven sidewalk.

I didn't harbor much hope that we'd be allowed anywhere near the chain-link fence. It had been unapproachable when we were there earlier. We could already see the red-and-blue-flashing lights from police vehicles and more than one ambulance. I recognized the medical examiner's long black van—always an ominous sign. Jim handed me my mic. "You might as well start talking," he said. "We can use some of the intro you did earlier. We'll edit later." Jim, walking backward, aimed the camcorder toward me and, with his free hand, gave the usual countdown hand signal. "Three, two, one." He pointed and I began.

"Lee Barrett here," I said, "I'm approaching the entrance to Gallows Hill Park, where Paragon Studios has leased much of the area while they are filming final scenes for *Night Magic*, a motion picture based on witchcraft in Salem. Early publicity releases tell us that the plot involves time travel, as the characters move back and forth between the 1692 witchcraft days in Salem to Salem today. As we get closer to the fenced area, we can see indications of police activity. Several Salem Police Department vehicles are here, and there's an ambulance parked close to the front of a building marked 'Soundstage,' where a replica of an actual room in the Witch House has been built. The Witch House, also known as the Jonathan Corwin house, was the scene of actual trials of accused witches back in 1692. The medical examiner's van has just moved in through the gate in the fence."

I moved aside, so that Jim could focus on the assorted vehicles. I wondered which of the vehicles Pete had arrived it. His personal car wasn't among them. I was sure that he must be inside one of the buildings.

How much could I say? I knew for sure I wasn't going to be the one to announce Darla Diamond's apparent current nonbreathing condition. That would be up to somebody with real official status—not somebody in charge of dog costumes and souvenir teaspoons. It would probably fall to Police Chief Whaley to make the sad announcement from the podium in front of the police station. Hopefully, Scott Palmer would be back from North Salem in time to cover it.

I turned off my mic for a moment. "Jim, if the medical examiner is there because of a death," I whispered, "they wouldn't bring the—uh—the body out with all of us watching, would they?"

"They'll just back the ME's van right up to the soundstage door," he said. "I've seen this kind of thing before." He continued filming.

"That's good," I said, not wanting to see what I'd already been imagining. Sure enough, the ambulance pulled away from the soundstage and the black van backed up to the doorway, its back double doors opened wide, completely shielding whatever might be removed from the building from curious eyes. The other vehicles began to leave the premises, one at a time, leaving behind a uniformed officer at the gate of the chain-link fence. A priest holding a Bible, his head bowed, remained close to the van. Onlookers and media types, including Jim and me, figuring that nothing further was about to happen, prepared to leave. Turning the mic back on, with my back to the site, I signed off. "The medical examiner's van has left the area," I told my audience. "Stay tuned to WICH-TV for further updates on this continuing story."

Jim and I walked back to the VW. If there hadn't been people watching us because of the station's logo on the VW, my jacket, and the mic, I'd have gladly made the trip barefoot. As soon as we were inside, I kicked off the cruel shoes and pulled down the sun visor so that I could check my hair and makeup in the vanity mirror.

Big mistake. Very few people know a secret about me. Pete, Aunt Ibby, and my friend River North know that I'm what's known as a scryer. That means I'm a person who can *see* things in shiny, reflective surfaces—see things that others cannot. River calls me a gazer, and says it's a gift. I don't think it's a gift. Everything it's ever shown me has been something to do with death. As I looked into that mirror, the familiar flashing lights and swirling colors appeared—as they always do before a vision. The still picture came into focus. I leaned closer to the visor. Was I watching the scene Jim and I had filmed earlier in the day at Gallows Hill Park inside the chain-link fence? I recognized the soundstage, the galley, and the costume department, the cars and limos and fancy trailers, before the vision blinked away. What could it mean? River told me a long time ago that the visions could show the past, the present, or the future. This could be any one of the three. I returned the visor to the up position and hoped that Jim hadn't noticed my momentary distraction. If he had, he didn't say so.

"Can you drop me off at the dollar store where I left my car, Jim?" I asked. "I need to go home and change clothes; then I can easily cut across the common and walk back to the station. It's really quicker than driving these days."

"No problem," he said, and with a minimum of stops and starts, he let me out beside the Jeep, where I was happy—and lucky—to find no parking ticket or warning note on the windshield. I proceeded to drive, unashamedly barefoot and with only a few minor detours, to my house on Winter Street. O'Ryan didn't greet me at the door, so I assumed that he'd left for greener pastures—and a better brand of cat food—down the street at Aunt Ibby's. I changed quickly, and wearing my most comfortable old sneakers, elastic waist jeans, and one of Pete's big T-shirts, I actually enjoyed my unencumbered walk across our lovely common, with seasonal flowers in bloom and not a Paragon Productions truck or camera in sight.

I entered the station through the front door, walked across the black-and-white-tiled floor and rode up to the offices on the vintage, brass-doored elevator, known fondly, and deservedly, as Old Clunky, and checked in with Rhonda. She took in my casual appearance with a long, up-and-down, appraising look. "Well, at least your hair still looks good," she said. "Scott got back, but now he's on his way to the police station. Chief Whaley called a presser. Scott wants to know if he can use your Gallows Hill footage for the late news tonight."

"I guess it'll be okay," I said. Ordinarily, I'd hold out for a late-night news spot myself, because it was my stand-up, but I was darned if I was going to get dressed up in on-camera clothes again today. "Is the presser on yet? I'm dying to see exactly what was going on at Gallows Hill myself."

She turned on the monitor over her desk. "He should be on in a couple of minutes. Doesn't Pete know all about it?" The screen showed a close-up of the podium in front of the police station. The chief hadn't yet appeared.

I dodged the question. "I'll watch it in my office. If anybody needs me, that's where I'll be." I hurried for the metal door and raced past the newsroom to my own glass-walled cubicle and clicked on my monitor.

Scott appeared on camera, looking very serious. He gave his trademark long stare, then used what I call his golf tournament voice—kind of hushed but excited at the same time. "We're expecting Chief Tom Whaley to appear momentarily to relate the details of a presumed death today on the set being used for the filming of an upcoming Paragon Productions motion picture about witchcraft in Salem starring Lamont Faraday and Darla Diamond. We have contacted the studio for comment, but they have not returned our calls. Here comes the chief." He stepped aside.

Everyone knows that Chief Whaley hates doing these things, and he gets them over with as fast as he can. He wore full dress uniform, complete with ribbons and medals. He placed one sheet of paper on the lectern and proceeded to read from it.

"'Salem Police received a 911 call at approximately twelve forty-five this afternoon. A person from Paragon Productions, a motion picture company that is making a movie in Salem, called and reported the dis-

covery of an unresponsive woman on a stage set built
to duplicate a room in the Witch House. The woman
was transported to the medical examiner's office, where
she was pronounced dead. The dead woman has been
identified as actress Darla Diamond.'"

There was an audible gasp from the reporters present at the briefing—including Scott.

CHAPTER 5

As usual after an announcement like that one, the chief was anxious to leave—dodging as many questions as possible. The assembled reporters would have to be quick on the draw, as Ranger Rob was fond of saying. Scott was fast—and first—with the obvious question.

"What was the cause of death?"

"The exact cause of death has not yet been determined." The chief picked up his sheet of paper, as though he was getting ready to dash inside.

"Has the movie studio been contacted?" The question came from one of the Boston radio stations.

"Yes. Of course. Someone from Paragon will make a statement soon."

"Have you talked to her costar? Faraday?" The film critic from the *Boston Globe* wanted to know.

"We're attempting to get in touch with Mr. Faraday. We'll update you here at five o'clock this afternoon. That's all for now. Thank you."

Shouted questions followed him as he ducked indoors.

Scott couldn't hide his disappointment when he faced Francine's camera. I felt sorry for him. I would have been disappointed too. Such a major story and so little information. Scott had the actress's bio, naturally—everybody on the staff had the studio-issued cast notes. I even had the bios in case I needed them for show prep for one of my programs. Scott did the best he could with what he had. He paraphrased what the chief had said, added information about where and when she'd been born. He mentioned a couple of her most famous movies and advised viewers of WICH-TV to stay tuned for more information as it became available.

I knew that the first thing *I'd* do in that situation would be try to track down and interview the costar, handsome Lamont Faraday, who'd made so many successful movies with his famously beautiful costar, who he may have loved, or—if one were a reader of grocery store tabloids—possibly hated.

The studio-issued cast list was in my top desk drawer. I pulled it out for a closer look.

"Hello. This is Lee Barrett." I was startled to hear my own voice coming from the monitor. Looking up, I recognized the chain-link-fenced area temporarily housing Paragon's mini-Hollywood setup at Gallows Hill Park. The station had chosen to use Jim's too-far-away-for-the-nightly-news-but-might-be-okay-for-the-documentary footage as a follow-up to Scott's too-brief coverage of the news of Darla's death. It was also the same scene I'd recognized in my recent vision in the vanity mirror.

I watched the now familiar video, peering closely at the background, thinking maybe I'd see something—anything—that would tell me why this particular footage had become a vision—something I needed to pay attention to.

I squinted at the screen, focusing on the big, beautiful house trailers. There were two that were bigger and more beautiful than any of the others. *One is his. One is hers*, I told myself, knowing instinctively that I was right. *Scott needs to get inside that fence.*

I forced myself to concentrate on the cast list. While I was sure the medical examiner's report would not say that Darla had died from natural causes, I wasn't sure exactly what I was looking for. Maybe those tabloid stories mentioned the name of someone linked with her in an unpleasant way. Not at all unlikely, considering her reputation.

My somewhat divided concentration was interrupted by a tap-tap-tap on the glass wall that separated my office from the busy newsroom. Scott was back and wanted my attention. With his thumb and little finger in the *phone-me* position, he gave me the long stare. I nodded *okay* and picked up my phone. "What's up?" I asked him.

"Hi, Moon," he said. "Did you watch the chief's presser?"

When I first came to WICH-TV I did a brief stint as a call-in psychic, using the name Crystal Moon. Scott still sometimes calls me that.

"Of course I did," I told him. "What are you going to do now? Try to grab an interview with Faraday?"

"I've made a couple of calls in that direction," he said. "Doan wants me to stay on the Darla Diamond story. But right now, I'm about to go across the street and grab some lunch. Want to come with me?"

"Are you buying?"

Short pause. "Okay. Yes. I'll meet you in the front lobby."

The Friendly Tavern is across the street from the station. It's superconvenient and the food and drinks are all good. Wishing then that I'd dressed differently, I pulled the bottom of the T-shirt into a knot on one side, making it fit a little better. Anyway, my hair still looked good. I picked up my handbag, walked down the short ramp back to the reception area, and told Rhonda where I'd be.

"If Scottie is buying, see if he'll go for a vegan wrap for me," she suggested. With that unlikely possibility in mind, I took the stairs down to the lobby, bypassing the shiny, reflective brass doors of Old Clunky, where visions sometimes lurked. Scott was there, as promised, and we crossed Derby Street together, dodging traffic both ways.

"Do you want to sit at a table or the bar?" he asked.

"The bar is fine," I said, and it was. The bartenders at the Friendly are almost as informative as some hairstylists. I was interested to learn if Leo or Pascal had had any of the movie people as customers yet.

Scott asked the question before I had a chance to.

Leo was quick to respond. "We've had a few of the

actors stop in—at least they said they were actors—along with quite a few carpenters and painters. One time we both thought Darla Diamond herself was here—but it turned out to be her body double. The girl looked almost exactly like her."

"You mean River North?" I was surprised at his description. Leo knows River as well as he knows me.

"No. Not River," he said. "River has black hair. The other one. The bleached blonde. The double Darla brought along with her from California. That one even has her hairstyle exactly like Darla's. Her name is Paulina something. River is prettier. But yesterday we got the big enchilada!"

Pascal chimed in. "Lamont Faraday. Big as life. He said he'd made a thousand-dollar bet with somebody that he could have a drink in every bar on Derby Street during the time he was here. Yesterday was our turn."

"What was he like?" I asked.

"Nice guy," Leo said. "He stayed for about half an hour. He signed autographs on cocktail napkins for everybody who was here at the time."

"Yep. He had a pen in one hand and a beer in the other," Pascal offered, "even though he said he wasn't usually much of a drinker."

"It was because of the thousand-dollar bet," Leo said. "The man loves to gamble. I'll bet he blew fifty bucks on lottery pull tabs while he was in here."

"Did he win anything?" Scott wanted to know.

"Nowhere near the fifty he spent." Pascal laughed.

"He was a good tipper anyway," Leo added.

"Did he have anything to say about Darla Diamond?" Scott asked the question I was thinking about.

"Not much," Leo said. "Of course, she wasn't dead, then."

"Right," Pascal said. "Somebody asked if it was true that they didn't like each other much. He just smiled and said, *We need each other.*"

I could see what Faraday meant. Movie audiences expected to see the two together—always in a happily-ever-after love story—and as long as the formula worked, Paragon would continue to make those movies, no matter what the real relationship was between the actors.

Scott ordered our burgers, and gave me a raised eyebrow when I suggested a veggie wrap for Rhonda. I thought about what Pascal had said about Faraday drinking in as many bars as he could find on Derby Street during the week or so he planned to be here. Scott was going to be busy. Just offhand, I could think of at least a dozen bars—probably more.

"It looks like you'll be doing some pub-crawling," I said, halfway wishing the Darla Diamond assignment was mine. If the star's death meant the end of the filming of *Night Magic*, it meant the end of my documentary too.

CHAPTER 6

As soon as we'd finished our burgers, Scott walked back across the street with me and dropped me at the front door. "See you later, Moon," he said. "I'm about to become an expert on Derby Street's saloons."

"Tough job," I said, "but somebody's got to do it." I knew Scott's totally smart iPhone would produce TV-worthy videos, and that even if he didn't find Lamont Faraday on his first try, he'd wind up with a nice little feature about Derby Street. I'd bought the veggie wrap for Rhonda because she deserved it. Wishing Scott a nice day, I stepped inside the lobby. Eyes downcast while the brass door slid open, I rode Old Clunky uneventfully up to the second floor.

A glance at Rhonda's whiteboard revealed nothing out of the ordinary for me, so I'd have plenty of time to work on some of the quite ordinary program director duties I'd felt guilty about neglecting lately. I handed over the wrap and told her I'd be working in my office.

It felt good to be in my little glass cube with no serious pressure. I emailed some of Salem's many antiques dealers asking about the availability of old-time Salem souvenirs for the *Shopping Salem* segment and very quickly found dozens of Daniel Low silver teaspoons and scissors bearing the traditional witch-on-a-broom-themed design. Ditto a Hull Pottery vase and assorted pin trays and decorative plates.

I called Pete to let him know that I'd already had lunch. Sometimes, if we're both free at lunchtime, we grab a bite together. "I had lunch at the Friendly with Scott. He wants to use my footage of Gallows Hill on the news tonight. I said okay. Now he's gone on a tour of all the barrooms on Derby Street searching for Lamont Faraday."

"I could save him the trouble," Pete said. "Faraday turned up sound asleep on Darla Diamond's bed in her personal trailer—all dressed up in character. Seems she'd sent him a note to meet her there."

"He didn't even know she was dead?"

"So it seems. He's pretty broken up about it."

"Did he have the note?" I asked.

"Yep. It's in her handwriting on her personal stationery," he said. "She said she'd left the door unlocked and for him to come inside and wait for her."

"Maybe he did love her," I said. "You say he was really upset when you told him she was dead?"

"He seemed to be. Of course, he's an actor. Maybe he was faking it, or maybe he's upset because without her and this movie, he's out of work, along with everybody else."

"That's right. I guess that means River won't have a movie credit on her résumé after all." I realized that my friend's opportunity as stand-in and body double for the star was over before it began. Anyway, if Leo was right about Darla having her original body double here in Salem, maybe they wouldn't have used her anyway. I glanced at my watch. River wouldn't be awake yet. Back when I was Crystal Moon I'd worked those midnight late-show hours myself. She wouldn't be up until after two o'clock sometimes. I'd call her later.

"Did the ME come up with a cause of Darla's death yet?" I asked.

"Poison," was the one-word answer.

"Can you tell me what kind of poison?" I wanted to know.

"Nicotine—and no, she wasn't a smoker," he said. "It was mixed with chocolate somehow."

"Straight out of an Agatha Christie novel," I said. "*Three Act Tragedy.* Aunt Ibby read it to me when I was about ten."

"Chief's wife spotted that too," he said. "Darla ate some special brand of liquid-center chocolates. Doc Egan says the poison must have been injected into the center of the candy."

"It must have tasted terrible," I said, "unless she swallowed it whole."

"That's possible. Apparently she was addicted to the things. There were bowls of them on every set, in every dressing room she used—even where they were only taking still shots."

"Suspects?" I wondered aloud.

"Just about everybody who worked on *Night Magic* knew where the candies were, but nobody dared to touch them and touch off a Darla temper tantrum. With her gone now, they're all out of work, so it wouldn't have made much sense for any of them to kill her."

"Did she have any enemies?"

A short, grim laugh. "Got a Los Angeles County phone book? I have to go, babe. See you at home tonight."

It was for sure a real life Agatha Christie mystery—one it wasn't up to me to solve. With my imaginary program director hat firmly in place, I returned my attention to the various productions under my care. I'd put Paco the Wonder Dog's needs aside long enough. Within a short time I'd found a sweet doggy pirate costume that would be perfect for one of the days when Captain Billy Barker, owner of the Toy Trawler and frequent advertiser, made one of his sea-themed appearances on *Ranger Rob's Rodeo* show. Because it was Halloween month, Paco's fans would expect some new duds. I was thinking that a pair of cat ears and a tail would be cute when caller ID showed River North's name.

"Hello, River. I was planning to call you."

"About Darla? I just heard about it from Doug Sawyer." Emotion showed in her voice. "Such terrible news."

Doug Sawyer. The name was familiar, but I couldn't quite place it. "Doug Sawyer?" I asked.

"Yes. I guess I forgot to tell you I'd met him when I was interviewed for—you know—for stand-in for poor Darla."

Who is Doug Sawyer? Memory suddenly clicked in. "The child star?" I asked. "The cute guy in the shows about the tame bear?"

"That's him," she said. "I recognized him right away. He's grown-up now, of course, but still cute. He's still under contract to Paragon too, but he hasn't had a major role for a long time. Anyway, he's been really nice to me, and he feels so bad about Darla dying. He had tears in his eyes when he talked about her." River sounded sad. "He's even taking care of her dog now. A sweet black lab. Doug and Darla have been friends since he was a kid. She'd always tried to get him a part in whatever movie she was making. She was always a bigger star than he was. Even back then, she had her own trailer on the set. I read that in a movie magazine. Even if there wasn't a part for him, she made sure he was part of the work crew. He's really knowledgeable about just about every aspect of making movies."

"Sure. *Adventures with Barney the Bear*. I remember him now," I said. "Doug must be in his twenties."

"Twenty-seven," she said. "He's a little older than I am." I knew without asking that there was no romantic interest there—at least on River's part. Her main man is the WICH-TV, drop-dead gorgeous, night news anchor Buck Covington. River dropped her voice to a near whisper. "Darla may have been poisoned," she said. "She might have eaten poisoned chocolates."

Astonished that she already knew about the poisoned chocolate, I managed to form a question. "What makes you think that?"

"My hairdresser, Jenna, does one of the prop guys.

He had to show the cops where all Darla's bowls of fancy chocolates were stashed. Then the cops picked them up with gloves on and put each bowlful in a red plastic hazmat bag."

Amazing. Chez Jenna had come up with more detailed information than my detective husband had shared.

CHAPTER 7

I clocked out at five o'clock, realizing that about half of the working people in Salem were heading home at approximately the same time. I realized too that between police vehicles investigating Darla's death, Paragon Productions' cars, trucks, and trailers moving from place to place, assorted witches, princesses, flying monkeys, and superheroes darting in and out between vehicles, and the ever-present lookie-loos driving aimlessly around Salem looking for movie stars, the traffic was nearly gridlocked. Derby Street seemed to be one long, unmoving line of vehicles in both directions. I was glad I'd walked to work, leaving the Jeep safely in our backyard. Ducking between the cars and walking across the common to Winter Street was the quicker and undoubtedly more pleasant option.

Aunt Ibby had invited Pete and me to join her for dinner at her house and we'd happily accepted. My aunt, among her many other talents, is a wonderful cook—a talent I most assuredly have not inherited. As I retraced my steps across the common, enjoying once again the pleasant oasis of well-maintained grass, sturdy trees, bright seasonal marigolds and daylilies, comfortable benches, and the handsome bandstand, I felt relaxed and happy. I'd caught up with my program director duties, I didn't need to prepare dinner, and chances were, with Darla Diamond's unfortunate passing, maybe I wouldn't even need to don the executive documentary producer hat. I could just enjoy being married and living in our new home. No worries.

As soon as I inserted my key into the green door on our side of the duplex house, I heard O'Ryan's welcoming "Mmrrup" from inside the front hall. How does he always know which door I'm going to use? Once I stepped inside, the big cat, purring loudly, made figure eights around my ankles, letting me know that he'd missed me.

"I missed you too, dear cat," I told him. "Pete will be home soon and then we'll go to Aunt Ibby's house. I'm sure you're invited too." He gave an acknowledging swish of his tail, then, ears alert, dashed away toward the sunroom, where the back door opened onto our backyard parking spaces—indicating that Pete was already home.

It didn't take long for Pete and me to shower and change clothes for our dinner date—Pete opting for something more casual than his business suit, me choosing something dressier than my T-shirt and baggy pants ensemble. By seven o'clock, Pete, in tan slacks and Tommy Bahama shirt, and me, in a Lilly Pulitzer print midi and low heels, walked down Winter Street to my aunt's house. "Look," I said. "There's Betsy Leavitt's Mercedes out front. The Angels must be here too."

Aunt Ibby and a couple of her senior citizen girl-friends who share an interest in mystery-solving call themselves "the Angels." Picture a cross between *The Golden Girls* and *Charlie's Angels*. My aunt, her high-school classmate Betsy Leavitt, and her close friend Louisa Abney-Babcock get together every week to watch an episode of *Midsomer Murders*. They discuss—and critique—the plot, especially the crime-solving methods.

"This isn't their regular TV show night," I said. "They must have called an emergency meeting."

"Because of Darla Diamond's death, I suppose," Pete said. "That's a mystery the Angels would find worth solving."

"There's apparently no shortage of suspects," I said.

"Tell me about it." He shook his head. "I'm halfway hoping the Angels can narrow the field a little."

I wasn't surprised at the comment. The three women, with their unique talents and connections, have more than once come up with solutions the professionals have missed. Betsy Leavitt, beautiful at sixtysomething, still occasionally models for both print and television advertisers. Also, Betsy admits to knowing everybody who is anybody in Salem and beyond. Louisa is the financial wizard in the group. Wealthy in her own right, she sits on the boards of several area banks. Aunt Ibby has spent a distinguished career as an expert research librarian and still serves part-time in that capacity at Salem's main library. In addition to that, she's a technology whiz. My aunt was talking about artificial intelligence a couple of years before the term AI became a thing. Her home office is crammed with enough gadgets and gizmos to make MIT envious. I've often heard her admit to having a master's degree in snooping.

Pete and I approached the front door of the handsome old house and rang the bell. A smiling pumpkin sat on the top step and an autumn wreath decorated the door. I'd returned my own keys to the house when my aunt turned my onetime upstairs apartment into a couple of really cute bed-and-breakfast suites. O'Ryan's fuzzy face appeared at the side window just as the door chimes played "The Impossible Dream." Through a series of cat doors and a fast trip through several Winter Street backyards, he'd beat us there.

Aunt Ibby pulled the door open. "Come in, come in, my dears," she said. "I knew you were on your way when O'Ryan appeared in the kitchen a few minutes ago."

"Something smells amazing." I craned my neck toward the kitchen and sniffed audibly.

"Chicken marsala," she announced. "When the girls said they were coming over I threw in a couple of extra chicken breasts. It only takes half an hour to make, start to finish. No big deal. I'll give you the recipe. It's not our regular meeting night, you know. I think Michael may drop in too, at least for dessert."

Michael Martell, an antiques and collectibles expert who lives in the other side of our house, is sometimes invited to join the Angels at their meetings. Michael is also known by his pseudonym, Fenton Bishop. Under that name, he writes a popular series of mystery books—

Antique Alley Mysteries—and teaches creative writing at downtown Salem's Tabitha Trumbull Academy of the Arts. I used to teach a class in television production there myself. It's an excellent community school. Everyone calls it the Tabby. The "girls" have long recognized Martell's unique qualification for murder investigation. He'd served twenty years in prison for killing his wife. (Scott Palmer insists on referring to Michael as *your friendly neighborhood murderer*.)

This seems like a strange friendship, I know, but as Pete says, the man willingly served his full twenty-year term, never accepting offers of earlier release, always displaying sincere repentance for his crime. Anyway, the Angels trusted him completely and valued his opinions.

In addition to an always delicious menu, the guest list promised to be unusually interesting as well. The Angels' meetings usually involve watching the TV show, followed by a discussion about the murder of the week, along with a yummy dessert. This time, though, the death was both real and recent, and the participants didn't wait for a sugar rush to get started with the clue-chasing.

The chicken marsala had just been served when Betsy began the unofficial meeting with a surprising statement. "The eighth episode of the tenth series has nothing to do with it."

"May 8, 2008," Louisa nodded. "That was the first one I thought about too."

My aunt passed a basket of hot rolls to me. "It's always been one of my favorites," she said, "but it's definitely the wrong chocolate box."

Pete and I looked at each other. Were the Angels speaking in some sort of television show code? They occasionally lapsed into British-sounding metaphors when discussing the weekly adventures of the Devon county of Midsomer's brilliant Detective Chief Inspector Tom Barnaby.

Recognizing our confusion, Betsy hurried to explain. "There was an episode years ago called 'Murder in a Chocolate Box.'"

"Like Darla's death," I said. "I get it."

"But that episode had nothing at all to do with chocolate," Betsy said. "It happened in what the Brits call a chocolate-box building—one of those thatched-roof, cutesy houses—overdecorated like a chocolate candy box."

"Darla's death was more like the chocolate candy murders that really happened in Dover, Delaware, back in 1898," Louisa said. "Two women died after they received a poisoned box of candy sent by mail."

"It reminds me more of John Dickson Carr's book, *The Black Spectacles*," my librarian aunt commented. "A wonderful locked-room mystery about poisoned chocolates."

"Interesting." Pete used his thoughtful-cop voice. "Were all of those solved? Did the police in Delaware and the cops in the book figure out who the killers were? And why they killed with chocolates?"

"The Delaware one was the first case of the US Postal Service being used to commit a murder," Louisa said. "And I remember that the killer was a woman. I'm sure you can look it up."

"I will," Pete promised, scribbling a note in the

small notebook he always carries. "What about the mystery book, Ibby?"

"It appears that a woman is the likely killer there too, Pete," she said. "It was based on a real murder that happened in England in 1871—Christina Edmunds was known as the Chocolate Cream Killer. I'll get you a copy of the book from the library. I think you'll enjoy it."

The conversation among those gathered around Aunt Ibby's dining room table didn't dwell for long on murder or movies. Topics ranged from high school soccer and fall gardening tips to local building codes and the price of gasoline. As my aunt had suggested, Michael Martell arrived just as after-dinner coffee and slices of Aunt Ibby's Dark As Night devil's food cake were being served. He was greeted affectionately by the group. He's not only one of the Tabby's most popular instructors, he's part of a new outreach group working with prisoners about to reenter society that Pete says is already showing positive effects.

After dessert I stood, joining my aunt and both of the Angels in carrying cups and dishes to the kitchen while Pete and Michael arranged the living room chairs in their usual meeting-night places, facing the darkened TV screen. It was obvious that even without Inspector Barnaby's weekly adventure for focus, the group was prepared for an evening of crime solving.

"Dinner was wonderful, as always," I told my aunt. "The invitation was especially welcome today. Things at both the TV station and the police station have been crazy lately and meals at our house have been strictly haphazard."

"We're hoping you two can stay for our meeting," she said as we began the usual dishwasher-loading procedure. "We've all been doing a little investigating into the Darla Diamond matter and we'd welcome some input from both of you."

We'd occasionally joined the group, who were always respectful of the fact that Pete was constrained in what information he could share but welcomed his input on points of law. My position at WICH-TV offered me some close-up insight into the varied aspects of newsworthy local current events that most people don't have. The information gleaned from the brief conversation while having lunch with Scott at the Friendly Tavern came to mind. I wasn't sure where Louisa and Betsy had their hair done, and I wondered if they'd heard as much as I had about the alleged money problems at Paragon. The idea of joining the meeting suddenly seemed appealing. "I'll check with Pete," I said, hoping he'd want to stay for a while too.

CHAPTER 8

We stayed later than we'd meant to at the Angels' unscheduled meeting. Louisa's information on the state of Paragon's finances was particularly interesting. Louisa's sources had told her that the estimated budget for *Night Magic* was $220 million, not an unusual amount for a film featuring big-name actors and an appealing paranormal plot. The movie, which so far had been filmed mostly on sets in the California studio, had run into quite an astounding number of delays—from a fire that had consumed a replica of the Witch House kitchen, and had to be rebuilt, to power outages, labor disputes, which a broken water main that had flooded the executive offices. "*Night Magic* is already more than a million dollars over budget," Louisa said, "and they still had on-site filming to do in Salem when Darla turned up dead."

Betsy had some worthwhile tidbits of information— admittedly of the gossip variety—but, she insisted, from *totally credible sources*. According to Betsy—whose reputation for knowing everybody who is anybody extends across the nation and sometimes across the world—there were rumors rampant in the film community that Paragon would be close to bankruptcy if this movie didn't turn out to be box office dynamite. "Even without Darla, though," Betsy confided, "one of my most reliable West Coast contacts says that if they have enough bits and pieces of film, along with artificial intelligence manipulation for her voice and maybe a body double for distance shots, they can try to save it." Betsy's far-reaching network had informed her about Lamont Faraday being found asleep on Darla's bed too, and about his being dressed for his leading man part in *Night Magic*—information she willingly shared with the group. I was pleased about that because I was sure Pete wasn't about to mention it, and as far as I knew, it hadn't appeared in any of the local media so far.

My movie buff aunt performed some fast, on-the-spot research about films that were released in theaters and failed to break even by a lot of money—known in the trade as box-office bombs.

According to my aunt, *Cleopatra*, starring Elizabeth Taylor and Richard Burton, had darn near bankrupted 20th Century Fox because of huge production and marketing costs and numerous delays. "*Cleopatra* gets the blame for a decline in big-budget epic films," she said, "and *Waterworld* was another one with high expectations and disappointing results."

"It will really be good for Salem if they can save it," I said. "The publicity would boost tourism for sure." It would also put me back into the documentary business. I had mixed feelings about that.

Michael hadn't contributed much to the Angels' conversation, except to note that the field of suspects would be hard to narrow down. He stressed the importance of being careful not to tarnish an innocent person's reputation while trying to determine who the actual killer was. Pete agreed wholeheartedly. Like Pete and me, Michael had walked the short distance down Winter Street to Aunt Ibby's house. When Betsy and Louisa left in Betsy's car, it seemed natural for Michael and Pete and me to walk together to our shared house. We parted when we reached our front door. "Good night, neighbors," Michael said. "It was an interesting meeting, wasn't it? I'll be especially interested to hear what Lamont Faraday has to say about being asleep in Darla's bed while she was across town being poisoned."

We'll all be interested to hear that story! We wished our next-door neighbor a good night, and Pete unlocked our door. As always, it felt good to be in our own home—even though we'd only been away for a few hours and only a few houses away. I wondered if we'd always feel that way, or if the novelty would wear off someday. I hoped it wouldn't. Pete turned on the bedroom TV while I changed into pj's and cold-creamed my makeup away. "Time for Buck Covington and the eleven o'clock news," he said, "and your friend Scott is sitting right beside him."

"No kidding?" I rushed back into the room. "He's in the second banana seat at the beginning of the show?" Usually the field reporter gets called to sit at the news desk beside Buck for only the few minutes it takes for him or her to tell a story. Then he's dismissed. Scott must have learned something new—something besides my little video about Gallows Hill Park—something important.

Buck did the usual introduction, highlighted some local headlines, and dropped a teaser reminder to stay tuned because Scott Palmer had some breaking news to share after a commercial message.

"Breaking news," I muttered under my breath as I climbed into bed—feeling the teensiest bit of envy. At one time that would have been me in the seat beside the nighttime anchor.

Pete joined me in our big bed. The commercial ended and Buck turned on his perfect smile. "Folks, I'm sure you all know WICH-TV's top field reporter, Scott Palmer. Scott, I understand you've done a bit of recent special investigation involving local bars. Tell us about it."

Scott has a pretty good smile of his own. "Thanks, Buck. Some of your viewers may already have heard that shortly after the news of Darla Diamond's death became public, Lamont Faraday, her costar in *Night Magic*, was discovered sound asleep in her luxury trailer." Here, Scott paused for one of his trademark long stares into the camera. "According to several sources, members of the Paragon crew who've been working inside the Gallows Hill Park facility, Faraday had a note, handwritten on Darla's personal stationery—blue, with DD in tiny script letters on one corner—telling him to come inside and wait for her there. Did Faraday have such a note? If he had it, did Darla write it?"

Jim's zoom picture of Gallows Hill Park appeared on the screen. "Here's the area Salem people are calling 'little Hollywood,'" Scott announced. "Look closely and you'll see two luxury trailers side by side. These were the ones at Gallows Hill Park occupied by Darla Diamond and Lamont Faraday." He drew an arrow pointing to the one closest to the fence, using the green-screen technique he'd learned from Wanda the Weather Girl. "This was Darla's," he said, then, drawing another arrow, "here's Lamont's, right next door."

I thought about my recent vision, showing me the same zoom picture but without the arrows. What did it mean? I tried to concentrate on Jim's picture, but it popped away and we were looking at Scott again.

"Now, about those local bars, Buck." Another pause and the long look. "I'd heard that Lamont Faraday made a thousand dollar bet that he could have a drink in every bar on Derby Street while he was here in Salem. He figured he could take time off from working to go to one bar every day. Those of you who know the area can understand the challenge." Big smile. "I began on Monday morning at the corner of Lafayette and Derby. I crossed back and forth, covering both sides of the street. Apparently, Faraday used the same method. Each of the bartenders I spoke with that afternoon remembered his visit. Just about everybody recognized him. The script for *Night Magic* calls for the actors to move between the seventeenth century and the twenty-first. Faraday had been wearing one of his very up-to-date, twenty-first-century *GQ* suits from the movie—kind of out of place in Derby Street bars, if you know what I mean." Scott gave a broad wink before he continued. What a ham. "Anyway, he tipped heavily and signed autographs in each place. Later in the day, though, I had to wait for the second-shift bartenders to arrive. I lucked out with one of the afternoon bartenders in a place just past the Custom House."

The screen showed a still shot of a small mom-and-pop bar named Mahoney's Place. It had been there for as long as I could remember. The owner's daughter, Mary Catherine, used to tend bar. Pete and I went there sometimes when we were first dating. They had great corned beef sandwiches.

"The bartender here remembered him." Scott had changed to his network announcer voice, so I knew something important was about to be shared. "Most importantly," he said, "she remembered the note. Faraday was nursing a light beer at the bar for a while when a uniformed courier arrived with a message for him. The fellow handed an envelope to the bartender, asking her to give it to Faraday when he came in. She said that the messenger didn't seem to recognize the actor even though he was seated nearby."

Is Mary Catherine still working there? "Pete!" I tugged at his elbow. "Maybe we should stop by for a corned beef sandwich tomorrow afternoon sometime."

"Good idea," he agreed. "I wonder if Mary Catherine will remember us."

"Great minds," I said and returned my attention to the nightly news and Scott's breaking news.

"The bartender watched as Faraday tore open the envelope and pulled out a single sheet of blue paper, read it, stuffed it into his pocket, and left." Scott's tone had turned breathless. He held up a blue envelope. "Lamont Faraday left the envelope on the bar. Here it is."

"Shouldn't the police have a look at that?" I asked.

"I don't know what use it would be," Pete said. "We already have the note. As far as we can tell, it's authentic. The handwriting matches, and she's used the same notepaper for years. It has that tiny monogram with her initials on it—both for answering fan mail and for short, personal notes like the one Faraday got."

"Scott will probably give it to you if you want to see it," I said. "It's already served its purpose for him."

Pete smiled. "A good visual prop for the nightly news breaking story, right?"

"Right," I agreed, returning my attention to the TV just in time to hear Scott offer to turn "this valuable piece of evidence" over to the police. "More than just a prop." I pointed to the screen. "He's made it into a valuable piece of evidence. The man is a self-promoting genius."

Buck Covington thanked Scott for joining him, went to a sixty-second spot for an oil change company, and Scott was gone when the nightly news returned. *Tarot Time with River North* follows the news, and Buck sometimes stays to introduce River's show and to shuffle the tarot deck for her. Because the audience knows that River and Buck are definitely an *item*, Bruce Doan likes the lead-in from one top-rated show to the other. It's a fact that occasionally River's late show has actually drawn better ratings than the network late night shows. So after Scott left and Buck announced that he'd be heading over to River's *Tarot Time* set, we left our TV on.

As soon as River's theme music, *Danse Macabre*, began to play, O'Ryan joined us on the bed. Neither of us was surprised. O'Ryan loves River, and the fact that he'd left Aunt Ibby's and traveled down Winter Street in favor of the midnight spooky movie and card readings wasn't unusual.

Ever since Buck began shuffling the beautiful tarot deck, he's been getting better and better at it; some viewers compare him to a professional casino card dealer. After he'd finished with a final flip and cut the cards for River, he pulled the blue envelope from his pocket. "Scott Palmer left this in the newsroom, River," he said. "I thought maybe you'd like to see if the cards can pick up anything from poor Darla through it."

"What a good idea, Buck!" River, beautiful as always, wore a red satin gown. Tiny silver moons and stars were woven into her long black braid, and a large, jeweled spider brooch was pinned to one shoulder of the gown. She leaned forward in her fan-backed wicker chair, accepting the wrinkled blue oblong. She bowed her head, placing one hand on the cards and the other on the envelope. "I consecrate this deck to enlighten myself and others more fully. May those who have used and touched this envelope know the love of Spirit and be drawn into the Light of Spirit." She smiled into the camera. "Tonight's movie is a true classic. *The Spiral Staircase* is a 1946 psychological thriller starring Dorothy McGuire. If you'd like me to read the tarot for you during commercial breaks in the film, call the number at the bottom of your screen. I'll begin tonight's readings with Darla Diamond's blue envelope."

She lifted the envelope to her forehead, replaced it

on the table. When she reads for me, she always begins by placing the Queen of Wands in the center of the table. That card, with its fair-haired, blue-eyed woman sitting on a throne, is the card she uses to represent me. The card even has a cat in the foreground.

The overhead camera zoomed in on the card she'd placed in the center this time. It showed a sculptor carving in what looks like a church with two people looking on. "This is the Three of Pentacles," River explained. "It's a card I often use to represent a master craftsman—like a skillful artist or a writer or—as in this case—an actor. The craftsman is approved and applauded by the audience—as Darla Diamond is." She shuffled the cards and cut the deck into three piles and then lay nine face-down on the table in a familiar pattern. The first card she turned face-up was the Six of Cups. She placed it across the Three of Pentacles. "Here's a little boy offering a little girl a cup filled with flowers," River said. "This card sometimes means a meeting of a childhood acquaintance who offers a gift."

The next card turned up was one I recognized—the King of Cups. It shows a man with brown hair and hazel eyes. "Here's a man with an interest in the arts." River tapped the card with one finger. "He is someone who may have helped Darla in her work. He keeps his emotions to himself. Is he perhaps Lamont Faraday? We'll see."

She turned over another card. "Here's the Nine of Cups." She shook her head. "It's reversed, meaning mistakes, and plans that may not turn out the way she'd thought they would." The card showed a well-fed man with nine cups in a neat row. "It often points to overindulgence in food and drink." I thought about the burst seams in the designer dress and all those chocolates. Next came the Two of Swords. "Tension in relationships," River announced, pointing at the card with the blindfolded woman holding two swords. "She may have been blind to her situation."

The next card she turned face-up was the Ten of Pentacles. The overhead camera showed a family scene, complete with dogs, with a fine, tall house in the background. "Interesting," River said. "This card often indicates family matters, perhaps an inheritance. In this case, though, I believe the house on the card represents the house central to the movie plot. Salem's old Witch House."

There were four more cards in the reading—the Six of Swords, which might mean a trip, was followed by the Temperance card, indicating a need for moderation. I thought again about Darla's recent weight gain, and the split seams on the designer dress, along with the consumption of chocolate. The Ten of Wands showed a man struggling to carry ten long poles toward a city. "It looks like a difficult test, doesn't it?" River asked the audience, "but it could mean a problem is solved." The next card was a pretty one—the Page of Swords. A young person holds a sword with both hands. A flock of birds flies overhead. River said it could signify an imposter.

She turned over the final card, revealing the Seven of Swords. "Someone, like the thief on this card, who is stealing five swords, is getting away with something. But he's only partly successful." She swept up the cards with one graceful hand and returned them to the deck. "After these commercial messages, stay tuned for to-night's totally creepy movie—*The Spiral Staircase.* Dorothy McGuire plays a young, mute woman being stalked and terrorized in a rural Vermont mansion by a serial killer targeting women with disabilities. At the break, phone lines will be open. I'll be back to read the tarot—maybe for you!"

Pete usually calls the tarot reading part of the show "River's hocus-pocus." I was surprised when he actu-ally made a comment about the reading. "That was in-teresting," he said. "I mean the part about the Witch House on that card."

"It makes sense to me," I said. "The whole movie is about that house—its past and its present."

"I mean about the picture on the card. It shows a new house, not an old one. Darla's body was found in a brand-new replica of a room in the old house. I've been over every inch of that replica room. We'll take the crime scene tape down as soon as we can so that they can continue using it. Everything in there is new—even reproduction furniture."

"You're right," I said. 'I think you read that card bet-ter than River did. I can hardly wait to tell her."

Pete didn't comment further on the reading. "Do you want to watch the creepy movie?" he asked.

"I don't think so. I've seen it before—totally terrify-ing."

"Lights out, then?"

"Lights out," I agreed. But even in the darkness of my comfortable room and cozy bed, I lay awake, thinking about the vison I'd had duplicating Jim's video of the fenced-in Paragon Productions area—with its replica room, where Darla was found. I thought too about the blue envelope that had changed hands so many times today. It had moved from Darla, to a nameless courier, to a bartender, to Lamont Faraday, back to the bartender, then to Scott, then to Buck Covington, and finally to River. "It wouldn't be of much use anyway." I spoke into the darkness.

Pete answered in a sleepy voice: "That's a whole lot of fingerprints."

CHAPTER 9

I'd planned a busy day for myself and meant to get an early start on it. I woke to the sound of country music and the smell of coffee coming from the kitchen, ensuring an excellent beginning for my day. I climbed out of bed, popped into the bathroom for a quick splash of cool water on my face, brushed my teeth, and hurried for a good-morning hug from my husband.

"My documentary on the making of a movie may turn into a news feature after all," I said. "Scott's getting quite a lot of mileage out of all that's happening so far."

"The blue envelope." Pete poured coffee into my New Hampshire Speedway mug. "He used your footage of the trailers. Will you and Old Jim be trying for some more pictures of Gallows Hill Park?"

"I'm going to see if my TV press pass will get me a little closer to the action. I might at least find someone who'll talk to me over there."

"There's a gate tender—kind of a uniformed security guard there—who admitted us when Darla's body was found," he said. "Of course, he didn't have any say about letting the police in, but I have his name, if that would help."

"It couldn't hurt," I said. "What's his name?"

"Wait a sec. It's in my notebook." He went back into the bedroom, returning with the worn leather pad.

"Here it is," he said. "Doug Sawyer."

"You're kidding! Doug Sawyer is the security guard?" I couldn't keep the amazement out of my voice. "*The* Doug Sawyer?"

He frowned, then smiled. "Wait a minute. Wasn't he some kind of kid star on TV a long time ago? I knew the name sort of rang a bell, but I couldn't place it."

"*Adventures with Barney the Bear*," I said. "Every Saturday morning. I had a wicked crush on him. He was so darned cute. River says he still is."

"River knows him?"

"She's met him. She said he was close with Darla. She tried to find parts for him in her movies. He's still under contract with Paragon."

A childhood friend who offers a gift?

"*Barney the Bear*?" Pete couldn't hide an amused look. "You watched a show called *Barney the Bear*?"

"Sure. Didn't you?"

"No. I think my sister Marie might have. Too girlie for me. I watched *Power Rangers*."

"I didn't watch that, but one of my middle grade boy friends gave me a watch with the Pink Ranger on it," I admitted.

"Kimberly," Pete said. "Gotta go. Will you be home for dinner?"

"Was that the Pink Ranger's name? I think I'll be off at five." We exchanged a goodbye kiss. "Dinner in or out?"

"Let's decide when we get home. Do you still have the watch?"

"Maybe. It's probably somewhere in Aunt Ibby's attic. It could be a collectible by now. Maybe someday I'll venture into the attic and put it in Marie's Christmas stocking, just for fun."

We decided on breakfast at home. I'm still not much of a cook, so we shared some Eggo toaster waffles with some excellent Vermont maple syrup, along with our coffee and orange juice. I put some dry cat food in O'Ryan's red bowl—instead of the kind I keep in the refrigerator—along with a bowl of water just in case he dropped by during the day.

"If you're free for lunch," I reminded him, "remember we talked about dropping in at Mahoney's for corned beef—and a chat with Mary Catherine, if she's still there."

"I'll make time," he said. "I'd like to get her impression of Faraday. He's on his best behavior—cooperative and movie-star charming, with a lawyer at his side when he talks to us. Daytime drinking at Mahoney's may make a big difference in his personality. It's right down the street from your station. How about meeting me at Mahoney's at noon?"

I agreed and we left together through the sunroom for our cars parked in the backyard in the shade of a red maple tree. I followed Pete's cruiser onto Winter Street and headed for Hawthorne Boulevard, planning to get together with Old Jim for another foray to Gallows Hill as soon as I got my daily program schedules nailed down.

As soon as I unlocked the studio door and entered the cool darkness of the long, black-walled room, I could hear the chorus of excited children's voices. Ranger Rob's *little buckaroos* had arrived. I drew closer to the commotion, watching as Rob's sidekick, Katie the Clown, accompanied by Paco the Wonder Dog, herded them into a line, allowing each kid to pat Paco and give him a tiny treat. I so admired the gift Katie had for calming a roomful of children, making the little ones love her. Would I, I wondered, when Pete and I started a family, be that good with our own little buckaroos? I fervently hoped so. It appeared that the schedule for *Ranger Rob's Rodeo* was working fine. I knew the special guest for the show that day was a talented mime from the Tabby's actors' studio and was always a hit with audiences young or old.

I clattered up the metal staircase to the second floor, interested to see what awaited me on Rhonda's whiteboard. I couldn't help thinking about the TV shows of my own childhood—like the recently discussed *Adventures with Barney the Bear*, starring Doug Sawyer, and Pete's happy memories of the *Power Rangers*. I remembered exactly what young Doug had looked like and wondered what changes the intervening years had brought. With a little bit of luck, I'd find out soon. I remembered too that the Pink Power Ranger on the watch wore a mask. Maybe Pete had no idea what she looked like unmasked. I planned to ask him. I also planned to try for an introduction to Doug Sawyer. I've heard that you're always only seven steps away from connecting with anyone else in the world. Between River and Pete, I was already two steps closer to my child star idol. With a little luck, I could skip some steps and walk right up to the current uniformed security guard at Gallows Hill Park and maybe, through him, get a step closer to Lamont Faraday and the interview everybody wanted. I'd have to do it without Jim and the WICH-TV mobile unit, but the camera in my own phone took good enough video for television.

Rhonda greeted me with a happy "Good morning." I looked for my name on the whiteboard. It was there beside an underlined order: "See Mr. Doan about the Witch House tour."

"What Witch House tour?" I asked Rhonda.

"The one he wants you to head up. He thinks viewers will line up for a free tour of the old house with you leading the pack. You'd be a WICH-TV pied piper. Cool, huh?"

"No way," I declared. "Not me. Uh-uh." I marched toward the station manager's door. "That's one thing I'm not going to do. I don't even like going on guided tours of anything, let alone leading one myself." I tapped on the slightly ajar office door.

"Come in, Ms. Barrett," Bruce Doan invited me casually. "I have an assignment for you that you're going to enjoy."

I don't think so.

Naturally, the meeting didn't turn out the way I wanted it to—even though what the boss had in mind for me actually did sound a little bit interesting. The storyline of the nearly finished movie involved the lead characters having past lives at the time of the real witchcraft trials—some of which happened within the walls of the very house we were discussing—and later living in present-day Salem involving the same building—renovated and carefully furnished with period pieces. Doan's idea involved me doing a show escorting a smallish group of selected regular viewers of WICH-TV on a tour of the Witch House, room by room. The fact that one of the stars had died in a replica of one of the rooms made the idea timelier in a bizarre sort of way. I'd give the story of Judge Corwin and the sad goings-on of the actual trials, then talk about how much those bad old days have influenced life in Salem today.

This led to the point of the whole walking tour. I'd guide them to downtown Salem, visit the Witch Museum, some of the witch stores, the statue of Samantha, a bookstore, the site of the actual hangings at Proctor's Ledge, the museum, and more, winding up again at the Witch House, and making sure to include mostly places that already advertise with us. "The present advertisers will love it," Doan promised, "and they'll promote it to their customers and business associates. The whole show is a promo pitch to get more WICH-TV advertisers."

Sneaky but brilliant.

Reluctantly, I agreed with Doan. "It would probably work," I said.

"You bet it will." He pounded on his desk. "The viewers will like it, the advertisers will be thrilled, the historians will eat it up. I can get Howie to do it if you turn it down, but I'd rather have you. The viewers know you better. We'll run it more than once, so it'll be extra airtime for you and Old Jim."

I liked the idea of working with Jim. "This will take some time. Are Jim and I on the clock for this thing?"

Thoughtful pause from Doan. "Whenever the camera is running," he agreed.

I considered the answer. It was not entirely unreasonable.

"What about Scott?" I asked. "Did you talk to him about doing this?"

"Sure. He's not interested in the least. He likes the hard news stuff, not historical buildings. He said I should give it to you."

"I'll think about it," I told him. "I'll talk it over with Jim, and with Pete. It's a matter of fitting it into my regular schedule."

"You can do it in one day," he assured me. "Of course, if it's a big hit, we'll do it more than once, with different shops, different old houses."

Mr. Doan has a way of making things sound much easier than they actually are. "The event itself can be shot in one day," I agreed, "but the planning, the lining up which stores, which houses, where the tour begins and ends—all that takes time to figure out. Some of those places charge admission. Who's paying?"

"You're right," he allowed. "Maybe we'll have to charge for the tour—or get a serious sponsor."

"If I have to do the planning, lining everything up so the timing works, it'll take a while. That has to be on the clock too—if I decide to do it," I warned him. "I have a life besides working here."

"How about if Rhonda contacts everybody, sets up the times, the entrance fees, all that—then you and Jim just have to lead the pack and get the video."

That sounded more reasonable. I was beginning to warm up to the idea. "Because the theme of the movie is the main idea behind it, maybe Paragon would pick up the tab," I suggested. "Then we could even throw in lunch at one of the good restaurants."

"I've heard that Paragon is having money issues," he said.

"We're not talking about a lot of money," I insisted. "Some admission charges and a few sandwiches. It would be good promotion for them."

"So, you're on board with the idea?" His smile showed that he was pretty sure he'd talked me into it. Somewhat surprised, I had to admit to myself that maybe he had. I tried to shove the walking tour idea to the back of my mind while I concentrated on my program director's job and allowed a few thoughts about the proposed documentary to flit around at the same time. Was I trying to take on too much? Was I stretching myself too thin? I had a husband and a home to consider now. I'd made a lunch date with Pete for Mahoney's. Between asking questions about Lamont Faraday, trying to get a step closer to Doug Sawyer, and eating a big, thick corned beef on rye sandwich, I'd run the new idea by Pete.

CHAPTER 10

Pete and I arrived at Mahoney's within minutes of each other. Mary Catherine was there but busy. "It's so good to see you two." She escorted us to a booth and handed us each a menu. "I heard you got married. Congratulations. Listen, as soon as I get a break, let's catch up with each other. I just got engaged myself. It's corned beef on rye with hot mustard and Diet Pepsi for both of you. Right?"

I hoped her memory about her conversation with Faraday was as sharp as her recollections of menu items. We confirmed the order and sat in the cozy booth, facing each other. I took the opportunity to bring up the walking tour idea.

"Mr. Doan has a new idea about a special feature for me to think about," I said. "It's kind of interesting, but I'm not sure I want to invest the time it could involve."

"Tell me about the interesting part first," he suggested. "The time would depend a lot on how much you'd like the challenge."

"*Challenge* is the right word for it," I told him, and proceeded to spell it out as closely as I could remember—the boss's plan for the Witch House walking tour.

"There's no doubt that you and Jim can make a success out of this. I'm sure you realize that," he said. "Doan certainly knows it." We paused in the conversation when our thick, hot sandwiches arrived.

"That's true," I said after my first bite. "But I don't want to pile too much onto my TV career plate and not leave enough time for my married lady plate."

"You know I feel that way about my job too." He took a bite from his sandwich too, chewing thoughtfully. "Oh, wow! I'd forgotten how good this is. We need to come here more often. Lee, when you talk about the Salem history part, there's excitement in your voice. You light right up." He reached across the table and squeezed my hand. "I've always worried about spending enough of what the magazines call *quality time* with you."

"Every minute we spend together is quality time," I said, knowing how corny that sounded but meaning it anyway. "Every single second."

"I know that," he said. "If the challenge of this particular assignment gives you pleasure, I think you should do it. It's not as if it's a long-term commitment, you know."

So it was decided. If the details could be worked out—and that was a big *if*—like finding a sponsor to back the Witch House walk idea, and making the whole thing financially feasible for me and Jim—I'd do it.

By the time we'd finished eating, Mary Catherine

cleared our dishes away, then came back and slid into the booth beside me. It was time to bring up the second topic of the day. What did Mary Catherine think about Faraday, and did she have anything to add to what we'd seen on television—any details about the actor himself, or anything special she'd noticed about the blue envelope that had been handed around so carelessly from the moment the courier delivered it?

After a few minutes of welcome catching up, congratulating her on her upcoming wedding and telling her about the high points of ours, we got down to business. "I saw the news report about Lamont Faraday coming here to Mahoney's for a drink and the bartender handing him a blue envelope," I told her. "We wondered if that was you."

"It was me for sure," she said. "It happened just the way that reporter told it. A courier in a fancy uniform came up to the bar and said that if Lamont Faraday came in, I should give him this note. Then he handed me the blue envelope." She held up an imaginary envelope. "Faraday was sitting right here, not two stools away from him, but the guy must have been from someplace else because he didn't recognize a movie star whose picture had been in all the papers and TV around here for weeks."

"So, did you point him out to the courier?" Pete asked her.

"No. None of my business. I just said okay. He didn't offer me a tip or anything like they usually do. I stuck the envelope in my apron pocket and as soon as he left, I gave it to Mr. Faraday. *He* gave me a tip." Big smile. "Sweet man. He only had a beer and a bowl of chili, but the tip was double the tab."

"So he opened the envelope right away?"

"He held on to it for a minute, turned it over once or twice, then he tore it open—real carefully, like, an inch at a time, and pulled out a note, read it, and stuffed it in his pocket. He left the envelope on the bar, finished his chili, said goodbye to everybody, and left. That's all. The reporter asked if I still had it and I gave it to him."

"You'd saved it?" Pete asked. "Why?"

She lifted one shoulder in a little shrug. "It was silly, I guess, but I never had anything from a movie star before. I'd stuck in under the cash drawer. Then, when that Scott guy offered me twenty bucks for it, naturally I gave it to him. I heard later that he showed it on TV. He said it was a *valuable clue*." She looked at Pete. "Was it?"

"Not really," Pete said. "We had the note itself, which proved that Darla Diamond had written it. After he'd used the envelope on TV, Scott Palmer had no further use for it and it wound up on the WICH-TV late show. I guess that's where it still is." He looked up at the ceiling. "I see you have a security camera. Is it possible that you might have a picture of the courier?"

"Maybe," she said. "It's an old machine. Pretty grainy. My dad takes care of it. I could ask him to see if we still have anything from that day."

"Would you let me know if anything shows up?" Pete handed her his card. We thanked Mary Catherine, gave her our new address so she could send us an invitation to the upcoming wedding, and left for our re-

spective jobs. Pete gave me a lift back to the station
and, during the short trip, I managed to squeeze in a
question about my plan to meet Doug Sawyer. "You
met him," I said. "Do you think, if he's the gate tender
and I sort of dropped your name, it would get me onto
the property?"

"I don't think meeting me was a big event in his
life," Pete said, "but we exchanged business cards. I
can give you the one he gave to me if you think it will
do any good." He parked and let me out next to Ariel's
bench—a special seat beside the seawall overlooking
the spot where Ariel Constellation drowned in Salem
Harbor. He pulled a card from his wallet and handed it
to me.

"Thanks," I said, secretly kind of excited just to have
my childhood idol's card, let alone a meeting. "That
could be my ticket into the Paragon inner sanctum.
I'm going to ask River about it too. She already has a
way in."

I tapped my code number into the studio door, wondering if the well-traveled blue envelope was still on
the table in the *Tarot Time* set, or if Chester, the jani-
tor—who, in keeping with Doan's many hats theory is
also the nighttime security guard and the wardrobe at-
tendant—had disposed of it.

I walked down the dark corridor of the black-walled
room to River's unlighted set. The envelope was on the
floor under the wicker table. I stuffed it into my old, favorite Jacki Easlick hobo bag and took the metal stair-
way up to the second floor. As usual, I checked in with
Rhonda. I never know what might happen if I'm away
from the station for an hour or so. Sometimes there's

something new written on the whiteboard, and sometimes there's just some new gossip waiting to be shared.

"Guess what just happened?" Whispering, Rhonda looked from left to right. "Doan just got a call from his buddy in Hollywood. You know how he leaves his door open all the time? I couldn't help hearing him yelling! It looks like Paragon Productions is a goner for sure. He had a chunk of money invested in the new movie and they were calling to see if he wanted to pony up a little more!"

I couldn't help whispering back, "Did he?"

"Not a chance. He called Buffy to come over and pick him up, then he slammed his door shut. That's all I know."

"Wow. Bad news all around, I guess—not just for the Doans, but really for the whole city. Salem was so excited about this movie. Do you know if they're going to finish making it after all?"

"Oh, they'll have to finish it," she said. "It's just that the whole thing is so far over budget it'll never make a profit. All of the investors will lose money. Our movie reviewer says that so far they've spent almost three hundred million dollars because of all the delays—and that doesn't count what marketing it will cost."

"Did they think it would be a big enough hit to make it worth it?" I wondered.

"They were counting on the star power. People love seeing Darla and Lamont in those love scenes—and they knew the story was strong—witches and time travel and star-crossed lovers."

"That's true. My aunt and her girlfriends never missed any of their movies."

"At least River will get a movie credit for her résumé," Rhonda reported. "She called in and said they shot a few scenes this morning with her in Darla's costume. She said it was creepy—wearing the dress that still smelled of Darla's perfume."

"This morning? She worked until two o'clock this morning on her own show." I was surprised. River had known she'd be working in the daytime for the film and had an agreement that they'd respect the late hours of her regular job. So far they'd never scheduled her before noon. I wondered for a brief second why they hadn't used Paulina Something, the body double Leo had told us about. "She must be exhausted."

"As well as creeped out," Rhonda said. "They were shooting on the set where Darla died."

CHAPTER II

The whiteboard held no instructions for me, but I knew that the assortment of colorful sticky notes on the glass wall separating my office from the newsroom comprising my to-do list would keep me busy for the rest of the day. As usual, being inside my own space—even though all four walls were glass—gave me a feeling of security. As videographer Marty had pointed out: *Even a goldfish is probably happy in a bowl where the other fish can't get at him.*

It was true. Once inside, I locked the door behind me and sat at my desk. I pulled off a pink sticky note from the glass at random. The host for *The Saturday Business Hour* needed a new package of yellow-lined pads. I made out a requisition slip and pulled another sticky. This one was green. Chris Rich, from Christopher's Castle, wanted to confirm his appearance on Ranger Rob's show to tell the little buckaroos about some new Harry Potter games. I texted Rob to confirm the date. One after the other, I unstuck notes from the glass, taking time every so often to squirt a shot of blue window cleaner onto the surface to clean up the gluey streaks. By four o'clock I'd taken care of almost all of them. I was about to reach for another when the only other fish who ever knocks on the wall of my personal fish bowl rapped sharply on the glass with his phone.

Call me, Scott mouthed, then smiled his cheesiest smile.

He knew I couldn't pretend I didn't see him. I sighed, not returning the smile, and hit his number. "What?" I said.

"What's going on with Buffy Doan? She just steamed past me in the corridor like a streak of purple lightning. She practically had smoke coming out of her ears."

"Mrs. Doan doesn't consult with me," I hedged. "Why don't you ask Howie?"

"I did. He says he doesn't know. He says she gets upset easily and not to worry about it."

"Take Howie's advice," I suggested. "Is that all you want? I'm busy."

"Now that you mention it, I heard that your friend River had my blue envelope on her show. I heard that she told its fortune, or something like that. That true?"

"Yep. It's true. Since when is it *your* blue envelope?"

"Since I paid a barmaid twenty bucks for it," he growled. "I tried to call River, but she didn't answer my call."

"She works until two in the morning, dork," I said. "Of course she didn't answer your call." I didn't mention her early morning filming in Darla's dress. "I thought you were all through with the envelope anyway."

"I thought I was too, but it looks like there's still some mileage in it. If you talk to River, will you ask her if she still has it? I guess I can go for another twenty if I have to."

She doesn't have it. I do.

"Okay," I agreed. "What will you do with it if you get it back?"

"I'm not exactly sure it'll work, but I have a plan that might get me another seat at the nightly news desk." The cheesy smile again.

"Are you going to tell me about it?"

"Of course not."

"Then I guess I can get back to work now. Bye." I put down the phone on my desk, pulled another sticky note, and spun my chair around so that I faced the door on the opposite side of the cube, pretending to be intent on the small pink square in my hand. *"Colin's Birthday,"* it read. The date on it was one day away. Colin is Pete's nephew, his sister Marie and her husband Donnie's oldest boy. (Yes, Pete's sister and brother-in-law are Donnie and Marie.) Too late for Amazon to bail me out. If I left work right now, I'd have just about enough time to buy and wrap a gift and get home by five. Then Pete and I could drop it off at his sister's place in plenty of time for the boy's birthday.

I remembered the new Harry Potter game that was going to be introduced on Ranger Rob's show. I called Rhonda. "I'm going to leave early. I have to stop by Christopher's Castle about a game they're going to feature on the morning kiddie show." *True enough.*

Chris Rich is always glad to see me—not just because I'm a good customer, but mostly because he's a genius at figuring out how to get free airtime on the station. For instance, he'll make a guest appearance on Rob's show and talk about Harry Potter—showing the kids how to play the new game and giving one or two games away, and it won't cost him a penny. He sells costumes and magic tricks too, so he's sort of a professional guest.

The chimes over the door played "It's Magic" when I entered. "Hi, Chris," I said. "I'm here for one of those Harry Potter games for Pete's nephew's birthday."

"Good choice, Lee. They're selling like Hedwigs."

"Hedwigs?"

Chris shook his head in mock dismay at my ignorance. "Hedwig is Harry's pet snowy owl. I have maybe the world's best collection of Hedwig-themed toys, books, and games. If I remember correctly, Pete has two nephews. Surely he doesn't gift one boy and ignore the other? I'd suggest a modest owl-themed surprise for the younger boy. Kevin, is it?"

"What an amazing memory you have," I said. "And yes, an owl would be good."

"A Hedwig key chain, then," he said. "Gift wrap for both?"

"Thank you, yes. How has all this news about the movie impacted your business? I noticed your *Night Magic* window. It looks beautiful. The Witch House model kit is amazing."

"I ordered those for this shop exclusively. We already had the *Hocus Pocus* house and *The House of the Seven Gables* models anyway. Darla Diamond and Lamont Faraday each bought one. Not together, of course. I understand they barely spoke to each other off-screen." He boxed and deftly wrapped the two gifts in different gift-wrap papers and handed me two tags. "Here you go."

While I wrote names on the tags and signed them from Uncle Pete and Aunt Lee, Chris grew silent for a moment, then asked an odd question. "Has Pete figured out how they got the poison into the chocolates?"

"I don't know. Why?"

"Strange thing. Before that thing happened to Darla, maybe about a week before, a guy came in here looking at jewelry making supplies." He pointed to a section of the store devoted to gems and chains and findings. "He said he needed a glue injector. Something to inject a thick substance without making a big hole."

"Is there such a thing?" I asked.

"Sure, several of them. They're not expensive. He paid cash." Chris handed me my purchases. "When I heard about Darla's death it occurred to me that a glue injector like that could put something into a piece of candy. It's probably a crazy idea, but do you think maybe you should tell Pete about it?"

I thanked him for the Harry Potter gifts and told him that I would definitely tell Pete about the glue injector. I agreed that it was probably a crazy idea, but I've seen crazier ideas than that one turn out to be spot-on.

CHAPTER 12

I'd just parked in my usual space and locked the Jeep when Pete's cruiser pulled in. He backs into his space so that if he gets called away, he can just zoom out of the yard. He joined me on the back steps.

"What do you think? Dinner in or out?" he asked.

"It's such a nice night," I said. "We could take a ride down to the Willows. Maybe grab some chop suey sandwiches and walk on the beach." The Salem Willows Park is a favorite destination for Salem people of all ages. It's not a big tourist attraction—nothing fancy about it—but there's an arcade with all the old-fashioned games—pinball machines and Pac-Man. The iconic chop suey sandwiches have been a favorite treat for generations of Salemites. The ownership of Lowe's Chinese Restaurant on the boardwalk has changed, but the sandwiches remain the same—the original chop suey recipe served on a soft white hamburger bun, wrapped in waxed paper with a tiny fork.

"Sounds good," he said. "Let's change and get there in time for the sunset."

A walk on the beach would be a good time to tell my husband about Chris Rich's crazy glue injector idea.

It didn't take us long to change from work clothes to walk-on-the-beach duds. Cargo shorts and Boston Red Sox T-shirt for Pete, Lulu-B shorts and Tampa Bay Rays T-shirt for me. (Pete and I agree on the Celtics, the Patriots, and the Bruins, but baseball—not so much.) I tossed my hobo bag over my shoulder, said "So long" to O'Ryan, who was curled up on a red cushion on the wooden bench in the sunroom, and we were on our way.

We chose a bench facing the ocean under one of the famous white oak willow trees and enjoyed our sandwiches in companionable silence, watching the boats pass by, luminous in the sunset's pinkish-orange glow. Pete put our paper cups, forks, and waxed paper into a nearby recycling bin and we started our walk along the shoreline. We paused, watching a row of plovers scooting along at the edge of the water.

We talked a little bit about my decision to do the Witch House walking tour. "It could be quite successful, I think."

"I agree," he said, "I'm behind whatever choice you make."

"I know you are. Thanks for saying so. Meanwhile, there's the documentary too. Even if Darla's gone, the movie will undoubtedly get finished and released somehow. I'm concentrating on the moviemaking, Scott is covering all the hard news parts about her death," I explained. "But I can't ignore it. If the documentary is going to be honest, I need to talk to Lamont Faraday about his feelings toward her. I need to dig into what other people in the cast think about all this. You know I want to meet Doug Sawyer because he's known Darla for so many years. And what about some of the other people around Darla? What about the wardrobe people who had to repair that dress she ruined? What about Paulina, the original body double? What about whoever it is who was responsible for keeping Darla supplied with chocolates?"

"One thing at a time, babe," Pete said. "When you get a little deeper into the documentary, you'll know how much time you'll have for other projects. Hey, the Witch House has been there for a few hundred years. It'll still be there for walking tours if and when you get around to doing them."

"You make so much sense," I told him. "What would I do without you?"

"You'll never be without me."

"I know it. One more thing, though. When I was at Christopher's Castle, Chris told me something that's kind of crazy, but I promised I'd mention it to you."

"Sure. What's it about?" We'd nearly reached the parking lot where we'd left Pete's car.

"It's about Darla's chocolates, and the way the killer got the poison into the center," I said.

"He—or she—must have used a syringe of some kind," Pete said.

"Well, Chris found something in his hobby department—in the jewelry section, to be exact—that he believes could have been used to do such a thing."

"Really? What would that be?"

"A glue injector. A customer a while back said he needed an instrument to inject some thick glue into a tight space. It would need to have a really skinny little needle," I explained. "Chris showed one to me. It makes sense in a crazy sort of way."

"Interesting," Pete said. "I never would have thought of that. I'll visit Chris's store tomorrow."

"Not so crazy?"

"A little bit crazy, maybe, but murder is a crazy business most of the time."

We headed out of the park and toward home. It was a pretty time of day. The streetlamps had started to come on, and the old streets looked mellow, any shabbiness or Halloween litter obscured by the kindly fading light. We turned onto Derby Street, where costumed buskers posed with visitors for selfies and hoped for tips. Neon signs already glowed from storefronts— quite a few of them spelling out the names of various beers and cocktails. "No wonder Lamont decided to do his day drinking around here," I said.

"I know," Pete agreed. "When you drive down this street practically every day, you don't notice how many gin joints there are. It must look like one-stop shopping to him."

We reached Winter Street and Pete had just backed the cruiser into his usual space when our next-door neighbor Michael Martell's Lincoln moved smoothly into his own space on the opposite side of our wide, shared yard. Michael's half looks bigger than ours because we have a tall, slim maple tree on our side. Pete says that someday it'll be a perfect tree for climbing, and that when we have kids he's going to build a tree house in it for them.

"Hi Pete. Hi Lee," Michael called. "Beautiful day, isn't it?"

We agreed that it was indeed. I could tell that Michael had just returned from teaching one of his creative writing classes at the Tabitha Trumbull Academy. He wore dark slacks, a tweed jacket with leather elbow patches, a white ascot tie, and polished cordovan ankle boots. He teaches under the same pseudonym he uses on his Antique Alley mystery books—Fenton Bishop. He's always Professor Bishop to his students, even though most of them know his real name. When he's not teaching, his appearance is quite different. He favors khaki slacks, expensive sneakers, shirts with rolled-up sleeves, always open at the throat, exposing a well-muscled chest and a couple of gold chain necklaces. Sometimes, on weekends, he sports an attractive stubble of beard.

We stopped to chat for a moment, midyard, comparing notes on our respective cats—O'Ryan and Frankie. Frankie, Michael's white cat, had for several years been an occasional visitor at Aunt Ibby's house. But when Michael moved into his place, Frankie had shown up one day, moved in with him, and apparently intended to stay.

Pete unlocked the door to our sunroom and we went inside, accepting O'Ryan's welcoming purrs and enthusiastic ankle rubs, returning the favor with head pats and ear scratches and loving words.

"You can always tell when Michael's just come from school," Pete said.

"I know. I was just thinking that—a change of clothes can almost create a different person."

"It can. I get a much different reaction from people when I'm in police uniform. I guess all cops do."

"But you're still you. Michael is still Michael," I reasoned.

"Of course."

"I wonder how it works for actors," I said. "They have to change into someone else for every job."

"If you get a chance to interview Faraday," Pete suggested, "you could ask him about that."

"When you interviewed him, you said he seemed genuinely upset about Darla's death," I recalled. "I guess you don't think he's a suspect, right?"

"It's not my job to decide who is or isn't an actual suspect," he told me for the millionth time. "I'm just a fact-gatherer."

"He wasn't very far away from the Witch House set. The trailer dressing rooms were in the same fenced area," I said. "He was in her trailer. On her bed. They didn't like each other. It looks bad for him."

"It's a fact that he was in her trailer and on her bed. It's also a fact that he had a handwritten invitation from her, inviting him to meet her there. We don't know what their relationship was at that moment," he pointed out. "There are over a hundred people at one time or another behind that fenced area, and quite a few of them admit to not liking Darla Diamond."

"Everyone's a suspect."

"Just about."

"Not everybody who worked on the picture stays behind the fence," I reminded him. "One of the wardrobe ladies goes to Rhonda's hairdresser, Jenna. That's how I found out about the ripped dress. Jenna told me about it."

"That widens the suspect pool. I'm not surprised."

"It must be a terrible feeling—knowing that so many people don't like you." In that moment, I felt sorry for beautiful, famous Darla.

"She had a lot of fan mail from people who love her movies—boxes of it," Pete said. "She surely felt loved by the fans."

"It's what we were talking about earlier," I realized. "I mean how a change of clothes or attitude or even location can create a different person. She must have been a regular chameleon—changing color with every movie."

"I suppose that's an occupational hazard of the acting profession."

"I don't think on-camera, WICH-TV Lee is much different from eating-chop-suey-sandwich-at-the-Willows Lee, do you?" I wondered. "I hope not."

"Not much different." He reached over and ruffled my hair. "I love both of you."

CHAPTER 13

The very next morning, when I got a glimpse of Rhonda's whiteboard, I remembered my conversation with Pete about how some people change attitudes with a change of clothes or location. Bruce Doan had thought of another job assignment for me. This one looked like it might be fun—even if it came with a change of attitude.

Home for retired show-business animals.

"No kidding? Where is it?" I asked Rhonda.

"Not too far. A guy over in Topsfield started it. He bought an old farm and started a petting zoo, and he has a bunch of baby goats you can take pictures of, and he's made a space especially for retired show animals. No lions or gorillas, but he has some showbiz chimpanzees and trained monkeys, a llama, and even dogs and cats who've worked on TV and movies and commercials, besides some team mascot animals who have outlived their usefulness. Doan says it looks like it's going to be quite an attraction. None of the wild ani-

mals can be released—too imprinted by human associ-
ation—and he's found new homes for most of the do-
mestic animals. But their show business jobs are over
and you can't very well keep an out-of-work llama or
bear or emu in your house, you know? This guy didn't
like the idea of putting these older animals down, so he
bought this big old farm for them. They're all safely
fenced or caged, but he's made the habitat as friendly
as he can. And guess who one of his star attractions is?
Your old friend Barney the Bear!"

"Barney the Bear *and* baby goats? Who could resist?" I took a step toward Doan's office. "Shall I go in
now?"

"Yep. Go right on in. Doan thinks it will be a refreshing break from all the movie blah-blah-blah that's
been going on lately, along with the usual Halloween
craziness."

"I guess he's still not too happy about the financial
prospects of *Night Magic*."

"Buffy must have calmed him down. He seems to be
his old, normal self today."

"Whatever that means," I whispered, and tapped on
the partially open door.

"Come in, Ms. Barrett," he called. "How is our documentary coming along?"

"Well—er—I'm having some problems contacting
some of the people I want to interview, but we're gathering really good footage of the relevant areas around
the city. I'm sure when it all comes together the audience will enjoy watching." I attempted to change the
subject. "Rhonda says there's a new animal attraction
in the area."

"Yes indeed. The Family Farm looks to be a winner. I think it might make a cute, onetime feature for you and Old Jim to cover, and maybe you can arrange for some of the animals to appear on the morning kiddie show. Rhonda has all the contact information."

"That sounds good. I'll get right on it."

"Back to the documentary. I may be able to open some doors for you there." Big smile. "It turns out that perhaps *Night Magic* is in a better financial position than we'd thought it might be—after all the—um—unpleasantness about Darla."

"Oh?"

"Yes. My Hollywood contact has some good news. It appeared that the entire Paragon Productions enterprise was in danger of collapsing after investing so much capital in one movie—but enough of us minor stockholders have come up with sufficient funds to complete the movie—and even better—to assure its box office success."

"That's wonderful news," I said.

That meant he'd invested more money in the film. I *hoped* it was wonderful news. "I've been trying to get an interview with Lamont Faraday," I said. "And maybe Doug Sawyer too, and I'll get with Rhonda today about scheduling the Family Farm visit." It was good news all around. Maybe Bruce Doan's investment could unlock the Paragon Production gates to WICH-TV. All of Salem was interested in what was going on behind the chain-link fence—and cute animal stories are always a hit with WICH-TV viewers.

I took the long ramp to my see-through cubicle and hastily slapped two new sticky notes onto the glass wall.

"Prepare interview questions for Faraday and Sawyer" was the optimistic message on a pink square, and *"Schedule Family Farm visit"* was on a green one. I leaned back in my chair, feeling comfortable about the way things were moving along—marriage-wise, certainly, and now career-wise as well. The warm feeling of well-being didn't last long. I became aware of a lot of sudden activity in the newsroom on the other side of the glass.

I watched as Scott bounded across the room and slid into his chair in an almost cartoonish move. His frown told me this was no cartoon. I tapped on the window with my phone. *What's up?"* I mouthed, and held up the phone. *Call me.*

Still frowning, he pulled his own phone from his pocket and mine buzzed. "Trouble over at Gallows Hill." He stood and moved away from the window. "An explosion of some kind. I'm on my way."

I saw Phil Archer, the daytime news chief, take his place at the central news desk. In one motion I put down my phone and turned on the TV monitor. The breaking news graphic banner swirled onto the screen.

"Good afternoon, viewers," Phil said. "There has been an explosion in one of the kitchens on the movie set at Gallows Hill Park, where much of the anticipated film, *Night Magic,* is being filmed. Thankfully, no one was injured, but there is significant damage to the facility. Paragon Productions, the Hollywood-based studio producing the Salem Witch–themed production, has been plagued with accidents and misfortune throughout the filming of the movie. This appears to be another such incident. Several fire department units have responded to the outbreak of flames. We anticipate bringing you live coverage of this misfortune momentarily."

Phil began to read from a list of the events that had befallen the production so far. The California film crew had experienced a fire on the set of the 1692 courtroom, an overturned truckload of antique furniture was damaged beyond repair, a flooded soundstage, an outbreak of food poisoning attributed to one of the studio's food trucks, among other lesser, but time-consuming happenings, and so far the Salem-based staff—both actors and technical crews—had faced some bad luck, including a power outage, an overhead camera falling and destroyed, brake failures on a truck, and even an escaped pet snake causing panic in a women's dressing room.

Phil introduced a short video, credited to the Salem Fire Department, showing flames erupting from the doorway and window of a small outbuilding. "Unfortunately, this kitchen is the one used during the summer season as the Snack Shack operated by a local Salem charity organization. Paragon has promised to repair or replace the damaged facility. Field reporter Scott Palmer has just arrived at the scene. What's going on over there, Scott?"

Scott appeared, using a hand-held mic like the one I favored. Another man, wearing the denim jumpsuit of a construction worker, his face smoke-blackened, and with one hand swathed in white bandages and holding a red fire extinguisher in the other, stood beside him.

"I'm here with onetime child star Doug Sawyer." Scott extended the mic. "You did your best to put out this fire, and got second degree burns in the process. How are you feeling now?"

"Not bad, thanks, Scott. I guess it started with the gas stove. I was working outdoors, putting a coat of paint on the outside of the Snack Shack, and the explosion almost knocked me over. I knew exactly where the fire extinguisher was, right inside the door, so I grabbed it, tried to knock the flames down."

"You probably saved the building, Doug," Scott told him.

"Actually," Doug Sawyer said, "I wasn't worried about the building. I wanted to save the dog."

"The dog?"

"Toby. Darla's black lab. I take care of him now. He'd gone inside the shack." He smiled. "He's a nosy little guy. It smelled of food in there, so he had to investigate. I got him out. Want to see him?" He put the fire extinguisher on the ground and gave a low whistle. A silky black lab ran to his side. He bent and petted the dog with his free hand, holding him close. The lab licked the man's smoke-grimed face.

Scott nodded approval. "Good job. But how did an actor like you happen to be working as a painter?"

"Oh, I'm still acting. I'm in the new movie—*Night Magic*." The man wiped his forehead with the bandaged hand, leaving behind a patch of pale skin. "I have a contract with Paragon. I do what I can to support the company in every way I can. They've always been good to me."

"I'm sure they appreciate your loyalty and work ethic," Scott said. "Thanks for talking with us. Back to you, Phil."

My respect for my childhood idol increased. If I thought Bruce Doan's many hats theory was a bit much, a company that expected an experienced actor to do extra duty painting scenery had the WICH-TV system beat by a mile. I liked the fact that he'd risked his own safety to save Darla's dog too.

I turned down the sound on the monitor and returned my attention to the home-for-retired-animals feature I'd agreed to produce. Barney the Bear was lucky to be at the Family Farm in Topsfield. Paragon would likely have had poor old Barney hitched up to one of those old-fashioned horse mills, where the animal goes around and around in an endless circle to generate electricity.

I thought about Doug Sawyer's loyalty and work ethic, realizing that I too could do more than one thing at a time. There was room for more than one field reporter here. With one visit, Old Jim and I could produce at least two interesting reports about the Family Farm—maybe even three. I wrote out three sticky notes, all in hot pink: *"Family Farm overview," "Family Farm retired animals,"* and, finally, *"Family Farm—baby goats."* Each one of those topics would easily provide an excellent segment for *Ranger Rob's Rodeo* as well.

"Doug Sawyer," I said to the wall, "you are an inspiration." I was more determined than ever to get an interview with the child star/actor/construction worker/dog lover. That would provide material for yet another field report. I posted a green sticky: *"Interview Sawyer,"* and pulled the business card Pete had given me from my wallet. "I don't need to wait for Doan and Buffy to set up an appointment. There's no time like the present," I quoted to the wall, put on my green WICH-TV jacket, put the press card on the lanyard around my neck, and headed for the door.

CHAPTER 14

Meeting my childhood crush face-to-face turned out to be far easier than I'd ever imagined it could be. I parked in the same dollar store parking lot I'd used before, with a vow to go inside and buy something this time for sure, and began the uphill climb to Gallows Hill Park. I was sure that if I showed up here today with the mobile unit, or even Old Jim toting his shoulder-mounted camera, I wouldn't get within a mile of the place. But on foot, with only my phone camera, I believed I had a chance.

Before I'd even reached the entrance to the fenced area, I saw the bright white bandaged arm on the uniformed security guard. It made perfect sense to me that because Sawyer was at the moment unable to perform any of his usual duties, Paragon would justify his pay by utilizing him in a job he could do one-armed.

I approached the gate. In the distance I could see a small building marked "soundstage." They'd already removed the crime scene tape that had been festooned around it when Scott did his report. River was right about the gatekeeper. He was still cute. Smoke-free, his face still had a youthful, smooth, unlined complexion. I'd thought of two ways to begin a conversation if I was ever lucky enough to meet him. Now was the time to use both of them.

With the card Pete had given me in my hand, I stepped up to where he stood behind the barred gate and introduced myself. "You met my husband, Detective Pete Mondello, recently," I told him, displaying the card. "I hope you have a moment to talk to me about Barney. I'll be doing a special broadcast about him and the other retired animals for WICH-TV." I lifted the press card to his eye level. His answering broad smile and the instant sparkle in those deep blue eyes told me I'd chosen the right topic.

"Sorry I can't let you inside the gate," he said, "but sure, I can talk to you about Barney. Have you seen him yet? Is he okay over there? I haven't had time off to go over to visit him." He held up the injured hand. "I guess you know about this."

"Yes. I'm sorry about that. I haven't met Barney yet, but I will soon. Is your hand healing well?"

"Doc says it'll be good as new. What would you like to know about my bear?"

I pulled the camera from my hobo bag and affixed the collapsible selfie stick. "Mind if I record this?"

The slightest frown crossed his face, then the smile returned. "Sure. Why not?"

I moved closer to the gate, focusing the camera on the two of us. "Lee Barrett here, at the gate of Gallows Hill Park. My guest is Doug Sawyer. You may remember him as the star of a children's show called *Adventures with Barney the Bear.* I have to say right off, Doug, that I was a big fan of the show. I never missed an episode. I'm a big Barney fan too. I read that he learned to respond to your hand signals when you were filming the show? Did you train him yourself?"

"No. We had a professional trainer, but I learned how to do it from him. I'm trying now to train Darla's dog, Toby, with the hand signals."

"We have a very smart dog on our morning kid's show who does some pretty amazing tricks. We call him Paco the Wonder Dog," I told him. "Maybe someday you could bring Toby over to meet him."

"Sounds like fun," he said. "We'd enjoy that."

"Your old friend Barney is living over in Topsfield now at the Family Farm, along with quite a few other retired show business animals," I said. "That must please you."

"It was a lucky break for Barney and me both when they decided to shoot the rest of *Night Magic* here in Salem. There was so much bad stuff happening on the California set that none of us wanted to stay there. A lot of the original cast and some of the work crew got to make the trip. Darla and Lamont, of course, along with their stand-ins and body doubles, as well as the people who played the same characters in both old Salem and present-day Salem. That's how I got to come. At the same time things were going bad on the *Night Magic* set, things were breaking down at the facility where they kept Barney and some other TV and movie animals. Every once in a while they'd need a growling bear for a shot, so Barney was still working."

He scowled. "PETA got it closed down because the animals weren't getting proper care at exactly the same time the Family Farm opened up. Paragon shipped all of us East at once—probably saying *good riddance* while they waved goodbye. I wish there was a part in the new movie for Barney, though."

I laughed. "I'm sure he would have been great in it. Can you tell us about the character *you* play in *Night Magic*?"

"It's a nice little part." He gave a modest lift of one shoulder. "You know the story takes place in two different centuries—the seventeenth and the twenty-first—and most of the main characters appear in both centuries. I was lucky enough to play one of the witch-craft judges in the 1692 segment. We shot most of the interior scenes of the trials back in California—before that whole set burned down. I think we might need to reshoot some of those in the new Witch House court-room set here. Being in that old courtroom—even though it was just a reproduction of the place—felt real. I know that the extras who played a crowd of condemned witches were absolutely creeped out. I'm a trial lawyer in the current Salem story." He stood a little straighter and smiled. "No need to build a set here. We use the real courthouse."

A nice little part, *and they still have you painting a building and taking care of costume cleaning at the same time?*

I didn't ask the obvious question. Instead, I passed on a bit of news. "I've heard that Paragon's financial situation may have changed for the better."

The blue eyes widened. "No kidding? That's hard to

believe, with all the bad luck they've been having. Where'd you hear that?"

I had no intention of mentioning my boss. "Oh, you hear a lot of rumors around a TV station. I hope, though, that it's true, and that *Night Magic* will be a box office success after all."

"Thanks for stopping by, Lee." He glanced over his shoulder toward a man approaching from behind him. "I guess I'd better get back to business. I've volunteered to make sure that all of the costumes that need it get to the dry cleaner." A shy smile. "I'm kind of a stickler for cleanliness." His good hand shook slightly as he turned away from me, fiddling with the gate latch. I took the hint, whispered "Thanks," stuffed my phone back into my bag, and scurried away. I had no idea what his problem might be, but I sure didn't want to be part of it.

There are plenty of trees on Gallows Hill and I ducked behind one of them, daring a glance back toward the gate. The man stood beside Doug. They appeared to be laughing together. I squinted, studying the man's profile. No doubt about that classic nose and brow. It was Lamont Faraday.

I made my way back to the dollar store lot, remembering this time to go inside and make a token purchase. I returned to my car several minutes later with a good-sized bag full of useful items at prices I couldn't resist. Everyone can use sponges and pot holders and plastic measuring cups. I even found a couple of hardcover mystery books by authors whose names I knew. And I bought a yellow-feathered cat toy for O'Ryan.

On the drive back to the station I thought about

Doug. And Barney. The actor hadn't been allowed enough time to visit his pet/friend/companion/costar just a few miles away from Salem. Something seemed so wrong behind the chain-link fence at Gallows Hill—on so many levels. Doug had clearly been close with Darla Diamond for many years. She'd made sure he stayed working for Paragon ever since they were both young actors—Doug as a teenager on television and Darla beginning as a starlet in her midtwenties in the movies. It appeared that he was on good terms with Lamont Faraday too. So how was it that his time was not his own, and that some of the jobs he held didn't seem to fit his significant acting background?

There wasn't time in my own working day to ponder other people's problems. Next on my schedule was a visit to Topsfield, the Family Farm, Barney the Bear, and those cute baby goats. I texted Old Jim about it and asked him to meet me in the parking lot with the VW. He answered right away with a smiley emoji.

I called Pete to tell him I was heading for Topsfield with Jim and didn't know what time I'd be home. "They say traffic is tied up all over Salem," I told him. "Rhonda says they're doing outdoor scenes everywhere, from Chestnut Street to the courthouse, and there are tour buses on every corner."

"Okay. I'll see you when I see you. By the way, I found a guy online who's done the research on that Dover, Delaware, chocolate poisoning case. He's sending me the information—and guess what? They do a walking tour there that tells all about it. They call it 'the most romantic murder of the century.'"

"A romantic murder?"

"Yep. The suspect was a rejected lover looking for revenge."

"I can hardly wait to hear about it," I said. "Do you think it's possible that a woman might be involved in Darla's death?"

"Anything is possible," he agreed." I can't discard the possibility. Darla was rich and famous and beautiful. Some people—including women—might resent her for that."

"True but sad," I pulled into the WICH-TV parking lot, noting with annoyance that a cute, almost new Mazda Miata was parked in my designated space. There was a vacant space marked "visitor" nearby, so after a little annoyed huffing and puffing, I parked there. Jim stood beside the VW mobile unit, arms folded. I climbed out of the Jeep, closing the door a little harder than necessary.

"What's up with that?" I approached Jim. "Do you know whose car it is?"

"Didn't you notice what color it is?" He grinned.

The Mazda was purple.

"Buffy Doan," I mumbled. The boss's wife had intruded on my space.

"The visitor slots were all full when she arrived." Jim shrugged. "She said she'd just be a minute and she was sure you wouldn't mind."

I minded, but surely not enough to call for a tow truck to haul my boss's wife's car away. "I guess the baby goats and Barney the Bear can wait for us." I joined Jim beside the VW, my arms folded just like his, and waited.

CHAPTER 15

Considerably more than a "minute" had passed when Buffy Doan emerged from the studio door in an excited flutter of ruffled lavender silk. "Oh, there you are, dear Lee." She hurried toward me, arms outstretched. "I had such exciting news I simply had to come over and share it personally with Bruce!" She waved an amethyst ring–bedecked hand toward the parked Mazda. "I'm so sorry about that—but I see that darling Jim has kept you company."

"Yes, he certainly has," I agreed through gritted teeth. "Are you going to tell us your news?"

"I'm going to be in a movie. *The* movie! *Night Magic.*" She did a little skipping step toward her car. "I won't be a star, of course, but I'll be in a scene where Darla goes into the courthouse and stops to speak to me on the courthouse steps. Darla—I mean Paulina—says she'll have her back to the camera, but I'll be facing it—and the audience. Bruce is so proud of me!"

I was sure the offer of a part for Buffy had convinced Doan to invest some more money in the production. "I'm sure he is," I said. "You've met Paulina?"

Now maybe I'll learn Bleached Blond Paulina Something's real name.

"Yes indeed!" Buffy's smile was dazzling. "She's the one who told me about the part. When I met her I almost thought I was seeing a ghost. She looks that much like Darla."

"Where did you happen to meet her?" I walked along beside her toward my parking space.

"At my hairdresser's." Buffy patted her perfectly highlighted waves. "She was a walk-in. Can you believe it? Paulina Fellows simply walked into Chez Jenna for a quick blowout this morning and there I was. She said I'm perfect for the part." Buffy unlocked the Mazda and climbed in. I stepped out of the way as she joyously zoomed out of my space.

Jim, still leaning against the VW's front fender, rolled his eyes. "That's one happy woman," he deadpanned and got into the driver's seat. "Let's get a move on, Lee."

"Paulina Fellows," I repeated. "Never heard of her before. I guess I'll do a walk-in over at Chez Jenna myself." I backed my Jeep out of the visitor's space, put it back beside the seawall where it belonged, and joined Jim in the aging mobile unit. "Let's go talk to the animals," I said.

"It shouldn't take but twenty minutes or so," Jim advised. "We'll just go from here over to Summer Street; then it's pretty much a straight shot up to US1 and into Topsfield Center. Rhonda says we can follow the signs to the farm from there."

Jim turned the radio to an oldies station and the ride through Peabody and Danvers was a pleasant one. As Rhonda had promised, when we reached Topsfield the signs for Family Farm were prominent and attractive. One had a bear that looked as if it might be Barney on it, and I asked Jim to slow down so I could grab a picture for Doug.

The farm property was bordered by a long, white-painted, split-rail fence. A plain wood sign with block letters spelled out "Family Farm." It was a lot different from the Salem witchy-inspired Halloween flash and glitter we've become accustomed to—a refreshing change. There was a wide driveway with a gate made from the same rail material as the fence. A man in blue overalls waved to us from the entrance.

"Hey, there," he called as we drew up to the gate. "I'm Gino. Rhonda said you two would be along shortly." He pulled the gate open and pointed, directing us to the left. "Most of the critters are over that way."

We followed his direction, bumping along a dirt road. We heard the animals before we saw any signs of them. A cacophony of chatters, woofs, howls, and what might have been a hoot greeted us as we moved through a cluster of trees and bushes, finally opening onto a field, fenced with chain link. "Looks just like the fence at Gallows Hill," I remarked.

"Except that this one keeps the humans out instead of locking them in," Jim observed, "and look, there are a couple of big cages in there too."

He was right. I looked for a gate in the fence. Surely this wasn't going to be the only view we'd have of the rescued showbiz wildlife. And what about those baby goats? My unspoken questions were answered almost immediately. Another man in blue overalls ran toward us. Jim moved to the edge of the dirt road and parked the VW. Was this the same guy who'd greeted us earlier?

"Hello," he said. This wasn't the same man. "Hey there. I'm Greg. You must be the folks from the TV station. I'll slide the gate open for you so you can park. Then I'll walk with you to meet the gang. Anyone special you've come to see?"

"Barney!" I called, but he'd already moved away, pushing a wide section of fencing aside, easily admitting the VW. I noticed a wooden box with a slot in the top and a sign reading "Donations appreciated." By the time I'd slid from the passenger seat out onto the very green grass, Jim was already on the ground with the camcorder on his shoulder, my stick mic under his arm, falling into step beside our current blue-overalled guide. I stuffed a fairly large donation into the box and hurried to catch up.

The cages we noticed from a distance were really large. Big enough for the animal inhabitants to move about freely. Some even had small trees in them. The guide must have heard my shouted request because I recognized the soft-looking brown fur of my old TV friend, Barney the Bear. We moved closer, and Barney gave a soft "chuff-chuff" sound, just like he used to do when Doug Sawyer talked to him. I liked to think he was speaking to me, but of course that wasn't possible. I wiped a nostalgic stray tear from my eye.

"Wow! Look at that!" Jim pointed. "What's it doing in there with the bear?"

I followed Jim's pointed finger. Sure enough, there was a chimp sharing space with the TV star bear. There was a small sign affixed to the cage that answered my question. "This is Barney the Bear, star of his own television show—*Adventures with Barney the Bear*—a popular children's show in the late 1990s. His companion is Bodie, a trained chimpanzee who once worked with Barney in a short subject movie about smart movie animals. The two became great friends, recognized each other when they met once again here at Family Farm, and are now roommates."

I didn't need to tell Jim to get plenty of footage of the unlikely pals. Doug would be happy to see the furry companion of his youth had such a good friend to share his later years. I hoped that Doug had loyal friends too, now that Darla was gone. I spoke into my mic, telling the viewers about my own youthful admiration for this very bear, along with the story about the chimp. I promised the viewers too that I'd look up the movie Barney and Bodie had starred in together and try to get permission to show a few clips from it.

Our guide, Herbert, who clearly had some acting chops himself, told our audience how most of the cat and dog performers had been rehomed and now lived with their new forever families and that several of the dogs—two German shepherds, a border collie, and a golden retriever—now lived on the property with the founder and his wife and children and roamed the farm at will. Jim and I both laughed at the antics of caged monkeys who seemed to enjoy our applause and mimicked our hand clapping. "I expect you're anxious to see the goats," Herbert said. "Follow me."

By this time a group of people, mostly couples with children, joined us, and some of them recognized me, "Will we be on television too?" one asked.

"Only if you want to," I told them. Everybody wanted to.

Like a pied piper, Herbert led us to a long, grassy area. I extended my mic toward him as we approached a sturdy wire fence almost as tall as I am. "They're such tiny animals. Why such a high fence?"

"Goats are escape artists," Herbert explained as Jim focused the camera on the thoroughly adorable animals. "They can climb fences and crawl through little gaps."

"Pretty smart," I said.

"They are smart," Herbert agreed, "and they pay their own way with goat's milk. We sell it here. All the goats you see here are girls. Once they've been pregnant, they can give milk."

"No boys goats on the farm?" I asked.

"No. Males tend to be aggressive, and they smell kind of bad too." Herbert's smile was wry. "When it's time for a girl goat to breed, we send her for a visit with a boy goat—one from a very good family, of course—and then she comes home to the farm to raise her kid."

"Is it true that goats will eat anything? Like tin cans?"

"Those stories are exaggerated. Our goats eat grass, hay, greens, and a good brand of feed. Would you like to hold one of the babies?"

"Oh, yes, please." He clapped his hands, shooing the goats away from the narrow gate that admitted us to the enclosure; then, once we were inside—with no escapees—he handed me the baby girl goat. I hugged her and she nuzzled my neck. I wondered if the viewers could see the tears that welled up in my eyes. It was a very special moment.

CHAPTER 16

Much too soon, it was back to business for Jim and me—and the business on everybody's mind was still the death of Darla Diamond. I ticked off a few of the current topics on the fingers of one hand. "Scott's chasing Lamont Faraday around Salem's bars, looking for whatever connection he had to the crime. Pete, according to our most recent conversation, is working on the chocolates angle. Paulina Fellows, according to the beauty shop grapevine, is the person responsible for Buffy Doan's sudden movie career, who, in turn, is responsible for a financial boost to the production of *Night Magic* via husband Bruce Doan's monetary assist to Paragon Productions. Child star Doug Sawyer seems to be working around-the-clock trying to keep the failing movie studio afloat because it pays his probably significant salary, in addition to caring for Darla's dog." Also, as Jim—who is not prone to gossip—reminded me, Darla's assemblage of enemies was bicoastal and innumerable. "Should we," I wondered aloud, "pick up on one of these threads, or set out on a tangent of our own?"

"I'm kind of in favor of the chocolates," Jim offered, "but that might be because I'm hungry."

"We kind of skipped lunch, didn't we? Want to drop our morning's filming off for Marty to edit, then stop in at the Friendly Tavern and see if the guys there have come up with anything new?"

We fought the more-than-usual traffic back to the station, parked the VW, and walked across Derby Street and into the restaurant. Bartender Leo and several patrons greeted us by name. We chose two seats together at the end of the bar and each of us ordered a Friendly Burger with a side of fries and coffee. Jim ordered a slice of chocolate cake too.

"How's the TV business going?" Leo wanted to know. "Figured out the Liquid Centered Murder yet?"

"The Liquid Centered Murder? Is that what they're calling it?" I asked.

"Jeez, Lee, don't you watch your own station?" Leo teased. "Scott Palmer named it, I guess. At least that's what he called it on the morning news. Then, after that, he did one of those field reports where he walks around town shoving a mic in everybody's face, trying to get them to talk about the Liquid Centered Murder."

"Did he get any good answers?" Jim wanted to know.

"I liked one from the guy in front of the grocery store," one of the customers suggested. "He said his mother-in-law always pinches a chocolate before she eats it. He thinks maybe she suspects something."

Pascal laughed, then his expression turned sober.

"I'm just waiting for a copycat murder to turn up somewhere."

"I'd never thought about that," I said. "I guess it's possible."

"I'll bet Detective Mondello has thought about it," Leo said. "It wouldn't be too hard to do, I suppose."

"It's been done before," another customer put in. "My wife's got a book about it. It happened a long time ago, though."

I thought of Aunt Ibby's research into the topic, and at the same time about Chris Rich's observation about the jewelry glue injector. Leo was right. It wouldn't be hard to do.

"Now that it's all over the news because Darla was so famous," Jim said, "I wouldn't be too surprised if some nutjob somewhere might try it."

"I'll bet it won't be in Salem," one of the regulars said. "The Candy House has already taken all the liquid-center chocolates out of their showcase."

"What about the ones in the already sealed packages? Like the supermarket kind, with the chocolates all separated with a little map on the top?" someone asked.

"Nah. Liquid centers are expensive. They don't put those in the sampler boxes. Darla sent away to Europe for hers," Jim said.

"Just the same, I think I'll start pinching chocolates like that guy's mother-in-law," Leo decided, and Pascal nodded agreement.

"Yep. Darla should've squeezed before she slurped," the regular said. "Say, have any of you seen the new Darla double? I saw her shopping at Market Basket like a regular person. It was like seeing Darla again. Creepy."

"I guess if somebody is just a stand-in and not a star, they *are* just a regular person. That girl, what's her name? Paulina Fellows?" Pascal glanced around the bar. "She's sharing an Airbnb cottage with one of the sound engineers."

"No kidding. I heard that the man who takes care of her dog gets to move into Darla's fancy trailer as soon as the cops are through with it," another regular customer insisted. "He's one of the actors who came here from California. He has a long-term contract with Paragon."

"Where'd you hear that?" Jim beat me to the question.

"He told me so himself. Nice kid. Used to be a child star years ago. He's staying at the Hawthorne Hotel right now. I met him in the lounge over there."

"Doug Sawyer?" I asked.

"Right. You know him, Ms. Barrett?"

"I've met him," I admitted, and agreed that he was a nice kid.

"I guess it's like they say," Leo opined. "It's all about who you know."

Leo was right, and at that moment I was glad I knew Leo and Pascal and the Friendly Tavern regulars. I was glad I knew my hairdresser, Jenna, too. These friends and acquaintances had offered more information in a few minutes than Pete's officers could dig up in a week.

"I'll bet the Darla stand-in—that Paulina girl—isn't too pleased about Sawyer getting the trailer," Jim said.

"I'm sure the other double, River North, doesn't mind. She has her own place here in Salem."

"Right," Pascal agreed. "River only looks like Darla when they put the blond wig on her. Then she's a dead ringer."

"Dead ringer is right. The dead part, anyway," the guy next to me said. The remark was followed by a smattering of nervous laughter.

"Not funny, Bob," said another. "A lot of people really loved Darla."

"A lot of people didn't like her at all," Bob retorted. "I've met a few of the local carpenters and painters and regular folks like that, and they say she was a bitch on wheels. They had no use for her at all."

"I heard that even the costar, Lamont Faraday, couldn't stand to be in the same room with her when they weren't on camera," another of the regulars observed.

"Boy, some of those love scenes they did didn't look fake to me." The man next to me gave a shake of his hand, fingers spread. "Va-va-voom!"

"Yeah. And how come he was on her bed? That sounds like a pretty friendly visit," another regular offered.

"What does Pete think was going on there, Ms. Barrett?" Leo asked me.

"Come on, Leo," I said. "You know Pete doesn't discuss police stuff with me."

"You're married now. That makes a difference. Not even a little pillow talk?"

I thought about that for a moment. "He told me that

Darla had boxes of fan mail from people who love her movies. She surely felt loved by her fans."

"Yeah well, nobody she worked with around here liked her. Nobody I know had a good word to say about her." Bob sounded cross.

"So no pillow talk, Ms. Barrett?" came the question again.

"Pete doesn't discuss police business and he doesn't gossip," I insisted, "and I don't intend to share any 'pillow talk' with you guys."

I saw Jim smother a laugh. "You won't get any more from Lee than you would from Pete," he said.

"We need to get back to work now. Keep your eyes and ears open," I told the two bartenders. "Every little bit of information helps put the pieces together."

"We'd like to see you getting those late news spots again, Lee," Pascal said. "Scotty does a good job, but you're good too, and besides, you're prettier."

"Thanks," I said, "but like Pete always says, 'I just want the facts.'"

"It isn't that everyone has bad stuff to say about Darla," Leo recalled. "The guy who brings her black lab in here seems to have liked her."

"Doug Sawyer," I said. "The two have been friends ever since they were child actors together."

"He told us she'd done him a lot of favors over the years, and the least he could do was to take care of Toby. Cute dog. He's been teaching it tricks," Leo said.

"Toby is learning to take hand signal commands," Pascal said. "He'll sit and lie down and shake hands and even bark without Doug saying a word. All the man has to do is make motions with his hands."

"When Doug Sawyer was a kid, starring in the *Barney the Bear* program, that was how the bear trainer taught Barney all his tricks—even the fierce growl," I told them.

"I don't think Toby ever growls." Pascal grinned. "That dog's a little sweetheart. He's welcome in here anytime." He dropped his voice. "I heard a rumor that Darla just bought the dog because she thought she looked good with him on a leash. There are tons of pictures of her walking him, petting him, giving him a bubble bath. I even saw one in a magazine where she was in bed with him. I heard that Doug really took care of Toby most of the time."

Jim ignored the rumor about Darla. "Maybe Doug will turn Toby into a professional actor dog." Jim spoke thoughtfully. "I bet he could teach that dog enough so that he could do dog food commercials."

I was sure Jim was right—and I was sure Doug had something like that in mind. We said our goodbyes to the Friendly Tavern crowd and started across Derby Street. The purple Mazda was back on the parking lot—though, thankfully, not in my space. More surprising was the sight of my best friend, River, sans blond wig, long, black braid over one shoulder, in jeans and Salem State University T-shirt, waving to me from the front steps of the building. I checked my watch. It was only 1:45. Much too early for an after-midnight, late-show host to be awake. I knew that from experience. While Jim tapped his code into the studio door keypad, I waved and hurried toward her.

CHAPTER 17

"What's going on?" I gave her a hug. "This is the second time I've seen you in the daytime lately. More movie star stuff?"

"Movie star! That's a laugh. They called me to go over to the Gallows Hill set for about a half-hour shot of the 1692 heroine stripping to her underwear in anticipation of the hero's expected visit. It seems that Paulina Fellows didn't want to take the time to do it. The 1692 hairstyle is a lot different from the modern one, and it takes a while for the stylist to arrange it. I already have the blond wig with the proper Puritan bun in the back."

"So they woke you up instead?"

"Right. And it looks like I'll be getting some of the windup work on the film. Paulina says Paragon has told her that she and Faraday can take a week off before they're needed for anything again. She's finished with work here in Salem, and so is Faraday. Paulina is going up to Vermont to visit her mother for a couple of days; then she said she might come back to Salem. I don't know where Faraday is going."

"Wow. That's interesting. Mr. Doan says there's some more money being put into the movie," I said. "It must be for the final editing, and maybe the publicity campaign."

River smiled. "The extra money is good for me. We're saving for our wedding, you know. I don't mind losing a little sleep. I thought I might as well stop by here and check with Marty to be sure everything is all set to go tonight, so that all I'll have to do is show up." She pushed the door to the lobby open. "Come on in with me. I have something to tell you about your vision. Have you seen it again since we talked?"

"No. The scene in the VW's mirror was the last time. I've seen the actual video several times though, on TV." I followed her across the black-and-white-tiled floor to the metal door that leads to the studio.

"You know I don't claim to be a vision-reader," she said, "but it seems to me they must be something like waking dreams."

"That sounds like a good description," I agreed.

"I have quite a few books about dream images," she said, "and I'd like to tell you about a couple of possibilities I've discovered." We walked together down the center aisle of the long, dark studio toward the *Tarot Time* set. "Marty's going to meet me here in a few minutes." She pressed a button behind the star-flecked backdrop—the same one I'd used for my brief stint as Crystal Moon. We sat together at the wicker table she used for the tarot readings. She reached under the blue-velvet tablecloth and pulled up a thick book with a black cover. "This was one of Ariel's books," she confided. "It comes in handy occasionally." I leaned forward as she opened the book to a page marked with a red ribbon. "Since the first instance of the scene was one of the videos you and Jim made, I started by looking up 'Dream about video camcorder recordings.'"

"There's really a heading for that?" I was surprised.

"Sure. There are headings for almost anything you can think of. According to Ariel's book, it can symbolize that you need to be more objective in your decisions. Look carefully at your actions and reactions to the recorded situation in the dream—or, in your case, in the vision. Pay attention to small details. Make sense?"

"Yes, I think so." I spoke slowly, trying to concentrate on my reactions, other than confusion.

"Next," she turned to another red-ribbon-marked page, "because one of the visions was a still shot of the scene, showing the Gallows Hill movie site, I looked up 'photograph.' Here you go." She ran her finger across the printed words as she spoke. "To see a photograph in your dream tells you that there's a relationship that needs closer attention. You aren't looking deeply enough into a problem. Consider who or what is in the photo. The image might be trying to take you back to a particular moment in time." She looked up, then closed the book. "If it comes back again, try to zoom yourself into the picture. That might give you a close-up look at something important."

"I like that one," I told her. "I think that might be really helpful. I'm sure there's something there. Maybe it's too small to see in the video from where we were behind the gate." As much as I disliked the visions, at that moment I hoped there'd be another one.

As promised, Marty McCarthy arrived. She'd been my late show videographer too. "Glad to see you, Moon," she said. "You and Old Jim have been keeping me busy editing some good stuff. Love the baby goats. I heard you're going to be doing some kind of a Witch House special too. Is that right?"

"If everything falls into place, like sponsorship, it looks like a good possibility," I said. "It'll probably be a onetime thing."

She made a harumph sound. "Sure. One time. Like River, here, wasn't going to have to work daytimes on the stupid movie. Between Doan and those ghouls at Paragon, making a movie starring a dead leading lady—mark my words. Both of you girls are going to be totally exhausted by the time *Night Magic* is finished."

I had no answer. She was probably right. I decided to stick with the baby goats. "I hope I'll get to do another visit to the Family Farm," I said. "There's a lot of good material there. The goats are adorable, of course, and I guess you could tell that Barney the Bear is a favorite of mine. But the monkeys are fascinating, and the dogs and cats who've become house pets are worth a closer look too."

"I like the goats the best," Marty announced.

"Maybe the goat is your spirit animal, Marty." River spoke softly.

Hands on her hips, Marty gave another harumph. "What is that supposed to mean?"

"Goat spirit animals give some people a message

that the sky's the limit. It means you can allow yourself to reach your highest goals," River said. "You can trust your ability to land on your feet and have faith in yourself."

Marty's eyes widened. "No kidding? I like that."

I remembered what Herbert, our guide at the Family Farm, had told us about goats being able to climb fences and fit through tiny gaps.

If somebody was to have such a thing as a spirit animal, a goat would be a handy one.

Jim's voice boomed from the back of the long, dark room, dispelling all thoughts of misty baby goat spirits. "Lee? You in here? Rhonda says there's trouble over at Gallows Hill again. Let's go!"

I grabbed my bag from the top of River's table. "I'm coming!" I yelled, spoke a quick thanks to River, and began a dash up the center aisle. Jim held the door to the parking lot open for me, and together we ran to the VW.

I fastened my seat belt as Jim backed the old mobile unit out onto Derby Street. "Did Rhonda say what's happening over there?" I wanted to know.

"Yeah. Some durn fool ran a food truck into a fire hydrant and squirted water all over the sandwiches. A fight got started and they had to call the cops to break it up."

"Do you think we'll be able to get anywhere near it?" I asked. "Salem's even more of a traffic mess than usual."

"I called an old high school buddy of mine. He inherited his mom's house over on Aborn Street. We can park in his driveway and hoof it the rest of the way." He darted a glance toward my feet. "Not wearing the durn-fool high heels, I see."

Jim's high school buddy turned out to be much more than a source of a parking space. He knew a way to reach an overgrown row of bushes at the back of the park with a clear view of the area where the reconstructed Witch House stood. I grabbed my mic and followed the men. "This is where the swimming pool used to be, back when we were kids. We used to peek through the bushes at the girls," he told us. "Look. There's a police car. I heard the sirens a few minutes ago."

Jim aimed the camcorder through a break in the greenery and I pushed leaves and vines apart to make a peephole for myself. I was just in time to see a uniformed cop carefully conducting a handcuffed, rumpled-looking, Lamont Faraday into the back seat of a cruiser.

"Jim, if I move closer to you, can you get me in the frame so I can do the voice-over?" I whispered.

"Sure can." Pushing leaves out of my mouth and knowing my hair was completely messed up, mic to my lips, I stuck my face into the scratchy hedge. I wasn't about to give Scott Palmer the chance to use *my* footage of this arrest. If anyone was going to be front and center with a news anchor this time, it was going to be me. I lowered my voice. "This is Lee Barrett. I'm speaking to you from the edge of Gallows Hill Park, where police were summoned because of a disturbance within the area of the park being used by the producers of *Night Magic*, the motion picture currently being filmed in Salem. That's Lamont Faraday in handcuffs, being escorted into a Salem Police vehicle. Stay tuned to WICH-TV for updates on this breaking news story."

CHAPTER 18

I didn't hesitate to call Pete. If Lamont Faraday had really been arrested, it was a matter of public record and I could talk about it. Even better, we had pictures of it. All I needed to fill in the blanks was the reason for the arrest. I assumed that it had something to do with a food truck, a fight, and some soggy sandwiches. Jim and I were already on our way out of the Aborn Street backyard, heading back to the VW with the video of the arrest safely recorded and ready to air. As soon as we got to the station, I'd get going on the update.

"Can you tell me what Lamont Faraday was arrested for?" I blurted out, not bothering with the formality of saying hello first.

"A few things," Pete said "So far he's been charged with DUI, driving with a suspended license, destruction of public property, disturbing the peace, and assault. We're still deciding about grand theft auto. The food truck driver doesn't want to press any charges. He says Faraday paid for any damage he did to the truck, and he paid for all the wet sandwiches too."

"I've heard that he was drinking his way down Derby Street," I said. "So it looks like he got drunk, swiped a food truck, drove it into a fire hydrant, then got into a fight with somebody, probably the food truck driver." By then Jim and I had reached the VW and climbed in.

"Pretty good. Did I ever tell you you'd make a good cop?" I could hear the smile in his voice. "You're right. The fight was with the owner of the truck. Seems the guy left it running while he locked up his prep kitchen, Faraday climbed into the driver's seat and headed it straight down the road toward the Witch House set. He would have hit it too, if the hydrant hadn't been in the way."

"Do you think he was aiming at the set?" We started toward Essex Street, Jim phoning ahead to alert Marty about the video he was sending.

"I don't get to speculate on what a suspect is thinking. I'm just trying to put together what he actually did—besides ruining lunch for the movie crew."

"Gotcha. Thanks. I'm still planning to get out of here at five. How about you?" I said. "Jim got a good shot of Lamont getting into the cruiser."

""I'll plan for five then too. How'd you get that close?"

"Trade secret," I said. "Maybe I'll tell you later. Gotta go."

It took longer than we would have liked to get back to the studio of course, but it gave me extra time to jot down some notes covering what I'd say about the scene we'd grabbed. I had little doubt about my chances of having that coveted seat beside a news anchor with this one.

"Why do you think he'd be crazy enough to do such a thing?" I asked Jim. "The movie is already in big trouble."

"Drunks do crazy stuff." He shrugged. "It seems like some people are determined to wreck that movie every which way they can."

"I know, but Lamont Faraday is the star of *Night Magic*. Of all people, he should be the one who wants to see it finished and on the way into the theaters."

"Doesn't make much sense, does it?" We turned onto Summer Street, heading for Derby Street and WICH-TV. Jim pulled in behind Ariel's bench. I had my seat belt unfastened and my door open before we'd lurched to a stop. I hit the pavement in a dead run, barely pausing long enough to punch my code into the keypad. Marty was already waiting for me on the other side of the door.

"I've got a camera set up right now in the *Saturday Business Hour* area." She motioned for me to follow her to the already floodlit alcove. "Are you ready for the first follow-up? We've already shown your tease. Great stuff. Doan is loving it."

"I've got enough for a short take." With a quick pat to my hair, I slid behind the always neat *Saturday Business* guy's desk—surely a better choice of background than my own not-so-organized office—and the red light indicating that we were on the air clicked on. Marty ducked behind the cover of her camera. "Ready? Three. Two. One." She pointed to me and I smiled into the light. "Lee Barrett here," I said, "bringing you the latest exclusive information on the arrest moments ago of motion picture actor Lamont Faraday. According to sources, Faraday has been charged with driving while intoxicated and driving with a suspended license, among other charges pending. When a food truck driver left his vehicle running while he was loading it with lunch items for the cast and crew of *Night Magic,* it's alleged that Faraday got behind the wheel, drove the truck toward the movie set, and crashed into a hydrant, causing water to soak the food onboard the truck. The owner of the food truck and Faraday then exchanged blows. As many of you know who have been following the news regarding the many accidents and misfortunes that have plagued the production of the much-anticipated motion picture, a strange sort of bad luck has followed the cast, crew, and scenery involved with the film ever since the very beginning of the project at Paragon Productions in Hollywood. When the entire organization left California and came to Salem to shoot the necessary local scenes, the bad luck apparently followed them all the way here—culminating in the recent tragic poisoning death of leading lady Darla Diamond." Here Marty inserted a publicity still of the glamorous star.

"Is today's event, in which the runaway food truck seemed be heading for the newly built set—created to look like the place where Salem's long-ago accused witches were tried—part of the continuing run of misfortune that has befallen *Night Magic* since its beginning?"

Even as I spoke the words, looking into Marty's

camera, I felt that perhaps this was no random accident. "Stay tuned to WICH-TV," I advised, "for more updates on this breaking news story."

With a thumbs-up signal, Marty ducked out from under the camera's covering. "Good job as usual, Moon," she said. "Good working with you—and I have a feeling there's more to come on this one. Right?" She didn't wait for an answer. "This story's got everything. News value, of course. Murder of a famous movie star. A string of unexplainable bad luck. And, for frosting on the cake—the perfect Salem Halloween vibe! Witches, for God's sake. Could it be any more perfect?"

While I tried to frame an answer that wouldn't sound as if I was in favor of murder and bad luck, she continued, "And this one is all yours! You deserve all the news show exposure you can get!"

I couldn't disagree with that thought. "Thanks, Marty," I said. "It's great working with you too. It always has been. Ever since I tripped over O'Ryan on my very first day at WICH-TV and you saw to it that he went home with me."

"Yep. We go back a ways. Listen—you'd better get back to your regular job or Doan will be after me for taking up too much of your time. Shoo!" She waved one hand in my direction and wiped away what might have been a sentimental tear with the other.

She was right about my regular job—or jobs, as it had turned out. I opened the metal door at the rear of the studio and took the long ramp toward my own semiprivate fish bowl, where I could sort out the remainder of my working day—and look forward to going home at five o'clock to the true, welcome privacy of home and husband.

Once inside my office, I turned on the monitor. Marty already had my follow-up piece running. A peek through the sticky notes on the glass into the newsroom told me that Scott was watching it too. My voice sounded okay, even confident and professional, I decided. My hair was a mess, with a couple of small leaves caught in the uncombed curls, but the general effect was good enough for the on-the-fly story it actually was.

When the brief update ended, I turned off the monitor and buzzed Rhonda. I couldn't imagine that Bruce Doan could have come up with anything else for me to do today, but around here, one couldn't be sure.

"Nothing new on the board for you," Rhonda reported. "I liked the update about Lamont Faraday. Poor guy just can't stay out of trouble, can he? And what's with the wood nymph hairdo?"

"A temporary look," I promised. "The Faraday thing may be ongoing, though."

"Stay with it," she advised. "Doan is watching all of it."

"I'll be trying to catch up with my real jobs for the rest of the day," I told her. "Uninterrupted, I hope."

"Good luck with that."

I hung up and pulled down a baby-blue sticky note that was stuck near the top of the glass. Maybe it had been there for a while. *See if you can find any Paragon contacts who stayed in California for possible interview,* it said. I'd honestly forgotten that I'd written that one. I'd thought of it before any of the current drama had happened in Salem. It seemed like even a better idea now than it had when I'd first posted it. Did Paragon still have a California phone number? I checked on-line. A number was listed.

CHAPTER 19

An automated voice answered on the second ring. "You have reached the offices of Paragon Productions. All calls are being referred to a temporary location. Please call the following number and leave a message. Your call will be returned in the order in which it is received." The voice then recited a number twice—slowly and distinctly. I recognized the area code. It was a local number. I scribbled the numerals on a green sticky, then tapped them into my phone.

A new automated voice instructed me to leave my name and number and a brief message and promised that my call would be returned in the order in which it was received.

This could take a while.

Moving on, I reached for another sticky. Scott's face appeared, my hand covering one of his ears. Was that a hint of silver showing in his hairline? He gave the usual call-me signal. I couldn't pretend I hadn't seen him. He picked up immediately. "What's up?" I asked, knowing he'd just watched my Lamont Faraday exclusive.

"Did Buck Covington call you yet?" he asked.

"Buck? No. Why?"

"Why else? He wants you on his show tonight to talk about what you saw. How did you get that footage anyway?"

I gave him the same answer I'd given Pete. "Trade secret." Then I winked. "Gotta go. I have a call waiting. Looks like it's Buck. Bye."

The call was indeed an invitation to join Buck at the eleven o'clock nightly news desk. I was delighted to accept. My next call was to Jenna, who—once I explained the dire need for her help—agreed to keep Chez Jenna open for an extra hour. She'd do a quick shampoo and blowout at nine o'clock that evening. If I went straight home at five o'clock and fixed something simple for dinner, I'd have time to talk with Pete about the Lamont Faraday event and get to Jenna's by nine, then back to the TV station by ten to get some prep work done for the news spot.

Prep work. I was still supposed to be working on that Witch House tour idea. Sooner or later Doan would ask me how that was progressing—and so far I had zero progress to show for it. I remembered the media kit Paragon had sent. If I pirated some of the photos of the interior of the place from that material and cribbed a few quotes from some of the books in Aunt Ibby's home library, I'd have something to show him without too much time or effort expended. Not many home libraries are set up by the Dewey decimal system, but Aunt Ibby's is. I knew there was a hefty section of

Salem books on the shelves. If memory served, I'd find the information around 133.4. After dinner, I'd have time to run over to Aunt Ibby's house and grab a book or two before my hair appointment.

Does every married woman with a job have to schedule time for every little thing in her life?

I phoned my aunt to give her a heads-up on the books I'd need and scored an invitation to dinner at her house too. "Could you and Pete possibly stay for dinner this evening?" she said. "A fisherman friend gave me a lovely fresh haddock, so I made my grandmother Russell's haddock chowder yesterday. You remember—it takes me two days to make it, and there's more than I can possibly eat even if O'Ryan helps."

I remembered the chowder very fondly. It wasn't something she made often and it really took two days—sometimes more—to put it all together. Leftovers taste even better every day. I wouldn't miss this for the world, and furthermore, I wouldn't need to fix anything simple for Pete and me. I'd get my necessary research material for the Witch House tour at the same time and I'd keep my hair appointment with Jenna. Perfect multitasking. I happily and thankfully told her we'd be there at around six.

My phone buzzed. Caller ID showed the same local number I'd called earlier. Maybe I was about to learn some more about Paragon Productions. "Hello. Lee Barrett here," I said.

I'd actually expected another automated voice. But the voice that replied was warm, friendly—and definitely human. It was also familiar. I was talking to Doug Sawyer.

"Why, hello, Lee. It's Doug Sawyer. How can I help you?"

Surprised to hear his voice, I tried not to stammer. "I'm working on a documentary about the making of *Night Magic,* Doug. I wonder if any of the Paragon staff remained in California. I'd like to get the perspective from somebody who stayed after everything got destroyed out there. Do you know of anyone I could speak with?"

"There's a caretaker supervising the clearing of the property. Once it's leveled, it'll be up for sale, I suppose. There'll be nothing left except a huge empty lot. Do you want the caretaker's number anyway?"

I hesitated, but only for a moment. "Sure. Why not?" I said, and noted the number as he repeated it twice. The phone call wouldn't take much time, and it might add the human interest touch that Doan claimed to be so fond of. If the caretaker could take some pictures of the empty lot where a powerful studio once dominated acres of land, all the better. "Do you know the caretaker's name?" I asked the onetime child star.

"Roney," he said. "Roney McBiel. He used to be a stuntman before he wrecked his knee when the net that was supposed to break his fall from a giant crane failed. Bummer. He was one of the best."

"Another one of the Paragon unexplainable accidents?" I asked.

"Right. You'll enjoy talking to him."

"Thanks, Doug." I checked the time. Three o'clock in Salem. It would be just about lunchtime in California. I poked in the numbers. Roney McBiel picked up on the second ring.

"Roney here. How can I rock your world?"

A wrecked knee hadn't dented his sense of humor.

"Hello, Mr. McBiel. My name is Lee Barrett from WICH-TV in Salem, Massachusetts. Doug Sawyer gave me your number. I wonder if you could give me a few minutes of your time to talk about the clearing of the Paragon property. I'd like to record your comments, if you don't mind."

"Sure, honey. Call me Roney. Record away. What can I tell ya? The bulldozers and backhoes came and tore her all up. I'm running a big yellow Caterpillar grader back and forth to level her nice and flat so they can sell the whole mess to somebody else."

"How do you feel about that, um—Roney?" I asked.

"Kinda numb, to tell you the truth, sweetheart. Lotta good times here, you know what I mean? Good times—then a whole lotta bad times."

"I understand," I told him, although I knew in my heart that I didn't—couldn't—fully comprehend the extent of the bad times he and so many other people associated with Paragon had been through lately. "You stayed behind when the others came to Salem."

"Yeah. They invited me, you know? They said there'd be some kind of job for me to do over there, but hey, I'm a stuntman, you know? I used to roll cars over. Jump out of burning buildings. Take the punches for the pretty boy movie stars. That's why they gave me a nice, fat contract. If I couldn't do the job I was being paid for, I wasn't about to roll over and be Darla Diamond's lapdog—like poor old Doug had to do. I'm not complaining." I could tell from his voice that he wasn't. "I'm lucky to have a truck driver's license," he said, "and a job knocking things over. Breaking rocks. So I walk with a limp and I live in a one-room efficiency. At least I can face myself in the mirror."

That surprised me at first. But as I paused to think about it—Doug must have chosen to keep his big, fat contracted Paragon paycheck in exchange for doing whatever Paragon wanted him to do—including house painting and dog walking. What did he see in his mirror? That would be something to ponder later. I began recording.

"First, tell me about how you became a stuntman in the first place, Roney," I said. At the same time I looked up "Roney McBiel stuntman" on Wikipedia. The photo that popped up showed a good-looking muscular man— just about what I'd imagine a stuntperson should look like. Following was a list of motion pictures he'd worked in.

"It wasn't anything I set out to do," Roney said. "I played some college football and worked summers for my dad's construction company. I was hoping for a bid from a pro football team. Didn't happen. Right after graduation a talent agent took some pictures of me shirtless, working for Dad, hefting a pile of cement blocks, and Paragon made me one of those offers you can't refuse. It paid way more than my degree in business administration ever was going to earn me."

"You worked in a lot of major pictures, I see."

"Yeah. I did. Worked hard. Played hard. Lived high. I should have paid more attention to that business course. Spent every cent." He didn't sound regretful. "I always had a few side hustles going, though. Knowing all those movie stars came in handy. I got a lot of them to sign stuff for me. You'd be amazed at how much people will pay for something—anything a big star has signed—or even handled." He gave a short chuckle. "Clint Eastwood left an empty Luckies pack in my car once and I got a hundred bucks for it."

"You did a lot of fancy driving in those films. I'm a big fan of car chase movies. I guess I've seen you in a lot of them—even if I didn't know it was you."

"You like fast cars?"

"I was married to Johnny Barrett."

"Oh, wow. One of the great ones. I saw him race at Sonoma." His tone softened. "I should have caught the name. I'm sorry about your loss."

"Thank you. How did you learn to drive the way you did?"

"Messing around with my dad's big rigs. I wrecked a few, but I loved the big engines, the sounds, the speed, the danger, you know?"

"I know," I said, remembering riding with Johnny on a NASCAR practice track—the breathtaking thrill of hairpin turns, the heart-stopping, joyous exhilaration of a split-second two-wheel spin when it lands just right, the life-flashing-before-your-eyes fear when it doesn't.

"I can still roll a car," he said.

He must miss it terribly.

I changed the subject, "You've chosen to break the contract with Paragon and go your own way."

"Yeah. Paragon is still in business, you know, even if the main studio is gone. They'll be doing a lot of on-site pictures—like what they're doing up your way. They've got some scheduled for Georgia, I heard, some for Canada, and maybe even in some other countries. I'm back to working with my dad again. That's where the sweet Cat grader comes from. He calls what I'm doing 'the luxury of integrity.' He says he's proud of me."

"I understand," I said again. Only this time I meant it. Sometimes a person's integrity—that elusive something that makes facing oneself in the mirror possible—is worth a lot more than money. I learned that early from my Aunt Ibby.

"Tell me, Roney, do you think the Paragon bad luck streak is over? At least where you are in California?"

"Glad you asked me that one, Lee," he said. "I think maybe it's over out here. For a while it looked like somebody was trying to put Paragon out of business for good."

I remembered what Jim had said. "One of our video team people said almost the same thing. He thinks somebody is determined to wreck the movie. I guess if a big movie like this goes under it will be hard for Paragon to recover."

I was glad Roney'd started using my name instead of honey *and* sweetheart. I pressed the question. "Even with all the bulldozing and rock breaking, no unforeseen disasters out your way?"

"Since they shipped everybody but me back East to Salem, it's like a black cloud left and went with them. I mean, things are still falling apart over there, what with Darla dying and all."

"Do you miss them? The people you worked with for so many years?" I wondered.

"A few," he mumbled. "Good riddance to most of 'em."

"Want to tell me who you miss? Or don't miss? There's a lot of interest here in Salem about all the movie stars. My husband is a police detective, and of course he's interested because of Darla's dying the way she did."

"No. I don't want to talk about any of them. I don't like to make waves. Hey. Here's one. I liked that bear. Barney. I hated that they kept him in a cage. I used to sit beside the cage and share my lunch with the poor guy." He gave a short laugh. "He liked powdered sugar doughnuts."

"You'll be happy to hear that he has a lovely home now. He has a big enclosure to roam in, he's made friends with some goats, and his roommate is a chimp named Bodie he used to work with. Lots of people come to visit him—old fans like me and little kids too." I was glad I could share good news about Barney. "He's well cared for and looks fine. He's at a place called the Family Farm in Topsfield. They've made a home for retired show business animals. I'm working on a feature about the place. Next time I go there I'll try to smuggle in a powdered sugar doughnut. I'll tell him it's from you."

"Would you do that, Lee? I'm sure he'll remember me."

"I wouldn't be a bit surprised. He's really smart," I assured him.

"I'll bet old Doug was glad to see him again, huh?"

"Actually, he hasn't been there yet. Paragon seems

to be keeping him pretty busy lately." The excuse sounded pretty lame, even to me as I spoke the words.

Roney uttered a muffled expletive. "He sold his soul. First to Darla. Then to Paragon."

I try hard to think before I speak—especially when I'm being recorded or, even worse, when I'm live on the air. It sounded to me as if the stuntman was about to *make waves*. This time the words just slipped out. "His soul? Darla?"

Good thing this is my own recording. I can edit it if this leads to problems.

Roney didn't skip a beat. "Oh yeah. For sure. Doug and I are around the same age. Darla was about ten years older. Maybe more. That woman sure liked young guys."

I managed a noncommittal, "Oh?"

"For sure. The first time I met her she invited me over to her apartment. Not much doubt about what she had in mind."

Another "Oh?"

"She said she could help me in my career. That maybe there'd be a part for me in one of her movies. I turned her down cold."

"You said no."

"I didn't like her at all. Not in the way she was suggesting—or in any other way. I didn't need her help. I already had a good contract with Paragon that I'd earned by myself. Oh, she was beautiful all right." He paused. "But there was something almost evil about her—and I'm not the only one who knew it." Another pause. "But on the other hand, the woman loved animals—treated everyone she worked with like crap but took in stray cats, loved dogs, and she was plain crazy about Barney. Go figure, huh?"

I thought of what Jenna had told me about Darla's mean disposition, and about what some of the tabloids had long reported about her relationship with costar Lamont Faraday, but evil? Wasn't that a bit harsh? Especially in view of the kind-to-animals aspect. I didn't comment but waited for him to continue.

There was a sadness in his tone. "Doug fell for the big come-on, though. And he really fell for her too— but of course when the next young stud turned up from central casting she tossed Doug out of bed but kept the contract going to keep him around. He was like a pet for her, and, like I said, she loved the bear. The only civil conversation I ever had with the woman was when she showed up next to the cage when I was visiting Barney. She brought him some of those juicy candy things she used to eat—even though the vet said they were bad for his teeth. Anyway, she was outraged by the small cages, the awful conditions. You know, I wouldn't be a bit surprised if she was the one who called PETA on them for the way they were treating all those poor critters. Anyway, I called Doug after I heard about her dying like she did. He was devastated. I could tell even over the phone that he was crying. Poor slob."

By this time I realized that the only piece of this recording I'd ever use would be the part about Roney's new job grading the onetime Paragon movie lot, and his obvious joy in what he was doing. I asked him to send me a photo of himself on his grader in the empty space where the studio had once stood, thanked the man for talking with me, and wished him well with his construction career. He promised to send photos and videos of the finished project. Roney's comments about Darla Diamond intrigued me but needed a lot of fact-checking. I'd seen pictures of Darla with various pet dogs over the years, but other than that, this was the first I'd heard about her being a champion of animal rights. I'd strive to be more like Pete—to simply gather the facts and report them as accurately as I could. I'd leave the gossip for the beauty parlors and the super-market tabloids.

CHAPTER 20

I finished off a couple of easy stickies and thought about maybe getting a head start on the traffic so that I'd get home a little after five. I checked with Rhonda and got the okay to leave. I called Pete, told him I was on my way, that we didn't need to worry about cooking dinner, and hurried out to the parking lot, hoping to get away before somebody thought up something else for me to do. As I pulled away from the seawall, I thought about the conversation I'd had with the stuntman. His comments about the *luxury of integrity* stuck with me. At the same time, I thought about my husband's determination to simply gather the facts—to avoid making judgments about others. That required integrity too. I knew I'd give him an extra-big hug when he got home.

Even the extended time I'd given myself to get from Derby to Winter Street wasn't enough to avoid the more and more frequent traffic jam-ups at what seemed like every corner. I'd made it all the up to the statue of Nathaniel Hawthorne when the horns began blowing and everything slowed to a crawl. I rolled down my window when I saw a uniformed cop trying hard to make order out of impossible chaos.

"What's going on up there, Jimmy?" I asked.

"Darned movie people again." Long sigh. "Somebody said they saw Darla Diamond and Doug Sawyer in front of the Hawthorne Hotel up ahead. Shoot. Everybody knows she's dead, but this is Salem, and you know how some folks pretend they can see ghosts. And lately the rest of them are always on the lookout for movie actors—even the ones who aren't big stars."

"It must be Paulina Fellows," I said immediately. "She looks just like Darla."

"Sure, it's her. No ghost, just a stand-in." He waved me into the faster-moving outside lane. "Go ahead, Mrs. Mondello. Drive safe."

Pete's car was already parked behind our house when I got there. Our neighbor's Lincoln was in his regular space too. Does everyone know about Salem shortcuts that I haven't found yet? Glad to be home, even if it was already almost five thirty, I parked the Jeep, grabbed my hobo, and ran for the sunroom door. O'Ryan greeted me with ankle rubs and loud purring, and Pete welcomed me home with one of those long kisses that threatened to delay our dinner date with my aunt.

We were only a little bit late. We walked the short distance and arrived at Aunt Ibby's house at six fifteen. O'Ryan had left ahead of us and we expected that when we reached Aunt Ibby's, he'd greet us with a big cat smile when we got to her door, as he usually did. That cat has a warped sense of humor sometimes.

Haddock chowder with that noble fish fresh from a fishing boat, blended with rich milk, onions, potatoes, and a dash of cayenne, and topped with crunchy bits of fried salt pork and served with old-fashioned Common Crackers is a rich, tasty, wonderful New England meal at any time of year. Dessert was one of my favorites, a simple coffee gelatin with real whipped cream and shortbread cookies.

After dinner conversation turned to talk about the progress of the *Night Magic* movie. I mentioned what the officer had told me about traffic slowing down next to the hotel so people could get a glimpse of Darla's look-alike stand-in, Paulina Fellows.

"I suppose they thought they were seeing a ghost," my aunt observed. "The Fellows woman bears an uncanny resemblance to Darla, doesn't she?"

"She does," I agreed. "She was with Doug Sawyer. Remember him, Aunt Ibby?"

"Of course. The hero in the Barney the Bear show."

"Sawyer has a room at the Hawthorne while the movie company is working in Salem," Pete said.

"Isn't he staying in Darla's trailer so he can take care of her dog, Toby?" I wondered aloud.

"I guess he must have keys to both," Aunt Ibby said. "Betsy says he has a role in the movie. I think Paragon must pay him quite well."

"He's a lucky man to have keys to two places to stay, with rooms so hard to find in Salem in October," I said.

"I know. I have a lovely tenant for the whole month in my full-size Airbnb and I've got painters working on

the bathroom in the small one this week. It should be
ready in a day or so. I'll bet I'll have it rented as soon
as the paint dries."

My New England–thrifty aunt had made two attractive apartments from the large one she'd built for me
when I came home to Massachusetts after Johnny's
death, one with a full kitchen and the other a neat efficiency. Aunt Ibby enjoyed both the income and the
company her varied guests provided—and they, in
turn, enjoyed her gracious home and her delicious
breakfasts.

"I'm sure you will. No problem. By the way, I had
an interesting telephone interview with another onetime Paragon employee," I said. "He's a retired stuntman. Roney McBiel. He resigned from Paragon and
now he's working with a construction company in
California, leveling the lot where Paragon's main studio once stood. He's getting it ready for them to sell."

"That's a man I'd like to talk to," Pete said. "He may
have some information about the so-called accidents
that happened before the movie crew moved to Salem.
Want to share the contact number?"

"Does that mean we're working together on a case?"
I teased.

"Maybe a little bit, Nancy Drew," he admitted.

"I love the idea of crime solving together, you and
me." I pulled my chair closer to his and attempted
some eyelash-batting. "Not Nancy Drew, though. We're
married, so wouldn't we be more like Jonathan and
Jennifer Hart on *Hart to Hart*? Or Pam and Jerry North
on the old *Mr. and Mrs. North* show?"

"One of my favorite married detectives were Nick

and Nora Charles. *The Thin Man*. William Powell and
Myrna Loy starred in it." Aunt Ibby had a faraway look
in her green eyes. "My mother used to watch it."

Pete turned to face my aunt. "What can I do with
her, Ibby?" he asked. "I've always told her she'd make
a good cop, but no! She wants to be a fictional detective."

"I know, Pete. When she was little she wanted to be
Dora the Explorer. She carried a purple backpack and
a stuffed monkey around everywhere." My aunt smiled
at the memory. "She even learned some Spanish
words. Later, she read all of the *Encyclopedia Brown*
books and tried to solve the mystery from the clues before he did."

"I beat him to the solution more than once," I reminded her. "I used to close my eyes and think deeply,
just like he did."

"You still do that sometimes." Pete sounded surprised. "When you're trying to figure something out,
you always close your eyes for a minute. So that's
where that came from. Encyclopedia Brown, huh?"

"I'd almost forgotten," I said. "I loved those stories.
Thanks for the memories." We helped Aunt Ibby clear
the table, and with a covered plastic container full of
chowder and a foil-bagged stack of Common Crackers,
we started for home, once again with O'Ryan walking
with us. Pete unlocked the front door and stood aside
as I entered.

"I'm going to go upstairs and change into sweats
and slippers," Pete said, "to prepare for my evening of
watching mind-numbing TV while my busy wife works
late into the night." He handed me the plastic bowl.

"I'll just put this food away and meet you in the living room for a few minutes of shared mind-numbing before I have to go get my hair done," I promised, heading for the kitchen. The cat dashed ahead of me. I followed, put the chowder into the refrigerator and my handbag and the crackers onto the kitchen table and turned on the overhead lamp.

I saw the flashing lights and swirling colors reflecting from that foil bag immediately. I pulled up a Lucite chair and waited for the vision to take shape. It was the one I'd been waiting for. The one River had told me to move close to—to get myself into the scene if I could.

I did it.

Two women and a man stood between the trailers. The women looked like identical twins, each wearing a long, gray dress, each with blond hair drawn into a severe bun. "Darla and Paulina," I whispered. "In 1692." O'Ryan made a graceful leap onto the tabletop and positioned himself beside the shiny silver package. "Who's the man with them?" I asked aloud. He was tall, had a white beard, and wore a voluminous black robe. The answer came to me immediately. Doug Sawyer had told me, "I was lucky enough to play one of the 1692 witchcraft judges."

River had told me once that the visions could show me happenings in the past, the present, or the future. This one couldn't be showing the present or the future because Darla was now dead. So Doug Sawyer, Darla Diamond, and Pauline Fellows had met together between the two trailers—at some time between the arrival of the three actors in Salem and the day Darla died in the reconstructed Witch House room set in Gallows Hill Park.

More questions than answers.

Did the three duck into that narrow space to avoid being seen by others? Or was it simply a convenient, shady spot for a brief chat—like office acquaintances gathering at the watercooler? Had it looked like a friendly meeting? What were their expressions like?

I knew without asking what River's reaction would be. I'd need to revisit the vision and pay closer attention to faces and body language. Maybe I'd need to figure out how to stay longer at the scene, to see if they left one at a time, or had two paired up and left one of them alone?

The foil-wrapped crackers had become once again just that. A package of foil-wrapped crackers. No swirling colors or flashing lights. O'Ryan had lost interest and wandered away. Pete's voice issued from the living room. "Are you okay, love? Coming to join me?"

I shoved the crackers into an overhead cabinet. "On my way," I called and turned off the light.

CHAPTER 21

Even after eight in the evening the traffic in Salem was still busy. Stop and go. Stop and go. I couldn't very well close my eyes while I was driving of course. I hadn't told Pete about the recent vision, and between stops I couldn't help replaying the sight of the two trailers. Within the pages of supermarket tabloids I'd seen pictures of Darla posing on a huge, canopied bed. Did the bed in the trailer feature a ruffled white canopy above the satin-sheeted mattress? *Of course not. That's silly.* It would be a wasted space. I was sure Pete even had photos of the actual bed. Yet in my imagination, young Encyclopedia Brown saw not only a canopied bed within the trailer confines but, nearby, a smiling Darla relaxed in a swan-shaped tub—perky breasts peeking just above rainbow-colored bubbles. Certainly not an appropriate sight for young Master Brown. Maybe I'd tell River about it later, though.

Jenna was waiting for me, shampoo cape in hand,

when I arrived. "Take a seat, Lee. Let's get started." She ushered me to the pink reclining seat, and in moments her capable hands did their magic with massage and shampoo. By the time we'd reached the blow-drying stage, any tension I'd felt earlier had pretty much disappeared. I closed my eyes, remembering the conversation about Encyclopedia Brown. Pete was right. I did close my eyes like that clever boy detective when I was trying to recall a vision. Like the one I'd seen twice recently—the scene behind the fence at Gallows Hill Park. River had told me that if it happened again, I should try to move closer—to go behind the fence and try to discover just what it was the vision was trying to show me. Now I'd done that. I'd seen Doug and Darla and Paulina together between the trailers. *I still need to figure out what it all means.*

I hadn't talked to anybody except River about what I'd seen. Now I'd seen it twice and I knew there was a message for me in it somewhere besides the fairly vague interpretations from Ariel's dream book—like looking more deeply into a problem or being more objective in my decisions. Could Pete—or anybody—help with this one?

"Penny for your thoughts?" Jenna spoke softly.

I tried to answer her question without divulging too much. "It's about a dream I've had a couple of times lately," I admitted. "It's nothing scary. Just a bit of familiar scenery that we've used in some of my videos for the station. One of your customers was in it. Paulina Fellows. Buffy Doan told me Paulina was a walk-in. What did you think of her?"

"She was mostly pleasant to talk to. She needed a quick root touch up and blowout. One thing she said creeped me out a little, though."

"Oh? What was that?" I looked at myself in the mirror.

"We were talking about Darla. She said how much Darla liked being in Salem because when she was in California she'd had a few death threats and that everything was nice and calm in Salem. Do you want me to use the flat iron to tame some of these curls?"

"Yes, please. Death threats?"

"Yeah. But they stopped as soon as she got here, so she figures it was from some nut out there. Tell me about the dream she was in. Dreams usually mean something," she said. "Is it scenery from around here?"

"It was at the movie set over at Gallows Hill Park. Darla and Pauline and a man dressed like an old-time judge were in it."

"And you can't figure out what it means?"

"Not yet. My friend River North even looked in a dream book under *dream about video camcorder recordings*."

"I love River's show," she said, "and her hot boyfriend who shuffles the card. Is there really a heading for dreams about television cameras?" I heard the smile in her voice.

"Yes, there is. You'd be amazed at the categories in that book—and hers wasn't even the newest edition."

"Truly amazing," she said.

"I guess so. The dream book suggested that I be more objective in my decisions."

"What is that supposed to mean?"

"Beats me," I admitted. "I've been thinking about it, but none of my decisions about peeking through the fence at Gallows Hill Park have been anything except work-related ones. Like, facts about the Witch House rooms they duplicated there for the documentary I'm supposed to be doing about *Night Magic*, along with information on the real Witch House for a tour my boss wants me to do. How objective am I supposed to be? Both of them are just work stuff."

"I have a dictionary on my phone," she said. "Want me to look up *objective*?"

"I should have done that in the first place," I said.

With the dryer in one hand and the phone in the other, Jenna began to read aloud. "'Having to do with a known or perceived object as distinguished from something existing only in the mind of the person thinking about it. Being real, or actual, independent of the mind.'"

"Like Pete, my husband," I said. "The way he gathers the facts about a case without making any judgment. He's explained that to me a million times. He's totally objective about his work. He has to be."

"That's what makes him a good detective," Jenna pointed out. "On the other hand, you must have to use some imagination, some creativity, to make those documentaries you do sometimes so interesting. I loved the one you did about the seaports last year."

"So, if River's dream book is right," I reasoned aloud, "I'll need to step back from that bit of scenery and see only what is actually there—not what I'm thinking about what I'm seeing."

What had I been thinking about when I viewed that scene? I closed my eyes again—just like Encyclopedia

Brown—and willed myself back to the time Jim and I had done the brief stand-up piece outside the chain-link fence. A flood of thoughts inundated my mind.

How does my hair look?

My feet are killing me.

Did I lock the Jeep when I parked it?

"Focus. Focus," I told myself.

"Come on, *vámanos*!" whispered Dora the Explorer. "Let's go! I know that we can do it!"

Focus! I saw the trailers. Big ones. I assumed they belonged to the two stars of *Night Magic*. I recognized the brand name lettered on the end of each trailer. I'd seen similar ones when Johnny and I had traveled together on the NASCAR circuit. Top-of-the-line. Gear-head me visualized the massive Volvo D13 Powertrain with a smooth Allison B500 transmission lurking beneath that gorgeous exterior.

I saw chairs and tables beneath a striped awning. A dining area. Not a particularly objective conclusion. I saw the structure I'd assumed was the reconstructed Witch House movie set. I'd watched the uniformed man approach and then I'd run away. I opened my eyes.

"Anything?" Jenna almost whispered.

"Maybe," I said. Jenna spun me around and handed me a mirror so I could see the back of my hair. I pretended to look and handed the mirror back to her. I'd had quite enough reflective surfaces for now. "It looks fine. Thanks for fitting me in, Jenna." I paid, tipped her heavily, and started for the station and my long-over-due spot beside the night anchor.

With some luck I arrived in the WICH-TV parking

lot with some time to spare. I patted my newly arranged curls, buttoned the bottom two buttons of my green company-issued jacket, wiggled my toes in my flat shoes, glad that the news desk shot was always from the waist up and the dreaded high heels were not required. I pulled into my designated parking space beside the seawall, and climbed out of the Jeep. I locked the door carefully and started across the dimly lit lot. There were only a few vehicles there at this hour. Both mobile units, the aged Ford I recognized as Marty's, River's little orange Kia, and Buck's Lexus. As I passed the seawall, hearing the distant wail of the whistle buoy offshore, I couldn't help recalling the morning when I'd leaned across that wall and found the body of the witch, Ariel.

I had a few index cards in my handbag with notes about how Jim and I had happened to be on hand to film Lamont Faraday's fall from grace, along with some background observations about the ongoing bad luck Paragon Productions had endured—a streak that showed no sign of ending. I felt quite confident about the upcoming interview.

The sound of a vehicle behind me was startling. I recognized the SPD cruiser. The officer in the driver's seat rolled down his window.

"Is anything wrong, Officer?" I asked.

"Not at all, Mrs. Mondello. Pete asked us to take a ride by, knowing you'd be here so late by yourself—what with all the craziness going on in Salem and it's not even Halloween yet. I'll just hang here until you get inside, if that's okay."

Pete's worried about me. I don't mind that a bit.

"Thank you," I said. "I appreciate it." I tapped the code into the keypad and stepped into the cool darkness of the studio. The lights were on in the set midway down the middle aisle. River's area. I checked my watch. I'd like to stop for a quick visit—to tell her about my close-up view between the trailers—but there wasn't time just then. I crossed to the metal door and climbed the stairs to the second floor and the long ramp to the newsroom. There was no lack of bright lights and activity there. I pushed the door open and felt a homelike rush of familiarity. The usual personnel involved in producing a news show was present. The news desk was center front, a nighttime shot of the Salem skyline in the background. There were several cameras nearby, two main cameras on wheeled pedestals already manned and aimed at the desk. It takes quite a few people to produce a news show. Most of them are never seen on the TV screen. From where I stood in the doorway I could see the producer, Hiram Good, and his assistant at their desks, makeup woman Molly, two staff writers, and at least three other staff people. There was a large bank of overhead TV screens with half a dozen people watching them, where "Nightly News" was spelled out in neon letters. The green screen where Wanda would give the weather report was beside the main stage desk. In the far corner of the room I saw Scott's desk, and in the window across from his chair, a couple of forlorn bright sticky note squares identified my own glass cubicle.

Buck Covington was already seated behind the curved surface. I was pleased and a little bit surprised to see Jim there. He waved for me to come over to where he stood beside one of the pedestal-mounted cameras. I was glad he was there, and hoped maybe he'd be with me next to Buck to help tell our story. It had been, after all, his high school buddy who'd made it possible for us to be in the right place—at the right time—to capture Lamont Faraday's latest fall from grace—his arrest on camera.

I thought about the film we'd taken—the one we were about to introduce to the *Nightly News* audience, and felt a sudden pang of sympathy for Lamont Faraday. He'd not only lost his costar, *Night Magic* was apparently doomed to be a money loser—maybe to the extent of closing Paragon Productions for good—but now the world would see him disheveled and incoherent, being handcuffed and put into a police car. How had such a thing happened?

One of the producers walked to where I stood. "Hi there, Lee," he said. "Good to see you here. It's been a while. I saw the film you got. Fine work!"

"Thanks." I fell into step beside him. "It took a little bit of luck."

Luck! Leo had said that Faraday liked to gamble.

The realization of exactly how the movie star had become so drunk on the day he was scheduled to leave Salem slammed into my consciousness. There was a thousand dollars at stake and he had to have a drink in every bar on Derby Street. To win, he had to hit all the bars that remained on the list, and he had to do it all in the one day he had left. I knew I had to include the information when Buck asked me about the film Jim and I had shot. Was I being objective? Maybe not. But I was being fair.

I watched the large monitor screen to my left. The *Nightly News* banner and credits rolled, and I knew that a prerecorded voice-over was announcing the usual description of what was about to take place. A commercial for a Danvers automobile dealer followed. A tap on my shoulder broke my concentration.

"Hey there, Moon. It looks like we get to share the seats beside Buck tonight." Scott Palmer was all smarmy smiles. "I figured out how poor old Lamont got so drunk. Buck jumped on it. It's a perfect explanation of the video you lucked out with."

Luck again?

"The thousand-dollar bet," I said. "I don't need your help on that. Lamont's time in Salem was up. I have the story." I was darned if I was going to let Scott horn in on my turn in the *Nightly News* spotlight. "Just bow out gracefully, Scott."

I got the long look first, then he held up both hands in a sign of surrender. "Okay. I didn't know you'd figured out that part. Didn't mean to step on your toes." He motioned to one of the producers, pointed to Buck, gave a wave, and exited the long room.

Points for Scott for being a gentleman.

Good. I was going to be able to talk to Buck about how we'd happened upon the scene—without involving Jim's friend, of course—and how Lamont Faraday had managed to be so intoxicated at that particular time. If only I knew who'd made the bet with him in the first place, all the objectivity boxes would be checked. As it stood at that moment, the act that had set the whole scenario into motion was missing. I guessed that

I'd have to arrange an interview with the movie star to get the answer to that one.

Buck gave his introductory greetings to the audience, gave some traffic reports along with some live webcam shots of Derby Wharf. After a commercial about a special showing of the original *Hocus Pocus*, I was seated in the chair to the right of the newsman. "It's good to welcome our own Lee Barrett back to the news," Buck said. "Lee, I understand that you've been doing some investigation regarding the movie being made here in Salem—*Night Magic*—and you've come up with some interesting footage—most recently a video of one of the actors in a compromising situation."

"It seems to be a case of being in the right place at the right time, Buck," I admitted. "I'm working on a documentary about the making of the movie. There's been very little access to the area where a lot of the filming is being done over at Gallows Hill Park, and my videographer, Jim, and I were looking around, trying to find a spot where we could get a peek at whatever was going on behind that fence they've set up over there. We'd heard that Lamont Faraday had jumped into a parked food truck with its motor running, while the driver worked on arranging the food display. Apparently Lamont Faraday approached the truck and climbed up through the open driver's-side door and into the cab," I explained. "The driver ran for the truck's door and attempted to pull Faraday from the front seat. Faraday pushed the man away and steered the truck really fast down the road toward the replica room of the Witch House. He ran into a nearby fire hydrant. Witnesses say that the water spouted like a geyser and soaked the entire display of sandwiches meant to feed the movie crew. By then, with lunch ruined, the ticked-off food truck driver pulled Faraday to the ground and the police arrived."

I nodded to the director. "This is what I saw and heard from behind the fence."

"Roll film," Buck said. I looked up at the monitor and watched, along with the WICH-TV viewers, as the disheveled movie star, shouting words that were mostly bleeped, was escorted by two officers and handed into the back seat of the SPD cruiser. "Faraday was arrested and charged with driving while intoxicated," I said, "and has engaged counsel." I did my version of the long stare into the camera. "Some of you may remember that a short time ago, WICH-TV's field reporter Scott Palmer told you about a thousand-dollar bet Faraday made that he could have a drink in every bar on mile-long Derby Street while he was in Salem." Buck nodded in agreement. "Lamont's time in Salem was up. He hadn't finished his list of bars. I think it's likely that he visited several in a row in one day— accounting for his condition at the time of the arrest. He wanted to win the thousand-dollar bet. A caution-ary tale for all of us about moderation—in both drink-ing and gambling. Stay tuned to WICH-TV for updates on this continuing story."

Buck thanked me for sharing the film and the story, and I tiptoed out of the newsroom, anxious to get home—this time taking the ramp to the second floor and riding Old Clunky down to the entrance hall and out onto the sidewalk. I rounded the corner to the parking lot, and once again the SPD cruiser greeted me.

"Everything go okay, Mrs. Mondello?"

"Thanks, yes," I said. "I'm fine. Going straight home."

"I'll just tag along behind you, if you don't mind. There's still a killer loose, you know."

I knew that. It hadn't escaped me that Darla's murder involved Paragon Productions, and that my recent assignments had caused me to be digging around in all things Paragon. No wonder Pete was worried about me wandering around in the middle of the night. Was I getting too close to something that might worry a killer too?

CHAPTER 22

The cruiser was still behind me when I pulled into the narrow driveway beside our house. I opened my window and waved to the officer. "Thank you," I called softly, and drove into the backyard parking area. The spotlight over the sunroom door illuminated our half of the property. Michael Martell's half was dark. I locked the Jeep, scooted for the house, and stopped short when Pete opened the door, reached for me, and pulled me close.

"I should have gone with you," he whispered. "I've been worried. The cat has been pacing back and forth." Holding my shoulders, he looked into my eyes. "I sent the cruiser. Did you mind?" He didn't wait for an answer. "You did great on Buck's show. You didn't look a bit nervous."

"I wasn't nervous," I gave him a big smile. "I was with a whole newsroom full of friends and a quite large police officer was waiting for me outside." I paused and studied his face. His jaw was tight, eyes wary.

"Should I be nervous? Is there something going on that I should know about?"

"Chief called me right after you left. It seems that Paulina Fellows called to report that she saw somebody peeking into her bedroom window at the Airbnb she's staying in. The sound engineer she's staying with chased the guy off, but she gave a good description of the man. He wore a black hood and had scars on his face—like a pirate, she said."

"That's pretty scary." I felt the hair raising on my arms. It was *very* scary. I tried to sound calm.

"No harm done," Pete said. "But the boyfriend is leaving Salem in the morning, along with a bunch of the other people who worked for Paragon who've been told to leave town. It seems that there's nothing left to film that requires most of them—just some local scenery and distance shots using the body doubles. That means Paulina has to stay, and she's frightened. The thing is, what if *you* and maybe some others at WICH-TV have uncovered things a killer doesn't want known?"

"When you talked to Paulina did she say anything to you about Darla getting death threats when she was in California?"

"She mentioned it in passing. She said Darla got tons of fan mail and that Darla told her that most of her fans loved her and wanted her to make more movies, and one of them wanted her to jump off the Golden Gate Bridge. I guess it's not unusual for people in the public eye to get a certain amount of hate mail. Why do you ask?"

I tossed my handbag over the back of a chair and shook my head. "I heard just about the same thing from Jenna the hairdresser. She said the threatening notes only came while Darla was in California and she'd had none while she was in Salem. I didn't know if you knew about it, that's all. I don't even want to think about Paragon or killers or WICH-TV right now. We'll figure it out. We always do. For now, I want to take a shower, put on my soft, comfy nightshirt, climb into our nice, big bed, maybe watch some TV, and snuggle with my husband." O'Ryan hopped up onto the seat of the chair. I stroked his fuzzy head. "And maybe snuggle with my cat too."

"That sounds like a plan to me." Pete cupped my chin in his hand and kissed my forehead. "I'll meet you in bed. As Ibby would say, *Don't lollygag*. O'Ryan and I will be waiting for you."

I dashed for the bathroom. After a quick shower, hair towel-wrapped to protect the fresh hairdo, and clad in a Walt Disney World nightshirt featuring Goofy, I joined husband and cat in the bedroom. Pete was already in bed, pillows propped up just the way I like them, television tuned to WICH-TV. River's theme music began and the *Tarot Time with River North* logo flashed onto the screen. Pete patted the space beside him. "Buck's on the set. He'll be shuffling the cards for River tonight." I wiggled into my accustomed place beside him, giving O'Ryan a gentle shove toward the wall.

"I left before Wanda did the weather," I said. "Is tomorrow going to be nice?"

"She says we're in for some rain." Pete grinned. "She

was wearing a clear, plastic raincoat over a two-piece bathing suit. Perfectly symbolic of a change."

Bruce Doan's idea of what a TV weather girl should look like is amazingly retro. Our Wanda the Weather Girl has a degree in meteorology and has been nationally recognized for her cooking show on America's Hometown Cooks. But she often varies her regular professional wardrobe with some deliberately provocative outfits. The transparent raincoat over a swimsuit is a good example. Doan insists that it makes people watch WICH-TV weathercasts just to see what Wanda is wearing. Feminists in the audience don't like it, but the ratings are awfully good—which is, after all, the point.

I tried to concentrate on the TV image as River appeared on-screen. She was in glamourous, night show, movie host mode—quite unlike the gray-garbed Puritan of early Salem days she'd portrayed several hours earlier. Her long black braid was upswept and wrapped around her head with the trademark silver stars and moons glittering under the lights. The gown of the night was one I'd seen before—deep purple velvet with long sleeves, updated now with an amethyst necklace and matching earrings. Pete's information about the Peeping Tom incident at Paulina's Airbnb troubled me. I knew it had troubled him too, despite his assertion that there was no harm done, or he wouldn't have made sure I had a police escort for my brief nightly news stint.

As handsome Buck performed his ever-skillful card shuffling—including a new, over-the-wrist flip of half of the deck—I moved even closer to Pete. "Are all of our windows locked?" I asked.

"They are." His jaw was tight. "And the alarm system is working perfectly. I had it checked the minute I heard about Paulina's window."

"This is very serious, then, isn't it? You . . . the department . . . actually have no idea who—or where—the killer is?"

"Someone is determined to ruin Paragon Productions," he said. "We don't even know why. It may have nothing whatever to do with you, or what you've learned, but Lee—I can't risk for a minute having you in danger from some madman—or -woman."

O'Ryan turned, facing Pete, and gave a soft, puffing sound—one we've heard before and have determined usually means *Be quiet.* (A much louder puff would mean a no-nonsense *Shut up!*) The cat wanted to listen to River.

Silently, Pete and I watched the screen as Buck placed the shuffled deck face-down on the table, and River placed her right hand over the top card. She bowed her head. "I dedicate this deck to serving others with spiritual growth, for wisdom, knowledge, and to bring peace to all who seek its wisdom."

River's first call came from a woman who, like so many Salem citizens, was vitally interested in the making of the Witch House movie. "Have the cards told you what's going to become of *Night Magic* now that Darla is dead and everybody is saying that Paragon is going out of business? We all thought the movie would be good for Salem—like *Hocus Pocus* is, and like *Bewitched* was. I've got a small gift shop," she said, "and I depend on the tourists for my living. I've stocked a bunch of Witch House souvenirs—bracelets and earrings and little models of the house. I can't afford to get stuck with that kind of inventory if the movie is a big flop."

"I can offer you a reading for yourself, if you'd like," River offered. "The fortunes of Paragon will affect different people differently. Some may be greatly impacted, some not at all. Can you give me your first name and your birth date?"

River laid out the colorful cards in a familiar pattern, then began, one at a time, to turn them face-up. She explained to Gracie, a Capricorn, how the Ace of Pentacles indicated the beginning of material gain, and that the Two of Cups might mean the beginning of a friendship or partnership that could bring a balance of ideas and plans for her shop. As River's gentle voice continued to ease Gracie's anxiety, I wondered what the cards might hold for me at that moment. I wondered too how Paulina was faring after the fright she'd had. I was sure she was terrified to be alone in that apartment.

Pete and I, along with O'Ryan, had settled comfortably—and somewhat drowsily—in our big, cushy bed, watching our friend on-screen as she introduced the night's scary movie, when a persistent buzzing sounded from the direction of my antique bureau. Pete sat up straight.

"That's your phone. Who'd be calling at this time of night?"

My thoughts went immediately to my senior citizen aunt. I sped across the carpet, grabbing the phone, "Hello? Hello?"

The smooth male voice answered. "Hey, baby! It's

me. Roney McBiel again. I'll bet you didn't expect to hear from me again so soon. How you doin'?"

"Roney?"

"Yeah. Sure. Remember me? How can I rock your world?"

"Yes. I remember you, Roney." I gave Pete an it's-okay sign. "And you just rocked it a bit with your call." I looked at the clock on the bureau. "It's twelve minutes past midnight."

"No kidding? I'm sorry. It's only, like, a little after nine o'clock over here." He sounded oddly surprised by the usual time change between the coasts. "Well. Anyway, I wanted to let you know that I'm on my way to Salem. After all these years I'm on the Paragon payroll again. Expense account and everything. I'm at the airport right now. I'll see you sometime tomorrow. Okay? Maybe you can show me around town. I've never been to Salem before. Or even Boston. I'm excited! I'll call you when I get there. Tell your old man I may have something for him." And he was gone.

I replaced my phone on the charger. "Roney McBiel, calling from California. He's on his way here," I grumbled, climbing back into bed. "Calling me in the middle of the night! Durn fool," I quoted Jim. "And he says to tell my *old man* he may have something for you. Did you call him after I shared his number with you?"

"I did. We didn't talk about anything specific. He said he'd look around and see what he could find. Now I wonder why Paragon is flying everybody who's still in Salem back to California, while the guy who just finished leveling their main studio is heading here." Pete scooted over and welcomed me back into bed. "Of course Lamont Faraday has to stay here for a while longer to settle that drunk driving charge. He has no previous record and his lawyer got the charges down to just the DUI and some damage to the food truck. He'll pay a hefty fine and maybe have to stay around to do some community service."

"There hasn't been any mention of Doug Sawyer leaving Salem either," I said. "The last I heard about him, he was dividing his time between the hotel and Darla's trailer and trying to teach her dog to obey hand signals like Barney the Bear used to."

"We're keeping an eye on him too. He may know things the killer is worried about. He was always close to Darla. She trusted him—possibly with whatever secret got her killed."

"Have you warned him?"

"We warned all of the crew and cast members who remained in Salem after Darla's death to be aware of their surroundings and not to hesitate to call us if anything seemed threatening. That's why Paulina's boyfriend was ready to act when they saw that face at the window."

"So the boyfriend and some of the other Paragon people will be leaving in the morning."

"Right. Out of our jurisdiction." Pete sounded relieved.

"So just about everybody except Doug, Paulina, Darla's dog, and Lamont Faraday will be headed back to California—or wherever they want to go," I said. "Doug's part in the movie must be finished. I wonder why he wants to stay here. They'll surely be closing up the Gallows Hill Park site, won't they? I suppose that means the two trailers will get sent back to Paragon too."

"Their lease with the city will expire in a few days. The trailers will have to be towed away and the sound-stage will be dismantled. Say, I'll bet that's why your friend McBiel is coming here. To demolish whatever remains in Salem of *Night Magic*."

"I'll bet you're right," I agreed. "He seems to enjoy the leveling process. He sounds excited about coming here. And he's happy that Paragon is paying him. I wonder how long it takes to fly from Los Angeles to Boston."

"I did it once when I went to a police convention out there," Pete said. "It was around five or six hours I think. I'm still interested in talking to him about the California so-called *accidents*," Pete said. "Maybe that's what he has for me."

CHAPTER 23

There'd been no more surprise telephone calls by the time Pete and I left for our respective jobs in the morning, each of us leaving earlier than usual, each with a large to-go cup of coffee in our cup holders as we anticipated the slow going Salem traffic awaiting us. The annual Halloween Happenings jam-up, accentuated by the ongoing movie mania, had been made even crazier because of a sudden influx of leaf peepers, drawn by a particularly colorful autumnal display.

A line of buses crowded between the statue of Roger Conant and the Witch Museum partially blocked my access to Hawthorne Boulevard. "I should have taken the long way, down Bridge Street," I grumbled, taking a sip of rapidly cooling coffee, slowly inching—literally *inching*—toward the Hawthorne Hotel looming ahead just past the common. Seeing the hotel made me wonder if the soon-to-arrive stuntman, Roney McBiel, had thought to make reservations for his stay in Salem. *Lots of luck with that, Roney*. I lifted my coffee cup in a sarcastic salute. Accommodations in Salem during *any* October are hard to come by, and this particular October was worse than most in that department. I wondered if Pete was making better time than I was. Of course he had a siren and flashers.

I pulled into the WICH-TV parking lot, where nightwatchman-security guard Chester had taken on the duty of traffic cop—making sure no one who didn't have station business was grabbing the neatly sectioned spaces. "Good morning, Chester." I locked the Jeep and greeted him. "Intruders trying to grab our spaces today?"

"They sure are. Parking in Salem is bad enough any-time, but this month is the worst I've ever seen it."

"I hear you," I said. "Thanks for keeping them out of my nice seawall space."

"Some folks never give up. I throw them out and they drive around the block a few times and come back and try again."

"These days you could burn a tank of gas just driving around the block a few times," I told him.

"Yeah. There's this one guy. Big dude with a cowboy hat. He told me you were expecting him." He chuckled. "He's been here twice already today. I knew right away he was making it up about you expecting him. He told me he'd rock my world. Was that some kind of threat?"

Roney McBiel.

"I do know him, Chester," I said. "If he comes back, it's okay to send him inside. And no, it's not a threat. He's from Los Angeles. I guess they talk that way out there."

I used the side door to the studio and climbed the stairs to the second floor. Rhonda was already at her desk. Not a surprise because she has a gentleman friend who has an apartment nearby that he only uses in the summer. Rhonda gets to use it whenever she wants to—and she always wants to during Haunted Happenings. The whiteboard was blank.

"Doan isn't in yet," she reported. "He and Buffy are over at Gallows Hill Park. Buffy and some other local women are doing a quick cameo scene of the accused witches in the old courtroom, waiting to be tried. They have to do it in a hurry because they've got somebody coming to take the replica Witch House apart."

Roney McBiel. Again.

"Buffy was excited about having a part in the movie," I said, "and I'm pretty sure the man who's going to dismantle the Witch House set is already in Salem. He'll probably be showing up here before long looking for me. Tall guy wearing a cowboy hat. Roney McBiel. I'll be in my office."

"Got it," Rhonda said. "A cowboy hat? Like Ranger Rob?"

"Yep." I didn't try to explain but headed for the ramp leading to the newsroom and to my own private little fish bowl. It felt good to sit in my chair, monitor turned off and silent, looking past a few neglected stickies into the long roomful of desks and chairs, lamps, and TV screens where nothing much of significance was happening. It was sort of restful. I tilted my chair back and closed my eyes—not in an Encyclopedia Brown, searching sort of way but more of a Zen, enjoying-the-moment thing.

The buzzing phone interrupted. Rhonda. Doan and Buffy had arrived. "Buffy was so thrilled," Rhonda announced. "They did a close-up of her face while the women accused of witchcraft were gathered to hear the judges' verdicts. The director apparently told her that her look of anguish and barely controlled horror was absolutely perfect—encapsulating the feelings of those poor lost souls on that dreadful day in 1692."

"That's wonderful," I said. "Maybe she missed her calling. Maybe she'll do more acting after this."

Rhonda muffled a snicker. "Not likely. Doan told me that she was just royally pissed because the choice of wardrobe was a long dress in gray, black, or brown. She was sure that some of the women in those days must have worn purple."

I was still smiling when Chester arrived at my door with the expected man wearing a cowboy hat. I welcomed the two inside. "This the fellow you've been looking for, Ms. Barrett?" Chester stood in the doorway, blocking the entrance until I nodded my agreement.

"Roney McBiel?" I asked.

He doffed the big Stetson with a sweeping gesture. "At your service."

"Come on in, Mr. McBiel. Sit down. Tell me what's going on," I said, waving to the chair facing my desk. "Thanks, Chester. This is him."

The nightwatchman/security guard backed away, frowning, possibly unconvinced. "Call me if you need me. I'll be right outside."

I thanked him again and turned my attention to the stuntman turned demo expert now seated across from me, his hat covering about a third of my desktop. He still looked a lot like the Wikipedia photo—well-built and nicely tanned. It would be hard to guess his age. I picked up a motion on the glass behind him. My visitor had caught the attention of someone in the newsroom too. Scott Palmer had his nose pressed against the pane like a kid outside the candy store window.

Roney looked around the room. "Wow. They keep you on display, don't they? I guess you can't get away with much in here." He swung around in his chair, jerking a thumb in Scott's direction. "Big fan?"

"No. Just nosy. Tell me about your hurry-up trip to Salem. If I bring a cameraman in, can we do a short interview right now?" I hoped he'd say yes, certain that WICH-TV viewers would love to hear about the plans to take down the fence around the Paragon set at Gallows Hill Park.

"You sure can, sweetheart," he drawled, leaning back, extending his left leg, and putting a foot much too close to the edge of my desk. "Hope you don't mind. I have to stretch out the old injury after the cramped plane ride. Paragon flew me coach this time. It used to be first class all the way. The movie business ain't what it used to be." I saw Scott smirk at the foot-almost-on-the-desk ploy. I didn't comment but buzzed Rhonda.

"Can you round up a videographer for me? I need to do an interview from my office."

"Marty's free. I'll send her over."

"Perfect."

I stared pointedly at the offending foot. "We can do the interview outside if you'd be more comfortable stretching both legs after being cramped on a plane for such a long time." He pulled the leg back, putting both feet on the floor.

"Oops. Sorry. My big feet get in the way. That's a good idea. It's nice out in that parking lot. Smells like saltwater. Let's go." He glanced around at the four glass walls. "Too much reflection in here for proper camera work anyway."

"You're right."

I buzzed Marty. "Can you meet us out by the sea-wall?"

"Sure can. It'll make a better background than that clear plastic trash bag you work in anyway." I glanced around the room. The pile of yellow legal pads I'd promised to the *Saturday Morning Business* guy still languished on top of my printer. My wastebasket over-flowed with crumpled sheets of paper and needed to be emptied, and probably could do with a good washing. My green jacket hung over the corner of an open cabi-net door where a pair of high-heeled white pumps I'd used on a summer stand-up were in full, after–Labor Day view. I let the trash bag remark pass unanswered and made a silent vow to clean up my office really soon. "Come on, Roney. Let's go smell the ocean breeze."

"The fall leaves are nice too," he said. "I may stick around in Salem for a while. Is that big brick hotel I passed any good?" He reached for the hat.

"The Hawthorne? One of the best. Did you get a reservation somehow?"

"Not yet." He followed me into the corridor. "I'll call as soon as we finish the interview."

I didn't even try to disguise my laugh. "Lots of luck with that. They're taking reservations now for *next* October."

That brought a raised eyebrow. "Oh well, I guess a regular motel would be okay for a while."

"I don't think you get it, Roney. Salem in October is sort of like New Orleans at Mardi Gras. No rooms. Didn't Paragon make arrangements for you?"

"No. They just gave me a nice accommodations allowance, along with the plane tickets, the rental car, and a credit card for the equipment I'll need for the teardown. No rooms, huh? I hope I won't have to sleep in the car." A frown creased the Botox-smooth forehead. "An Airbnb maybe?"

"Maybe. Hey. I may know of one—if the paint's dry. I'll check it out after our interview. Give me your number and I'll get back to you." We stepped outside into the fall sunshine and good seaside smells.

CHAPTER 24

With Marty's expert instruction, perfect afternoon lighting, and even a couple of cooperative seagulls doing a flyby, I introduced Stetson-hatted Roney to the WICH-TV viewers, with a brief run down of his background as a stuntman turned contractor. He, in turn, gave a remarkably cogent, easy-to-understand explanation of exactly how the structures behind the fence at Gallows Hill Park would be safely and efficiently removed and, wherever possible, recycled. "Paragon has provided me with blueprints and schematics of all the buildings concerned." He spoke directly into Marty's camera with sincerity in his tone. "The city's property will be just as good or even better than it was when I'm finished. I promise." His smile was convincing. "My daddy taught me to drive all the right machines to do the job. That's probably how I became a professional stuntman." He gave a broad wink. "And I can still roll a car!"

With the video completed and ready to run on the next newsbreak, I thanked Roney, who'd by then wangled an introduction to Wanda and invited her to lunch at the Friendly on his Paragon account. I declined the invitation to join them and promised I'd check on the possible Airbnb efficiency apartment. He leaned forward and lowered his voice. "Don't forget to tell your policeman husband I may have something for him."

"He's looking forward to meeting you," I said.

"And I really want to go and visit Barney the Bear while I'm here. I'll bring him a powdered sugar doughnut."

I was sure Barney hadn't forgotten him.

"I'll give you a call just as soon as I find out about that rental," I promised and immediately called my aunt.

"The painters have left," Aunt Ibby responded to my phone call. "And it's a quick-drying paint. I'll need to give the place a quick going-over with duster and vacuum, but if your friend doesn't mind a small space, I guess it can be ready by this evening."

"He's not a friend exactly, but he's someone who might be helpful to both Pete and me in learning about the California angles of the Paragon problems," I explained. "He's a retired stuntman—kind of interesting, actually, even if a little rough around the edges. I just interviewed him. Watch the early news. You can see what you think." I gave her Roney's phone number.

My next call was to Pete, mostly to tell him that Roney had something to tell him and to see what he thought about the man staying at Aunt Ibby's house on

Winter Street. "I haven't actually told him about the apartment or where it is," I said. "I just told him I might know somebody who had one."

"How do *you* feel about him staying there?" he asked. "Do you trust him?"

"I think so." I hesitated. "But maybe it's because he's a Barney the Bear fan like me. When they were keeping Barney in a cage, Roney used to bring him powdered sugar doughnuts. He's planning to go over to Topsfield to visit him."

Pete's "Uh-huh" was noncommittal.

"That reminds me. Don't you think it's strange that Doug Sawyer still hasn't found time to go there and visit Barney?"

"He hasn't?"

"No. That's what he told me. He hasn't found time."

"I agree. It's damned strange. Look, I'll run a fast check on Roney McBiel, and if nothing criminal or suspicious turns up, I think it'll be okay for Ibby to rent to him if she wants to. Meanwhile, I'm curious to learn why Sawyer has time to walk somebody else's pet pooch but can't find time to visit old Barney."

"He's teaching the dog to obey hand signals like Barney used to do."

"There's something odd about Sawyer," Pete said. "Nothing really wrong. He's a solid citizen. No record of any wrongdoing."

"You checked on him?"

"Of course. We checked on everybody who had access to Darla. They were apparently very close."

"Roney says that Doug was in love with her. That he

was devastated when she died," I reported. "Roney said that she kept Doug around like a pet."

"No love interest? She just kept him around?"

"So Roney says."

"Strange woman," he mused. "She invited a man she reportedly hated to meet her in her private trailer. Then, a man who was believed to be in love with her and was said to have been treated like some kind of a pet, voluntarily takes full care of her *actual* dog, while ignoring the trained bear who was probably responsible for whatever success he'd enjoyed in his own career." It was a totally Petelike observation.

I could hardly wait to hear what he'd make of whatever it was that Roney had to share with my *old man*. Meanwhile, I still had a couple of jobs of my own to attend to. The documentary about the making of *Night Magic* was kind of in limbo at the moment. I was sure, though, that whatever the final fate of the movie was, I had plenty of footage to link together to tell the story that was still unfolding. It sure wasn't the story of glittery, glamorous moviemaking that Mr. Doan had expected, but it had a lot going for it—not the least of which was some unexpected acting chops for Buffy.

Pete and I agreed to a quiet dinner at home, he promised to get back to me about the Roney McBiel fast check, and I hung my green jacket on a proper coat hanger and shoved it into the narrow locker, which could use a thorough vacuuming due to a scattering of colored confetti on the floor left over from a stand-up I'd done at a ribbon cutting for the Pirate Museum. I made another quick vow before I closed the locker door: *Never let the house look like the office. Never!*

Rhonda sent out for a DoorDash pizza and a couple of Pepsis. We split lunch in the break room on the well-worn Formica counter with its rim of cigarette burns from back in the day when people used to smoke at work. After lunch I carried my wastebasket out to the dumpster, gave it a quick rinse with the hose, and began the process of putting together an updated folder of my progress on the *Night Magic* documentary in case Doan asked for a progress report. He likes paper folders so he can scribble suggestions on them. By the time I'd finished there were already several discarded, crumpled sheets of paper in the wastebasket and Scott was back, peering in at me, still smirking. I'm sure I glared, spread out both arms, and mouthed *What!*

He tapped his phone. Mine buzzed. "What?" I echoed the silent word.

"I grabbed a look at the interview you just did with the guy from Paragon," he said. "I wanted to talk to him, but Wanda got to him first. Good interview, though. Is he going to be staying around for a while?"

"Maybe," I hedged. "He's looking for a place to stay."

"Ha. Good luck with that."

"I know. He didn't make reservations before he got on the plane. Some people don't understand about Salem in October. What do you want to talk to him about?'

Big smile. "I want to hear about the stuntman days. He must have worked with some big names. If he's not going to be around long, I want to get him for at least a short take."

"When I talk to him again I'll give him your num-

ber," I promised. Gearhead, NASCAR fan me was
interested in those stunt days too—especially in the car-
chase, automobile-rolling scenes. If my plate wasn't so
full of other stuff, I would have tried for that interview
myself.

"Thanks, Moon," he said. "Get me that one and I'll
owe you big-time."

"I'll remember that," I promised.

By five o'clock I was more than ready to call it a
day. I said good night to Rhonda and took Old Clunky
down to the street level, where Chester was still on
parking lot duty, waving prospective parking lot prowl-
ers away. "Good night, Ms. Barrett," he said. "I need to
get inside pretty soon for my security job, so somebody will probably be trying to grab your spot. You
aren't on the eleven o'clock again tonight, are you?"

"Nope. Not tonight, Chester. I'm going to go home
and relax." I meant it too. But first I stopped at Market
Basket to pick up some of Pete's favorite dinner rolls to
go along with the steak I planned for dinner. While I
was at it, mindful of my recent vow to keep a clean
house, I took a quick trip down the cleaning goods
aisle for some spray cleaner.

The sun was just setting when I pulled into our
driveway and Pete called to tell me that he was on his
way home and that Roney had checked out okay. "No
record. No complaints. In fact, he's a volunteer with
Big Brothers and he donates time to the veterans' hos-
pital out there. I've already called Ibby. She says his
apartment is ready and she'll let him know he can
move in right away. I'm sure looking forward to that
steak dinner."

I was too. No cat greeted me at the door, so I assumed that O'Ryan had chosen to dine at the other end of Winter Street. I hoped Roney liked cats. I hoped O'Ryan would like Roney. I pulled the waiting steaks from the refrigerator and seasoned them just the way the cook on YouTube had advised. Nice, fat baking potatoes were washed and wrapped and ready to be microwaved. I'd heat up the dinner rolls in the oven. Peas and carrots came from a can, but the general effect was going to be fine. I was getting pretty darned good at this homemaker gig.

I had some time to spare, so I carried my new spray bottle of glass cleaner and a roll of paper towels out to the sunroom. *This is the room with the most windows*, I told myself, feeling quite virtuous as I polished the largest pane. I leaned forward, detecting a motion in the rapidly fading light. Was O'Ryan back? Had Pete arrived early? Or was someone walking across our backyard? I remembered the warning words I'd heard more than once lately—most recently from the kindly cop who'd escorted me home the night before.

There's still a killer loose, you know.

CHAPTER 25

The entire backyard seemed to light up at once. Our next-door neighbor's motion-activated outdoor spotlights turned on at the same time Pete's headlamps rounded the corner of our driveway. I squinted through my newly cleaned window. A cat yowled, and a fast-moving white blur told me that Frankie had just dashed across our yard. But was the dark shape just beyond the maple tree a person ducking out of sight or simply a swaying cluster of the last leaves of the season clinging to forked branches?

Pete was nearby, so I knew I was safe. I strained to replace fear with logic. Probably Frankie had tripped Michael's spotlights and I no longer saw—or imagined I saw—anything in either yard that resembled a human form. Still, I didn't unlock the door. I saw Pete's car back into his regular spot. He got out of the front seat just as Michael's outdoor spots turned themselves off, leaving only Pete's headlamps lighting his path toward the sunroom. Only then did I take the roll of towels from under my arm, put down my spray bottle, and turn the lock to welcome my husband into the house.

"Wow. That was an extra-special hug," Pete said. "Are you extra-glad to see me?" He put both hands on my shoulders and looked down at my face. "You okay? What's going on?"

"Probably nothing." I attempted a smile. "Something in the yard spooked me, that's all. I'm sure it was just Frankie racing around out there."

"Do you want me to go out and check?"

"No. I'm sure it's nothing. Just all this talk about Darla's murder and then someone peering in Paulina's window—and working next to a newsroom where they talk about it day and night."

"I know." He kissed my forehead. "And we live in a city full of Halloween ghouls and ghosts and witches. Let's forget all that and get that steak started."

"Everything's ready to go." I shook away the bad thoughts as we walked together into our bright, cozy kitchen. "Just make yourself comfortable and I'll get things started here."

Pete took off his jacket and tie, revealing his hol-stered gun, and started up the stairs. "I'll be back in a couple of minutes. You sure you're okay?"

"I'm fine." I popped the prepared potatoes into the microwave and began to preheat the cast-iron grilling pan when a knock at the sunroom door sounded.

"I'll get it." Pete bounded back into the kitchen and crossed to the sunroom doorway. "Stay right here."

I recognized Michael Martell's voice. "I'm glad you're here, Pete. Something's going on."

Disobeying Pete's instruction to stay in the kitchen,

I joined the two men. "Hello, Michael," I said, then, realizing that he held his white cat in his arms, "what's wrong with Frankie?"

"She's hurt. I think somebody kicked her or hit her with something. Do you two know where there's a vet open this late?" He stroked the softly mewing cat, one of whose front paws was extended at an awkward angle.

"I heard her cry out a while ago," I told him. "It was just before your spotlights turned on. Let me give O'Ryan's vet a call. His office is at his house, so if he's there, I'll bet he'll find time to see Frankie."

"I'm interrupting your dinner," Michael apologized.

"It's okay," I told him. "The phone only takes one hand. I can flip a steak with the other." I proceeded to prove it.

Dr. Henshaw agreed to see Frankie. Pete put away his gun and changed into sweats. Our dinner went as planned. My timing was good and everything was hot and tasty at the same time. Conversation should have been light and fun, and we both tried to keep it that way, but we couldn't ignore the fact that Frankie's injury confirmed the fact that there had been somebody—or something—in our shared backyard that was big enough to injure a very smart, very fast cat. By the time I served the usual dessert—ice cream—chocolate for me, vanilla for Pete—the troubling thought was foremost in my mind again.

There's still a killer loose, you know.

But what could I tell Pete that would possibly be helpful? I'd not seen anything real, concrete, solid.

We watched the Bruins-Blackhawks game on the

living room TV, each of us keeping an eye on the street outside, watching for Michael's car to make the turn into the driveway on his side of the house. As soon as those headlights showed the expected turn, together we left the couch—with David Pastrňák midassist—and raced for the sunroom door, anxious about the fate of poor Frankie.

Michael exited his car, the white cat cradled in his arms. "It's a hairline fracture," he said. "She's lucky the skin wasn't broken, so we don't have to worry about infection." Frankie did not look happy. There was a pink bootie on her right front paw, and she wore the dreaded Elizabethan collar in place of her usual rhinestone-studded, silver one. "She'll be on pain pills, but it looks like she'll be all right."

"Did Dr. Henshaw have any idea how it happened?" I wanted to know.

"Not really. He said she could have fallen from a height or she even could have been hit by something—or someone." Michael stroked Frankie's nose with a gentle finger. "No way she fell. Not this sure-footed lady. Imagine someone deliberately hurting this old girl."

"I heard her yowl and saw her run when it happened." I repeated what I'd seen. "She ran across our backyard, past the maple tree, toward your side of the house."

"That's all you saw out there?" Pete questioned. "Just the cat?"

"Well . . ." I hesitated. Had I really *seen* anything else—or just perhaps only *sensed* something—someone? "There was a movement—a shadow—maybe it was just branches—near the tree."

Pete wore his cop face. "You didn't tell me that."

"Because there was nothing to tell you," I alibied. "Nighttime shadows. Jitters from daytime news stories." I shrugged. "It wasn't worth mentioning. All I actually *saw* out there was Frankie."

Even to me, it sounded like a poor excuse. I should have told him about that lurking, shapeless thing behind the tree.

We both wished Frankie and Michael well and returned to our side of the yard. Pete's cop face was still in place. Silently, we went back to the living room and sat on the couch just in time to see the Bruins tie the game with a minute left in regulation. Disagreement about cats and shadows forgotten, we cheered in unison and shared a high five when Brad Marchand sent a pass to Poitras for the winning goal.

"I should have told you," I said as we climbed the stairs to the bedroom.

"It's okay," he said. "Like you said, you didn't actually *see* anyone—although there is still a killer loose, you know. Next time tell me every little thing. Promise?"

I promised, hoping hard there wouldn't be a next time.

CHAPTER 26

Aunt Ibby phoned before I'd even poured the coffee and put our breakfast strawberry Pop-Tarts into the toaster.

"Guess who I'm having breakfast with?" she asked.

"Who?"

"Roney McBiel. Scrambled egg casserole. This is a bed and breakfast, you know. He moved in last night and kept me and the other guests awake until after midnight telling Hollywood stories!" She laughed. "What an interesting man. He knows all kinds of movie stars. He wants to thank you for finding my place for him."

There was a little shuffling noise while the phone changed hands. "Hey, Lee. I can't thank you enough. What a great little apartment I have, and there's this cool, big yellow cat that likes me, and the food is fantastic. You have rocked my world. I'll probably see you at your work later. Scott wants to interview me. I'll bring along that thing I have for Pete. I told Ibby about it. See you later."

He was on a first-name basis with my aunt, had already set up an interview with Scott, had taken Wanda to lunch and entertained the other tenants at my aunt's house, all in one day. I was interested to see what his day at WICH-TV would be like. "See you there," I told him.

Both properly caffeine- and sugar-fueled, Pete and I set out for our individual workplaces. I reminded Pete that I'd be bringing home whatever it was that Roney had found worthy to carry all the way from California for him. "I'm betting it's something that used to belong to a movie star. He told me he collected any old thing somebody famous had used or even touched. People buy that kind of thing." I told him about Clint Eastwood's hundred-dollar discarded cigarette package.

"Maybe it's something of Darla's," Pete said. "He's got me guessing."

"Maybe it'll be useful, but I'm pretty sure it will be interesting anyway. See you tonight."

I knew that Pete was in for a busy day. It was Lamont Faraday's day in court. I couldn't help thinking that I should be there too, to cover it for my documentary on the making of the movie, but Scott and Howie had already spoken for the two mobile units—Scott for the big news story that it absolutely was and Howie for color, whatever he perceived that to be. I knew too that Scott would be happy to share his footage so he could check off that favor he owed me.

Pete headed out of the driveway first. I followed after taking a backward glance at the maple tree. The trunk was slim. It would be hard for an adult to hide behind it without being seen.

Chester was on duty in the parking lot again. He wore a green sweatshirt bearing the WICH-TV logo. The shirt covered all of his titles. Otherwise, I thought, he'd be changing uniforms all day from one of his duties to another. This time he'd set up a row of those orange witch-hat-shaped barriers so there was only one way in and one way out of the lot. He motioned for me to enter and held up a forbidding hand toward the car behind me. The system seemed to be working. The two mobile units were in place, along with vehicles I recognized as belonging to WICH-TV staff. I told Chester that the man with the cowboy hat would be back, and that it was okay to let him in. In anticipation of Roney's visit, I wore my best jeans, a white silk shirt, and almost-new brown loafers.

I told Rhonda the same thing. "Oh, you mean Roney. He already called me this morning. He promised to give me a jar of the expensive face cream Darla Diamond used to use. What a nice guy. Scotty is interviewing him this morning about stunt driving before he leaves for that dog-and-pony show at the courthouse."

I pasted on a fake smile. "I know. Cool."

The whiteboard had instructions for me. *"Lee Barrett. See the manager at the Witch House,"* it commanded in red marker. With an exclamation point.

"What's going on at the Witch House?" I asked her.

"Doan wants you to set up that tour he told you about. He's found a sponsor for it."

"Paragon?"

"He didn't say. But whoever it is came up with enough money to make everybody happy—the station, the Witch House, the restaurant, and the shops." Rhonda had already done the preliminary work. She'd figured out the costs, the number of guests the tour could accommodate, and the possible days and times it could be done. I accepted the neatly typed sheet of information. "The manager's personal number is highlighted," she pointed out.

"I guess I'll have to do it, then." I knew I sounded grouchy. It meant more time away from home. Away from Pete. "I'll get with Jim and see what we can figure out. I hope it's just a one-and-done promotion."

"I guess you'll find out today."

"Guess so." I took the ramp toward the newsroom, noticing through the glass that Scott was already at his desk, no doubt preparing for his interview with the coolest guy in town. I peeked inside my cubicle before I unlocked the door. It looked a little neater than it had the day before.

I pulled up the Witch House information to check their hours. With the Halloween month traffic, it was doubtful that the manager would even talk to me today, let alone take the time to set up a tour. I was wrong. He actually sounded happy about the idea and agreed to a meeting "to firm things up," the following week. I made a note of his name, number, and the time of the meeting on a lime-green sticky and slapped it onto the wall in front of me. During all the months I'd had the glass cubicle, I'd occasionally wondered, whenever I caught my reflection in the gleaming surface of my walls, why I'd never had a vision in there.

Wonder no more.

The flashing lights and swirling colors were all there, almost covering the wall. I whirled my chair around and stood, facing the doorway. Lights and colors there too, surrounding me, then fading. I saw the 1692 courtroom just as I'd seen it when I visited the Witch House before Darla died. This time, though, the judge was there— the same black-robed, white-bearded judge I'd so recently seen in another vision between the trailers with two women. He faced me, pointing an accusing finger.

I backed away, nearly tripping on my chair. Was I seeing a real judge? One of those Salem men who'd sent so many innocent women to their painful deaths? Or was I seeing one of Paragon's actors?

The thing faded away. I sat quickly in the chair. Now the figure in the doorway was someone else. The man pushed the door open. "Lee! What's wrong?" Roney McBiel grabbed my hand. "You look like you've just seen a ghost."

I wasn't about to explain what being a scryer involved to this darned-near-perfect stranger. "New chair," I explained weakly. "I must have spun it around too fast. The old one didn't have so much pep. Made me dizzy, I guess. Come on in. Have you finished your interview with Scott already?"

"Yeah. We had to hurry it up. Seems there's big doins' at the courthouse. Everybody's favorite playboy movie star has to face the music for drinking too much and stealing a food truck." He sat in the lounge chair across from my desk. "Poor guy. It wasn't like him to lose control of himself like that."

"Really? He was pretty well known in the bars while he was here."

"I've heard about that." Roney nodded. "The bet. But I'd always heard he knew how to pace himself. You

know? I've never heard of him getting arrested for anything before."

"Pete says his record is clean. No arrests," I told
him. "And nobody got hurt. He'll probably pay a hefty
fine, though, and some community service. I've heard
that he's going to teach a few acting classes at the college. I wish I could be there to record the proceedings
for the documentary I'm preparing about the making
of *Night Magic*. This is quite relevant, I think."

"Why don't you go?"

"Both mobile units and two videographers are already assigned to it," I explained. "I can use their clips.
It'll be okay."

"I've got a nice little Panasonic shoulder-mount
camera in my car. Why don't we take a run over there
and get you your footage?" He held out his hand.
"Come on. Let's go. Why not?"

Roney's spur-of-the-moment attitude was conta-
gious. Why not indeed? I grabbed my green jacket and
a clip-on mic, hung my press credentials on a lanyard
around my neck, and followed him outside, really glad
I'd worn sensible shoes.

"I'm a member of SAG," he said. "You can autho-
rize union pay for my time, can't you?"

I buzzed Rhonda and double-checked. "Doan says
yes, and says to thank you for the purple fountain pen
you gave Buffy. She loves having something so personal that belonged to Jennifer Lopez."

"Sure thing. Glad she likes it."

"Jennifer Lopez? For real?" I questioned.

"Of course for real." He sounded offended. "Would I
lie? She had a whole box of them for a book signing.

True Love. She wrote it herself—kind of like a diary. A good book. I just hung around until she was through signing, bought a couple of signed copies of the book, and asked her if I could have a couple of the pens she'd used." Again the boyish grin. "I sold the books for a lot more than I'd paid for them and I've just hung on to those pens thinking they might come in handy someday. Want one?"

"I'm not sure I can afford one. Why haven't you asked me for any money for the item for Pete?"

"I told you. Bad karma. It took me a while to figure out what it is. I don't want anything more to do with it."

CHAPTER 27

The steps to the courthouse were expectedly crowded. Roney moved ahead of me, the Panasonic already on his shoulder. Inch by inch, we moved ahead. Whether it was because of Roney's polite, smiling, slightly drawled, "Excuse us?" and "Beg your pardon, sir," or my press credentials or the security guard's "Hello, Mrs. Mondello," within five or six minutes we were in front of the courtroom door. There were already several reporters ahead of us. I recognized a top newsman from WBZ Boston. The double doors, which should probably have been closed, were partway open because somebody had stuck one of those triangular wedges under one side.

"How's your zoom on that thing?" I whispered to my companion. "We're not going to get much closer than this."

"We're good," he promised. "I'm not sure I can focus on you and Lamont at the same time. I'll take one shot of you right now while you introduce the piece, then as soon as Lamont shows up, I'll zoom in on what's going on up there."

"That'll work." He backed up as much as he could and aimed the Panasonic at me. I spoke as quietly as I could over the buzzing crowd surrounding us. "This is Lee Barrett, speaking to you from the Essex County Courthouse in Salem, Massachusetts, where motion picture actor Lamont Faraday is about to be arraigned on charges arising from a recent drunk driving incident. Faraday is one of the stars of *Night Magic*, a Paragon Production that has been plagued with bad luck and tragedies, including the death of Faraday's costar, Darla Diamond. Let's watch the proceedings together."

Roney nodded approval and focused on the scene at the front of the great room.

Things proceeded pretty much as Pete had told me they would. When Faraday and his lawyers were seated, things moved along quickly. The lawyers had apparently worked out an advantageous plea deal for the actor. He'd have to pay a fine, as expected. There was a collective gasp and a couple of low whistles throughout the crowded courtroom when the amount was mentioned. He'd also agreed to a week's community service, including teaching acting classes at Salem State University. I could only imagine how pleased those students would be. A course like that, taught by a famous actor, would cost a fortune anywhere else. I was surprised and amazed at the judge's next pronouncement. Faraday would teach, for an additional week, the same course at Salem's Tabitha Trumbull Academy of the Arts. How had Mr. Pennington angled that, I wondered, but then realized my own good luck. I was positive that I'd be able to sit in on at least one of those Tabby sessions.

"Got enough?" Roney had already turned off the Panasonic and was urging me toward the outer door. "Let's get this back to your film editor and see how it turned out."

"I'm sure it will be just what I needed," I told him.

"Good." He steered me toward the spot where we'd left the car. "Remind me to bring my briefcase inside when we get there. I have a little gift for Rhonda in it— along with the thing I promised you for your husband." Naturally I'd been wondering about that but hadn't wanted to come right out and ask if he'd brought it.

"We've both been wondering about what it could possibly be. Quite a mystery."

"Yep. Everybody loves a good mystery. I need to stop somewhere and pick up some flowers or candy or something for Ibby. She's invited me to join her and a couple of her girlfriends tonight to watch *Midsomer Murders* on TV."

"You're in for a treat," I said, somewhat surprised that he'd been invited to join that select group after such a short acquaintance. "Betsy and Louisa are delightful." I gave him a brief rundown on the two women. "Betsy is in her sixties and still works as a model. Louisa is a financial whiz and serves on the boards of several banks. You'll find them both interesting, I'm sure. Flowers would be nice. There'll be plenty of sweets available for snacking during the show, if I know my aunt."

"Thanks. I'll do that. I've watched that show a couple of times before. She says she and her friends try to outguess the detective. Right?"

"Right. They're good at it too. You'll enjoy meeting them."

"I suppose you're good at outguessing the detective, being married to one, I mean."

"I wouldn't even try—not about real cases anyway. I can outguess him sometimes on trivia games or watching *Jeopardy!*, though."

He drove us skillfully, if a tad too fast, back to the station. Chester made him roll down the window and took a good look before he motioned us into a space. Roney opened his door, then circled the car quickly to open mine. "Don't forget your briefcase," I reminded him.

"Curious about what's in it for your man, right?" he teased, smiling, picking up the case from behind the driver's seat, carrying his camera in the other hand.

"Of course I am!" We rounded the corner of the building and climbed the marble steps. Roney pushed the front door open, holding it for me.

"Want to try a guess?"

"I wouldn't know where to start," I told him. "Except that I know you collect things that have something to do with celebrities. So, I guess it's something you found when you were cleaning up what was left of Paragon." We crossed the black-and-white tiles and I pressed the button for Old Clunky. The doors slid open and we stepped inside.

"That's right. Of course they'd already removed every little thing they thought might be valuable. Chairs, tables, all the furniture, the pictures off the walls, naturally. They'd even pried the stars off the doors." Crestfallen look. "I was so hoping they'd left those. But they didn't get everything!" The smile returned. "I found something they'd overlooked behind one of those doors with the missing star. It was inside Darla's old dressing room."

The elevator began its slow and noisy trip upward. "It was a built-in thing," Roney continued. "It looked like a bookcase. All the shelves were empty, but what whoever did the earlier clean-up didn't know was that all the parts that looked like regular flat panels opened up if you pushed on them." He tilted the Stetson to one side. "Bonanza!"

"I know exactly what you mean," I told him. "I have an antique bureau like that. It has secret panels all over it."

"No kidding. Will you show it to me sometime?"

"Maybe." We got off on the second floor and entered the glass door to the reception area where Rhonda greeted us with a big smile—undoubtedly anticipating the promised movie star's face cream.

Roney put the briefcase on top of the purple Formica counter. "I have a little something for you, Rhonda," he said, slowly unzipping the top of the case. "I doubt that this can make you any more beautiful than you are already, but it must have been Darla's favorite. She had a little stash of them in her dressing room built-in cabinet." He pulled a gold-and-white jar bearing a top designer's label and handed it to Rhonda with a flourish.

"Wow!" she said, beaming. "I've heard of it, but you can't even buy it in stores. How can I ever thank you enough, Roney?"

He waved a dismissive hand. "No need for thanks. It's my pleasure, And here you go, Lee. Here's that package for your policeman husband."

I accepted a brown, padded envelope. "It may be a little messy," he said. "It all came from a small wastebasket in a compartment full of office stuff. Pens and pencils and receipt books and such—in the same built-in as the cosmetics. I messed with it for a while, trying to make sense of it. As soon as I figured out what was in it, I dumped everything into this envelope. It's sure nothing I want to have around. Bad karma for sure."

I sniffed the package, picking up a slight scent of chewing gum. I held the thing at arm's length. "Thanks— I guess," I said, not quite sure how to respond to his information. "I'll see that Pete gets it. There's nothing dangerous in here, is there?"

"Oh no. It's not a bomb or poison or anything. It's just—well—unpleasant. But I thought the police should have a look at it. Let's go drop off this video and I'll be on my way. I have a date with a bear over in Topsfield. . . . I need to pick up some doughnuts first. It'll leave me plenty of time to do the meeting with Ibby and her friends later. Want to come with me, Lee? I know you're a big Barney fan too."

"Powdered sugar," I said, remembering. I took a quick glance at the whiteboard. Nothing new for me there. "I guess I could take a long lunch hour," I said. "What about it, Rhonda?"

"Listen, Lee," Rhonda said. "Doan was talking about asking you to do another piece on that farm. You already have a cameraman, so you can visit the bear and the cute goats and dogs and cats and monkeys and be on the clock at the same time."

"Perfect," I said. "Let's do it. Come on, Roney. You can drop off this morning's footage and I'll put Pete's package in my office." He followed me down the ramp to the newsroom. I watched as he approached the editing department and I headed for my cubicle. Putting the package in the bottom of the locker, hoping the funky smell wouldn't affect the other items in there; then, remembering that it could be important to the police, I locked the metal door, caught up with Roney, and together, we hurried back to the parking lot. Once in the car, I texted Pete. **Roney's taking me to the Family Farm for a short shoot with Barney the Bear. Got your package from California and locked it in my office. See you tonight. Love you.**

He replied right away. **Do you know what's in it? Why Roney? A Barney fan too?**

Didn't peek. Smelly contents of Darla's wastebasket. Roney has video camera. Barney fan.

He sent me a happy emoji and I put the phone in my jacket pocket.

CHAPTER 28

We stopped at Dunkin for three powdered sugar doughnuts. I have a Dunkin card, so I picked up the tab for Barney's treat, along with a couple of coffees. Topsfield is only about ten miles away from Salem, so there was no need to hurry—a good thing when you're riding with a professional stunt driver.

"When will you get started on the demo of the Salem set?" I asked him. "And do you have to replace the landscaping, the grass, and everything that was there?"

"If I can get all the rental machines I need, I should get started for real in a day or two. I've already started stripping the rooms of the easily movable stuff. Paragon has rented a warehouse, and they've ordered a flatbed truck for the trailers—and yes, I do the planting, landscaping, and all. I've started to get pretty good at the grass-and-flowers part."

"Aunt Ibby says you kept everyone in her house entertained with your Hollywood stories," I said. "And I'm glad you got to meet O'Ryan. He's a really special cat. Did my aunt tell you we have a shared custody arrangement? He commutes between her house and mine."

"Real nice cat," Roney agreed. "After a while he sat next to me on the couch and purred a lot. I think that means he likes me."

"It does," I agreed. "You're going to like the animals you're about to meet at the Family Farm too," I promised.

"I'm still surprised that Doug hasn't gone over there to see Barney. They were like family, you know? He and the bear even took naps together on the set of the TV show." We'd reached the long, white fence that surrounded the Family Farm.

"There's a dirt road up ahead," I told him, "and I'll bet there's a big guy in overalls who'll direct us to the parking and the animals."

I was right. One of the seemingly interchangeable guides—I'm pretty sure it was Gino—pointed the way, and within moments we heard the sounds of the animals. Our guide asked the question I'd heard here before. "Anyone special you've come to see?'

"Barney," we chorused and climbed out of the car. Again, I tucked a bill into the donation box, stared pointedly at Roney, and waited for him to do the same. He followed my lead, but covered the bill with his hand so I couldn't see the denomination. Oh well, it's the thought that counts. "We know where he is," I told the waiting guide.

"Okay. He'll be glad to see you." He eyed the pink-and-orange Dunkin' bag in my hand. "A treat for the bear?"

I handed Roney the bag.

"Doughnuts," Roney announced. "He's eaten them plenty of times. I used to bring them to him when he was in that hellhole they kept him in in California."

"Okay. Ordinarily I'd say no, but that bear has an iron gut, I swear. Never been sick a minute since he's lived here." He pulled a pair of thick gloves from the commodious pants. "Here. You need to go behind the guardrail to get close enough to feed him. I'll have to go with you to unlock the gate."

"He won't bite me," Roney insisted. "He won't bite anybody. That was the first command Doug taught him. Never, ever bite a human."

"Even so." The overalled man held a cluster of keys aloft. "We have to be careful."

The chimp spotted us first, pointing and chattering. Barney looked up as the gate was being unlocked, then moved close to the bars, making his sweet "chuff-chuff" greeting.

"Do you think he remembers me?" Roney whispered, pulling one of the sugary treats from the bag and holding it with the gloves. Barney gave a much louder sound and reached both paws through the bars.

"I think he does, Roney," I told him—and I believed it.

Roney reached into the bag for another doughnut and fed it to the bear. He shook the bag and peered into it. "Hey, there's only half a doughnut left in here."

I had the good grace to blush. "Sorry," I said. "It smelled so good, I've been sampling little pieces of it."

It was really fun, visiting with that old bear. Roney talked nonstop, feeding him the doughnuts bit by bit, telling him about where he'd been and what he'd done since last they'd met. Barney seemed to understand every word, nodding now and then, never breaking eye contact, pausing to brush a dusting of powdered sugar from his snout.

When Barney had finished his treat and Bodie the chimp had licked up all of the dropped crumbs and morsels, we returned to a proper distance beyond the gate and I did a brief stand-up, talking about Barney and Bodie in their movie days and how much they were enjoying their new home. We omitted any trace of the treats, not wanting to encourage future visitors to disobey the plainly posted signs saying, "Do Not Feed the Animals."

We moved on to the baby goat display and did a short take there. I cuddled a brand-new baby, patted a few of the roaming dogs, and wound up the session with a few words from the guide, telling the audience about the days and hours they could visit, and noting that a donation to the organization was appreciated.

"That was fun," I said as we approached the parking lot. "I'm definitely going to bring Pete's nephews here."

"It's a great place for kids to have fun and to learn about animals." He smiled. "You and Pete planning a family?"

"We both love kids," I said, thinking it was kind of a personal question for such a short acquaintance.

"Thought so," he said. "I saw how you were holding that baby goat."

"Yep. I love that kind of kid too." Once again he held the passenger door open for me. I climbed in and tried for a change of subject. "So, you'll be planting grass and flowers at the park after you do the teardown. Have you decided what kind of flowers to bring to Aunt Ibby when you go to the meeting tonight?"

"I found a book about the language of flowers, so I ordered a bouquet with pink roses for *happiness* and purple sweet peas that mean *for a lovely time*, which I'm sure I'll have with such charming company. What do you think?"

"It will be really pretty. Will you tell her what they mean?"

"Oh, no. It's not necessary. They bring the messages with them. It's the giver's thoughts that are important." He paused. "Did you know that Doug has always believed that Barney responded to his thoughts more than to any learned hand signals?"

"I didn't know that," I said, almost adding, *but I believe it*. My years with O'Ryan have proven that *some* animals most assuredly respond to thoughts. I waited to see if he'd continue with this interesting-to-me topic.

He did. "Yeah," he continued, slipping slightly into a drawl to match the Stetson, "Doug was sure that the bear was a mind reader. He learned the hand signals, but most of the time he didn't even have to use them. Just thought of what he wanted Barney to do, pictured it in his mind, and the darned bear would do it. Crazy, huh?"

"Maybe not so crazy," I offered, pushing the envelope a little. "Sometimes if I just think about opening a package of O'Ryan's food, he shows up in the kitchen."

"That's because you feed him at the same time every day."

"Could be," I agreed, not about to share the many other times the big cat had displayed clairvoyant abilities. "You said Doug taught Barney to never bite a human. Hand signals? Or the other way?"

"I don't know. Ask him when you see him next time."

"Maybe I will." We'd reached Derby Street and could see Chester, on the sidewalk, using hand signals, warning prospective parkers away from the WICH-TV lot.

CHAPTER 29

For the second time that day the onetime stuntman and I dropped off video footage that I hoped might get me a little more field reporter time—at least the one about the Faraday trial. The Family Farm segment was what Doan calls evergreen, a clip that can run any-time—usually more than once. We'd done a good day's work. We stopped at Rhonda's desk on the way out. Nothing for me on the whiteboard.

Roney leaned against the lavender-topped counter and tipped that Stetson at an angle with one finger. "How about you let this hardworking reporter girl off a little early? You can check her out later, can't you?" He smiled the most boyish of grins.

Rhonda returned the smile. "I could do that," she said. "See you tomorrow, Lee."

Amazed, I murmured, "Thanks so much. I'll just run down to my office and pick something up."

'I'll be on my way, then, Lee," Roney said. "I need

to buy some flowers for a special lady." He walked with me to the metal door.

"How did you do that?" I whispered. "I'm supposed to stay here until five o'clock."

He shrugged. "A three-hundred-dollar jar of face cream can buy a few favors."

"Wow. I guess so."

"I have three jars left. Maybe I can sell them to the *Midsomer Murders* ladies, if that's all right with you."

"The face cream is the real deal? It's actually worth three hundred dollars?" I asked.

"Darla paid more than that for it. It's a bargain. From what you've told me about Betsy and Louisa, they'll know all about it. They'll want some—and I can tell from looking at your aunt that she takes really good care of herself too. Anyway, it didn't cost me a cent. I told you. It's a side hustle." He shrugged. "They get a real bargain. I make a few bucks. Everybody's happy."

"If they want some movie star face cream, who am I to object?" I reasoned. "Have a good time at the meeting, and thanks for the photographer duty."

"Just another side hustle." He winked, tipped the Stetson, and strolled away.

I waited until he was out of sight, then picked up the brown paper–wrapped package, holding it gingerly by the edges, and slipped it into one of the white plastic bags I use to line my wastebasket. I grabbed the extra-large can of antibacterial disinfectant we used to spray on everything back in the COVID days, gave the locker a good dose of cleanliness, and closed the door on it. Then I took Old Clunky down to the street level. A look onto the backup of cars creeping along Derby

Street gave me a clue of how long it was going to take me to get home. A good thing a jar of face cream had bought me some extra time.

I walked across the lot to my Jeep, put the trash-bag-wrapped treasure into the back seat, then, following Chester's hand signals, I drove to the indicated exit and watched for a break in the traffic. A courteous truck driver saw my predicament and paused long enough for me to wedge the Wrangler into the line. Once on my way I relaxed enough to gather my thoughts together, trying to figure out exactly how I was going to manage the next few days at work and at home without neglecting any aspect of either one. It occurred to me that Ranger Rob's little buckaroos might enjoy a visit from a real Hollywood stuntman. I hadn't broached the subject to Roney yet, of course, but I was pretty sure Rob would like it. I'd figure out how to do a tie-in with one of the Salem men's stores who sold Western wear featuring the wide-brimmed hats. Still on the movie topic, I wondered if Chris Rich would go for a commercial on some of the movie-themed games and toys he carried. I still had a lot of concern about turning out a good documentary on the making of *Night Magic*, considering that so far there'd been more problems than progress on the film.

By the time I'd reached the Nathaniel Hawthorne statue I'd figured out a mental shopping list to take care of groceries for most of the week and decided on updating my program director wardrobe for a more professional look without sacrificing comfort.

Winter Street was comparatively traffic-free considering its proximity to the Witch Museum and within minutes I turned into my own driveway and parked facing the maple tree. Pete's car wasn't there yet, and neither was Michael Martell's Lincoln. Frankie was at home, though. She sat on Michael's back steps, collared and not looking happy. O'Ryan appeared through our cat door and sat on our back step, apparently waiting to greet me.

"Hi, big boy," I said. "Why don't you go over and visit poor Frankie? She's had a couple of bad days." He turned, looking at his dejected neighbor, gave me a brief nod, and strolled over to the adjoining yard. Tell me that animals don't understand what you say—and maybe what you think! The incident reminded me of the recent conversation about Doug Sawyer training his bear with some kind of mental telepathy.

I removed the white bag from the back seat and went inside, leaving the cats to converse with each other by whatever means they chose. I had plenty of time to decide what to thaw for dinner. I stood in the middle of the kitchen for a moment, glancing around the room, deciding on where to put the package. *I don't know what's in it*, I thought, *but I don't think I want it near food*. I carried the thing back out to the sunroom and put it on the bentwood bench.

The cats selected that moment to join me. First, O'Ryan's fuzzy yellow head appeared at the cat door. He came in, followed by a hesitant Frankie, who seemed unsure about whether her collar would allow her inside, though she managed to fit through, pink-mittened paw first. I knew she could do it because our cat door was identical to the one on Michael's house. Both cats approached the bench in the cautious way that cats do when they aren't quite sure about what it is they're facing. Frankie was first to vocalize her displeasure with what she saw—or felt—or knew—with a low but resounding hiss. Unusual, because she's usually such an adventurous girl. She dropped her body into a low-slung slink, backing away from the thing.

O'Ryan moved closer to it, back arched, tail raised straight up, looking like one of those Halloween cat silhouettes so common in witch shop windows in Salem—and not just at Halloween. His remarks about it were louder than Frankie's disapproving hiss. He yowled at it, shaking a paw in a clawing motion, yet not touching it. Then both cats took positions in front of me, each in a protective stance. Clearly, they wanted me to stay away from it. Roney had promised that there was nothing inside it that was dangerous or poisonous and that it wouldn't blow up. Nevertheless, the cats thought there was something alien going on.

"Thanks, you guys," I said. "I won't touch it. Pete will be here soon and he'll know what to do with it. I'll tell him you don't like it."

I meant it too. I wasn't sure Pete would put much stock in the opinions of two felines, but he'd been with me long enough to know that O'Ryan was more often than not correct in his opinions—however masked they may be by his inability to speak English. In this case Frankie backed him up and, after all, she was the one who'd had a recent and painful encounter with whoever was lurking behind the maple tree.

I managed to keep myself busy with dinner preparations—which is usually a fairly simple process. I select the variety of frozen protein I'd decided on and pop it into the microwave on defrost, pick a canned veggie that looks good with it, and put together a salad—something I *do* know how to make. There's always ice cream for dessert and usually some cookies in the Red Riding Hood cookie jar. This night the choice was grilled chicken thighs, canned peas and carrots, and a nice salad with fresh Boston lettuce, sliced, big red tomatoes, some diced onion, bacon bits, and some shredded cheddar and croutons. The cats were apparently going to hang around in the sunroom for a while. I heard them talking in soft meows to each other.

Are they staying here until Pete gets home so I won't be tempted to open the white bag?

I didn't have to wait too long. I heard the crunch of his tires on the driveway and I went to the doorway between the kitchen and the sunroom. The cats by then had positioned themselves in front of that same doorway, so that's where I remained until Pete came inside.

"Well, this is quite a welcoming committee," he said. "Hello, my love. Hello, cats. What's the occasion?" He crossed the room and gave me a hug.

"I brought home the package Roney McBiel promised you, and for some reason these guys don't want me near it." I pointed to the plastic bag on the bench.

Pete frowned. "They don't want you near it?"

"It seems that way," I told him. "They haven't given me a hint about why. Roney has assured me that there's nothing dangerous in it. No explosives. No poison gas. Just the contents of Darla Diamond's personal wastebasket. It smells like chewing gum. Maybe Juicy Fruit."

Pete looked from me to the cats—still in protective stance—to the bentwood bench. "I'll tell you what.

Let's humor the cats. I'll lock it in my car and take it to the station in the morning." He picked up the bag—not by the edges as I had but carefully—and opened the door to the yard. The cats and I watched from the front steps as he returned to his car, unlocked the trunk, and placed the package inside. "Okay, O'Ryan? Frankie?"

Apparently it was okay because the two strolled away toward the other side of our house, just as Michael's Lincoln pulled into his parking space. He stepped out and, seeing us, came across the yard. "Some excitement at the school today." He bent and picked up Frankie. "How's my girl? Poor baby." He faced us. "The acting department is over the moon. Just think: Lamont Faraday will be teaching classes. He's already contacted Mr. Pennington about dates and times. I expect they'll hold classes in the main auditorium. Everyone wants to participate. I imagine you'll be attending, won't you, Lee?"

I hadn't thought about it, but yes, an acting session with Lamont Faraday would surely fit into my *Night Magic* documentary, and it might well work as a news story too. "I certainly will. I'll call Mr. Pennington in the morning and make a reservation."

"Good idea. There's no charge for the lessons, but Faraday is going to give the Trumbull Academy of the Arts one of the costumes he wears in the movie. They'll be selling chances on it to raise money for the school."

A little side hustle for a good cause!

Pete and I went back inside, where I put the finishing touches on the not-bad dinner while he set the table. "I caught some of the report you did on the Faraday trial," he said. "Good job. It looked as though you got a better look at it than some of the Boston stations did. How did you get that close?"

"Roney managed to get us up the stairs, and then one of your kind officers recognized me, and that helped with the positioning. Lucky breaks all around. Anyway, it was fun to do field reporting again, even for a little while. We did another piece on the Family Farm too. We saw Barney. He looks good."

"Do you know if Sawyer has gone over there to visit the bear yet?" Pete asked.

"Not that I know of. That makes me sad. It must make Barney sad too. Did you know that Doug tells people that he learned to do the hand signals the professional animal trainers use but that he could just *think* about what he wanted Barney to do and the bear would do it?"

"Just from thinking about it?"

"That's what I heard. I wonder if he's trying it with Darla's dog."

Pete shrugged. "I guess it wouldn't hurt to try it, but it's been my experience that dogs do best if you send them to obedience school when they're puppies."

"I think that's what we'll do if we ever get a puppy," I said, "but Toby is a grown-up dog. The bartender at the Friendly said that Doug has brought him there several times and that he is very well behaved and he's welcome there anytime."

"Good," Pete said, then gave me a questioning look. "Lee?"

"Yes?"

"When can we get it?"

"Get what?"

"The puppy!"

CHAPTER 30

A puppy? What is the man thinking?
I sidestepped the questions. "Someday, when we're not both so busy," I suggested. "What kind of dog are you thinking about? I mean, when we have the time to devote to training it—with or without mental telepathy."

"Maybe not a puppy, then," he said. "Maybe we should get a rescue dog. One that's older and trained and needs a home."

"That would be nice. Let's think about that." Visions of a golden retriever danced through my head. I picked up the dinner dishes and began loading the dishwasher. "Are you ready for ice cream? There are some of Aunt Ibby's Toll House cookies in the cookie jar too."

The topic of a dog for us was put aside, but the conversation remained on animals. "Poor Frankie isn't happy with that big collar around her neck, is she?" Pete asked. "And she's very careful about walking on that forepaw. People who abuse animals make me angry."

I scooped the ice cream into bowls and Pete carefully selected two cookies for each of us from the cookie jar. "I know. It makes me grateful that there are people like the ones who opened the Family Farm. The animals there, including the show-business dogs and cats, all seem happy with their new home. Say, did anyone tell you that Darla was an animal lover?"

"No. Where did you hear that?"

I repeated what Roney had told me about Darla.

"That gives a whole new facet to the woman's personality if it's true, doesn't it?" Pete mused. "I wonder if the contents of her wastebasket will tell us even more about her. Sometimes people judge one another unfairly when key pieces of information are missing."

"It's especially tricky when the person is an actress or actor," I said. "It must be difficult sometimes to get out of the make-believe world and back into the real one. Maybe if I get a chance to speak with Lamont Faraday when he's giving the class at the Tabby, I'll ask him about that."

"Faraday really seemed to regret the episode that got him arrested," Pete said. "He was embarrassed about it and willingly paid the fines and accepted the community service hours. I won't be surprised if he gives the school more hours than he has to."

"He already has a reputation as a nice person," I said. "So does Doug Sawyer. Not too many people have much of anything nice to say about Darla. Too bad she kept her nice side a secret—that is, if it's true that she *had* a nice, animal-loving side."

"She took good care of her lab, Toby," Pete pointed out.

"Maybe. Some people say Doug has been caring for

him all along. That Darla just used Toby for photo ops." I felt bad just repeating this bit of gossip. "I hope it's not true." I put the last of the dinner dishes into the dishwasher and wiped down the counters.

"It's still early," Pete said, "and it's a nice evening. Want to go for a walk?"

I agreed immediately. Even during the craziness of October's Haunted Happenings, Salem is a great walking town. We each put on light jackets and I followed Pete to the front door. The sun had set several hours earlier, but Winter Street's brick sidewalks were nicely illuminated by tall streetlamps. Smiling jack-o'-lanterns gleamed from several doorsteps on both sides of the wide street. Houses on our street open directly onto the sidewalk, like most homes in this section of Salem, with backyards for gardens or trees or the occasional pool.

Our front door sported a fall-themed wreath with colorful leaves and pine cones and tiny gourds with a gold bow. One of Michael's students had made a cute, white-flannel ghost with blinking blue eyes for his door décor.

"Left or right?" Pete asked. "The Salem Common or Beverly bridge?"

"Right," I said. "Too many good restaurants on Bridge Street and we just ate. Let's window-shop on Essex Street." I drive past Salem's main downtown street every day on my way to work, but because much of it is a pedestrian mall with lots of shops, walking it is a treat.

The air was cool, a bit nippy, and the fallen leaves made a pleasant crunchy sound as we made our way toward the giant, fifty-eight-ton granite boulder on the corner commemorating Salem's Civil War veterans. We passed Aunt Ibby's house, where the smiling pumpkin glowed from the bottom step. I couldn't help peering into the tall side window where O'Ryan often greeted me. "No cat," I said.

"Do you want to stop?" Pete asked.

"Nope. He'll undoubtedly catch up with us sometime later. Anyway, it's meeting night for the Angels. They must have parked in the backyard, and I'm sure Michael will enjoy the walk. Aunt Ibby invited Roney to join in too. Should be quite a gathering."

"You sure you don't want to stop?" he asked again.

"Nope. I'd much rather try to solve a real mystery with you," I teased. "Are you any closer to solving the Liquid Centered Murder yet?"

He made a sort of snorting noise. "The Liquid Centered Murder? Is that what they're calling it?"

"Scott Palmer named it."

"Well, to answer your question, we *are* making progress on several levels—including those liquid-centered chocolates. For instance, the chocolate that killed Darla wasn't one of the imported ones she always ordered. It was a local product. If she'd paused and looked at it before she popped it into her mouth, she would have rejected it."

"Why?"

"Forensics narrowed it down to one of three shops in the area that make liquid-center candy. We don't know which one yet, but you know how chocolates usually have that little squiggle on top? None of the local ones have the same designer squiggle as Darla's imported ones." He kicked a spiny horse chestnut out of the way. "If she'd just looked at it, she wouldn't have eaten it. And she'd be alive."

"Pay attention to small details," I said, remembering.

"What?"

"River found it in Ariel's dream book about being objective. It says, 'pay attention to small details.'"

"She's right." We crossed Washington Street and walked along the narrow sidewalk beside the iron fence that surrounds the common. "If you add up enough of those small details, a lot of the time you can come up with one big, fat, important fact."

"I'm going to try to do that," I promised.

"At work?" he asked.

"That too, but no, I was thinking more of trying to figure out the unfortunately named Liquid Centered Murder," I told him, sincerely meaning it.

"Okay, Mrs. Hart—or Encyclopedia Brown—I will welcome your help on this one." He draped an arm around my shoulders. "Seriously, you've already managed to be in touch with people the police department would never have connected with this case. Just be careful, my love." He tightened his arm, pulling me closer. "Keep me in the loop. Don't try anything on your own. Promise?"

"I promise. Anyway, I seem to be attracting conveniently located police escorts lately." I leaned into his shoulder. "It helps to have a friend on the force."

"Along with a couple of protective cats," he added.

"I know. That was strange, wasn't it? Those two rascals weren't about to let me near that package."

"Maybe tomorrow we'll know what made them so nervous about it. I know McBiel says there's nothing dangerous in it, but I think it's a good idea to open it carefully under safe circumstances."

I smiled. "Are you planning to involve the bomb squad?"

"Not quite *that* carefully!" Short laugh. "I mean, we'll use masks and gloves. Who knows what the woman threw into her trash? The chief thinks the whole idea is crazy. He says he's not really interested in going through some dumb blonde's garbage can."

"I never thought of it being dangerous," I admitted. "I guess that's what you call paying attention to small details."

We'd reached the hotel and prepared to cross over onto Essex Street. Traffic lights there are usually controlled by pedestrian-activated push buttons, but due to the crush of Halloween revelers, a uniformed officer did the job. Recognizing Pete, he immediately held up both white-gloved hands, stopped the four lanes of cars, and motioned us, along with several other people, across the busy street.

"It pays to have friends on the force." Pete grinned, and we stepped onto the sidewalk in front of Crow Haven Corner, the oldest of Salem's many witch shops. We took our time walking along the familiar street and soon approached the pedestrian mall where the serious window-shopping would begin. This fairly recently developed part of our city features art galleries, jewelry stores, and some more witch shops. Aunt Ibby says she remembers when this area was a thriving downtown, full of large department stores, elegant dress shops, and chain clothing stores, along with an assortment of sweets shops and specialty grocery stores and an assortment of restaurants.

We'd almost reached the entrance to the Peabody Essex Museum when I spotted a familiar couple coming toward us. Doug Sawyer and Paulina Fellows walked arm in arm. Paulina was stunning in a jacket and a slim pants outfit that surely bore a name designer label, and Doug was guiding a prancing Toby on a short leash. They paused in front of a jewelry store, and Paulina leaned close to the glass, blond hair and perfect profile reflecting in the glittering display window.

"Well, hello there," I greeted them. "Nice night for a walk, isn't it?".

"Perfect," Paulina said, taking her arm from Doug's and embracing me in a sudden, sweet-smelling hug. "Good to meet you. I've been enjoying your reports on TV." Doug and Pete shook hands, and at a slight movement of Doug's left hand, Toby sat down on the brick sidewalk, looking pleased with himself.

"I see that Toby is already learning obedience," I said, "and Paulina, you smell delicious."

"It's called Joy," she explained. "Doug bought it for me. It's the same perfume Darla always wore."

"It's lovely," I told her. *I wonder if Paulina's housing arrangements have changed along with the expensive new fragrance.* I wondered too about the obviously expensive outfit Paulina wore. One of Doug's residences now included the trailer, complete with Darla's closet, and Paulina was after all a body double. Maybe Doug had solved Paulina's anxiety problem about staying alone at the Airbnb, along with the dog-sitting duty, by moving her into the trailer.

We walked all the way down to the Witch House, stopping now and then to admire the costumed buskers who populate the city—especially during October—posing with visitors for tips. We turned and started back for home. It was nearly nine o'clock when we darted across Washington Street. "Want to cut through Aunt Ibby's yard?" I asked. "Less traffic that way." The front of my aunt's property is on Winter Street, while her garage and backyard face onto parallel Oliver Street.

"Less traffic, and you can see whose cars are there so we'll know if the meeting is still going on, Miss Nosy." Pete guessed correctly. He knows me so well. Holding my elbow, he steered me in the right direction. Betsy's Mercedes was there, along with Louisa's Audi, Roney's rental, and the other tenant's Ford.

"Michael must have walked over," I decided. "The movie takes two hours; then they'll have a discussion and eat dessert." I looked at my watch. "They'll probably be there until after eleven. Even longer if Roney gives his face cream sales pitch."

I explained to Pete about Roney's latest side hustle. "It's perfectly legal, isn't it?" I asked.

"If it's one person selling his own property to another person and there's no sales tax involved and it isn't stolen goods or an illegal substance, I presume it's okay," Pete said. We moved quietly through the yard, lighted by solar lights along the pathway, and exited onto Winter Street through the back wrought-iron gate.

It wasn't until we were at our own front door that it

occurred to me that we might have just seen the modern dress version of the vision I'd seen not long ago on a foil package. Then it was a black-robed judge and two blond women in drab long dresses. This time it was Doug Sawyer, Paulina Fellows, and her high-fashion mirror image in the store window. The only difference was the addition of the dog.

CHAPTER 31

It was too late to call River about the couple we'd seen on our walk and the resemblance to the trio who'd appeared in my vision. Maybe there was no comparison. Maybe my imagination was working overtime. Anyway, River could look it up in her dream book later. No hurry. *Why don't I just get a dream book from the library and look it up myself?*

"Good idea. I'll do it tomorrow."

"Did you say something?" Pete held the door open for me.

"Just thinking out loud, I guess." I told him. "The movie documentary is too much on my mind. Seeing Doug with Darla's double was kind of disturbing. No wonder people imagine they're seeing Darla's ghost."

"I know," he said. "I've been thinking about the package in my trunk. The contents of the woman's wastebasket might very well hold a message from her—well, from her ghost, because Roney seems to believe that whatever he saw there should be seen by the authorities."

"If I wear a mask and gloves, can I be there when you open it tomorrow?" The words spilled out. "After all, I sort of found it for you. If I hadn't contacted Roney, you wouldn't have it at all—and I'm the one who handed it over to you, unopened."

Pete turned on the living room lights. "True," he said. "You've put a lot of work into finding out all you can about what happened to Darla for your story. So far the chief's not even interested in seeing what it is. I think I can get you in—but definitely no news cameras."

I hugged him. "Thank you," I said, "but you'll have your own cameras there, won't you?"

"Of course. Now let's stop worrying about ghosts and trash cans and relax in our nice, safe, comfy bed." We climbed the stairs to our room, but not before Pete had checked the locks on all of the downstairs windows.

"Well, look who's here ahead of us. Hello, O'Ryan." The cat looked up at the sound of Pete's voice from the foot of the bed, where he'd been snoozing on the folded quilt. "I guess he's decided that you need his company day and night."

"I thought for sure he'd be spending the evening with Aunt Ibby and the Angels," I said, surprised. "He likes watching *Midsomer Murders* too." Pete turned down the covers and I headed for the bathroom. It would be good to get into silk jammies and—as Pete had suggested—stop worrying about ghosts and trash cans. Still, I couldn't help being excited by the idea that I'd be on hand to see the contents of one particular wastebasket. It was doubly exciting to realize that, for the first time ever, Pete and I would be working together on the same case. Kind of like Mr. and Mrs. Hart!

I phoned Rhonda in the morning to tell her I'd be late, but that I was working on an important aspect of the movie documentary. It was decided that I'd ride to work with Pete after breakfast, that he'd drop me at WICH-TV when we were finished, and I'd walk home at five, avoiding the traffic mess.

I don't go into the police station very often, and to me it always feels like a middle school trip—be quiet, act polite, and don't touch anything. I was greeted with the respect due the wife of a detective sergeant on the Salem PD, but I still didn't touch anything. I was handed a cup of very strong coffee. Before long, Pete and I, along with three officers, donned masks and gloves and entered a long, cold room. We sat in chairs around a steel table, the brown-wrapped package at its center. "My wife, Lee," Pete nodded in my direction, "acquired this item from an out-of-state source through thoroughly legal means. Her contact believes it contains something related to Darla Diamond that may be of interest to law enforcement. It may, or may not, be of importance. The contact says it contains nothing explosive or poisonous, but we'll take due caution in handling it."

Using a pocket knife, Pete opened the brown paper outer wrapping. There was what appeared to be a flattened tissue box inside, and from that, there issued what must have been hundreds of tiny, torn, scraps of blue paper. "What the hell is this supposed to be?" muttered someone behind a mask.

"Careful," said another. "Fingerprints."

"Right," Pete said. "We'll handle as little as possible, then check right away for prints."

Don't touch anything. I already knew that.

"Oops. Look at this." With gloved hands, Pete lifted a blue square of painstakingly pieced together, taped scraps. The message on the thing behind the transparent tape was printed in a childish scrawl with black marker. It was easy to read: DIE BITCH DO IT. Pete picked up one of the torn bits. We could all see parts of black marker letters on it. "Someone took the time to piece one of these together and to preserve the rest." He nodded in my direction. "It's likely that whoever taped this together had to leave some prints on the tape. Thankfully, my wife was able to get this to us for further investigation. I'm thinking there are other similar messages here. It looks as if we'll be doing some sorting and taping of our own for a while."

"I wonder who taped this one together," I wondered aloud. "It looks like Darla's blue notepaper. See the little initials?" I pointed.

"I'll bet you're right," another masked person spoke "But we'll need a comparison piece."

"We have the note she left for Lamont Faraday in the evidence room. I'll get it," Pete said. "Don't touch anything yet."

I already knew that.

He was back in what felt like only seconds, blue notepaper held between gloved thumb and forefinger. "Yes. It matches. The death threat note was written on her own paper, but it's extremely doubtful she wrote that one."

"Wait a minute," I said. "The colors don't match."

"What do you mean?" Pete asked. "What colors?"

"The letter in your hand is a much paler blue that the scraps from the wastebasket," I told him. "Try putting one of the scraps next to the Faraday note. There's a difference."

He did as I'd suggested, placing a torn blue scrap beside the note in his hand. "You're right. It looks as if the note she sent to Faraday is faded—older, maybe."

"Let's get the Faraday note tested as to its age," one of the masked officers offered. "Just looking at it makes me think Lee is right. They aren't the same at all. Can we do that?"

Another of the three raised his hand and responded, "I can do the analysis. Organic and inorganic both. I can find the mineral evidence in the pigment and ink, as well as find carbon-based organisms on either or both of them."

"Good," Pete said. "We'll set you up with a lab. Get back to me as soon as you can on this. I guess that's about all we can do right now. Having seen what it is, I'm going to ask McBiel to come in and give us the details about finding it and if it was he who pieced it together." He stood, indicating that the meeting was over. I stood too, beside Pete, and waited there until the others had left the room.

"Okay, I'll get you to your work as soon as we get all this safely stashed away," he said, waving a hand at the items on the table. Still gloved, he returned the blue scraps to the tissue box and wrapped it loosely in the original brown paper. "Want to wait in my office? You must be freezing in here. Want another cup of coffee?"

I declined the coffee, thinking I might find time to grab a cup of Dunkin' later, and followed him from the room into the nearby office. "I'll be right back," he promised, giving me a discreet peck on the cheek.

"I have an idea about volunteers to put the puzzle pieces together," I told him. "I'll tell you about it on the way to the TV station."

CHAPTER 32

I thought my idea for match-and-tape volunteers was a good one, and after a moment of thinking it over, Pete agreed. I'd suggested that Aunt Ibby and the Angels had the time, patience, and curiosity to do the job. "They're absolutely trustworthy," I backed up my idea, "and they'd probably wear masks and gloves if you want them to."

After a moment's consideration Pete agreed. "The Angels. Why not? I really don't have enough staff to take any of my officers off the street to work on this. Once the paper analysis is finished, they could get started. I'll have to get the okay from the chief of course. Do you want to ask them if they'd be interested in doing it? Or should I?"

"I think they'd love it if you made an official request," I said. "They already think they're detectives."

"I'll call Ibby today," he promised, "and get things started. The more of those notes we can get reconstructed, the better chance we have of identifying the writer of the death threats. And, possibly, the killer."

I felt a little glow of pride, thinking that if I hadn't made the initial call to California, the torn notes and the chilling threat wouldn't have found their way to Salem at all. I sipped my coffee as we wound our way through Salem streets and pulled into the lot behind Ariel's bench. "See you tonight," I said, "and thanks for an interesting morning. I love working with you."

"Glad to have you aboard," he said. The proud glow grew even bigger.

I entered via the studio door and climbed the metal stairs to the reception area. Rhonda greeted me with a smile and a note in red marker on the whiteboard. "Doan says to send you right in. Buffy's here too."

"I saw the purple Mazda outside," I told her. "What's up? Do you know?"

"Nope. Just that Buffy's in a real good mood, so it's nothing bad."

I tapped on the station manager's partially open door. "Come right on in, Ms. Barrett," Bruce Doan called. I pushed the door open and faced my smiling boss and his beaming wife.

"It appears that Buffy has an opportunity to further her acting career," Doan boasted, "and you have the expertise in television promotion that will be helpful to her. I believe you've even taught a course on the subject at the Tabby."

"Yes, sir. I did. It was some time ago," I admitted, thinking I was undoubtedly about to get another WICH-TV hat to wear.

"Paragon Productions has requested a video of Buffy

in the part of one of the accused Salem witches. A screen test, of sorts." There was such pride in his voice that I decided right away that I'd do all I could to further this new *career* for her. "I've received permission from the director of the Witch House to film it in the interior of the old house," he continued. "One of the actors still under contract to Paragon will take the part of the judge, and Buffy has been invited to go to the warehouse where the costumes for the Salem scenes are housed to select the proper clothing."

"I didn't know about the costume warehouse," I said. "That in itself would make an interesting part of the movie documentary we're doing."

"An excellent point, Ms. Barrett," he said. "I like the way you're thinking."

I wonder if Mr. Doan's financial contribution to Paragon has influenced this sudden interest in Buffy Doan, actress.

Whatever the reason, I was intrigued with the idea of a warehouse full of costumes somewhere in my city. "When would you like to begin?" I asked.

"The trip to the warehouse can be arranged anytime. The actual filming at the Witch House requires some planning ahead," he explained.

"Let's do it today, Lee." Buffy practically danced with excitement. "I'll bet we can find something really nice. After all, some of the accused women were from fine old Salem families. I tried to tell the director that not all the women who were hanged wore those awful gray and brown dresses, but he wouldn't listen to me."

"I'm sure you're right about that," I told her. "I believe the group shot of all the women in drab colors was done that way for artistic reasons—to illustrate the sadness and hopelessness of their situation."

"Then I'll be able to wear something a little more historically accurate—and more becoming, won't I, Bruce?" She aimed a confident smile in her husband's direction.

"Of course you can, dear. Wear whatever pleases you. I'll phone the warehouse and tell them you're coming," he assured her. "Ms. Barrett, see if Francine or Old Jim can go with you."

It didn't take long after that for Buffy and me to find ourselves in the converted VW bus with Jim at the wheel, on our way to a warehouse complex just across the Peabody line. I wore my green jacket, intending to do a brief stand-up in front of the place, along with a glimpse of a few of the costumes for a possible airing on the news, as well as a documentary-style recitation of what the viewers were seeing in regard to movie-making. Killing two birds with one stone, as the rather grisly old saying goes. In this case, it was three birds, including giving Buffy's newfound career a boost.

A woman met us at the gate of the place and directed Jim to the properly numbered building. "One of my associates will meet you there and unlock it for you," she promised, and after driving deeper into the property Jim parked in front of one of the many look-alike doorways and the three of us were admitted to Paragon's well-lighted, air-conditioned, off-site Salem costume department.

There were aisles in the place with signs identifying what was stored on rows of hanging racks. From where I stood in the doorway I saw signs indicating such categories as "Period dress women sizes P-S-M" and "Modern dress men sizes S-M" and "Uniforms, women sizes L-XL, XXL."

"Neat," I said. "Shall we go straight to period dress women, Buffy?"

We did so, with Buffy in the lead, Jim following with a shoulder-mount camera and me with my trusty hand mic. I did a fast intro, explaining where we were and what we were seeing. I realized quickly that even if this wasn't a newsworthy segment, it fit the evergreen category. Everybody likes costumes—especially in Salem—and especially in October.

I wound up the intro with "We're here with *Night Magic* actress, Buffy Doan, as she selects an appropriate dress for a dreadful occasion. She's looking for a dress that a condemned Salem woman might wear to the gallows."

Buffy quickly narrowed her choices down to the few dresses she found in size medium in shades of purple, and settled on a square-necked, narrow-waisted, full-skirted sateen dress in a pale lavender. We didn't follow her into the dressing room of course, but had the camera rolling when she emerged, looking lovely. There was no doubt in my mind that the WICH-TV audience would soon see a lot of footage of the lavender-clad accused witch.

"As long as we're here," I told Jim, "let's record as much of this place as we can. I'm amazed that there are this many costumes available for the scenes shot in Salem."

"I've seen the rushes from California," he told me. "They hired a lot of extras out there and made a lot of crowd shots. It looks to me as if they sent everything they had, whether they needed it in Salem or not. They're doing crowd shots here too, but mostly in modern dress, so extras can use their own clothes. We can walk up and down the aisles," he suggested. "That way we can give everybody a fast look at the variety of stuff, even if we don't show every costume in detail."

"Good idea." Jim, moving carefully ahead of me, walking backward down one aisle after another, filmed me as I pointed out the signs at the beginning of each aisle, pausing occasionally to pull out an item. "Here we are in a children's section." I pulled away a small sailor suit on a hanger from the rack. "I guess the sailor suit never goes out of style." We moved as quickly as we could from section to section. In women's modern dress I pointed out a really handsome business suit with a Halston label. In the men's uniforms department I showed a doctor's white coat, followed by a security guard's blue jacket and a short leather jacket marked CITY MESSENGER SERVICE, as well as a priest's vestments. We wound up the shoot with the warehouse door closing behind us. "When *Night Magic* is finished," I told my audience, "all of these very special movie props will undoubtedly go to another warehouse in another city for another movie. Perhaps you'll see a child actor in that cute sailor suit on the big screen someday, or see another actress wearing the full-skirted lavender dress that Buffy Doan showed us—at a party or in a garden—instead of on her way to the gallows."

"I liked your windup," Jim told me as we packed our gear into the VW. "Kind of creepy, though, how you went from the cute little kid's suit to the dress for the durned hanging."

"Contrast," I said. "Learned it when I was a home shopping host. It gives the audience an idea of the spectrum of merchandise you have to offer. Let's get back to the studio and get the Buffy footage edited for tonight's around town feature. Then, both of the Doans will be in a hurry to get Buffy back into that dress and off to the Witch House to be accused of witchcraft."

I'd no sooner closed the door to my office behind me when Rhonda buzzed me. "Doan wants to know how soon Buffy can get to the Witch House or the replica courtroom to do the screen test." I gazed at the wall, where a lime-green sticky practically called out *Pick me!* I reached for it and read the time and date the director had given me for a meeting about the planned tour I'd been assigned.

"They're already starting dismantling the replica," I told her, "but I have an appointment with the director at the Witch House tomorrow. Maybe we can set something up for a time when they're closed—like in the middle of the night."

CHAPTER 33

Sometimes, when I have a super busy day ahead of me, it feels as if everything moves along like a sped-up film, with time racing by at warp speed, situation to situation, place to place, scene to scene, problem to problem, with barely time to absorb each one before the picture shifts.

Pete and I both got up early. He'd scheduled a six thirty a.m. meeting with Roney McBiel to tie up loose ends about Darla's wastebasket. Roney had set the time because he needed to pick up a piece of heavy equipment for the demolishing of the Gallows Hill set at seven. Then Pete planned a meeting with Chief Whaley and my aunt to discuss the possibility—and the legality—of using the Angels to piece together what appeared to be death threats sent to Darla Diamond.

I needed to get to work early to make sure my program schedule was in place, along with my documentary duties regarding the making of the movie, as well as the planned meeting at the Witch House about the proposed tours. All that, along with trying to convince the Witch House people that it would be a good idea to open the place after-hours really soon to make Buffy's screen test.

Pete once again drove me to work via Dunkin's for coffee. It was my turn to stock the break room, so I picked up a dozen powdered sugar doughnuts. We'd watched Buffy's around town segment on the news the night before, as well as some clips from my filming of Lamont Faraday's trial and a teaser from the shoot we'd done at the Family Farm. I felt as though I'd been darn well represented, considering that Scott Palmer did the introductions on each piece.

I dropped off the doughnuts, then, once I'd settled myself in my glass cube, made a call to the Tabby, reserving a space in the upcoming Lamont Faraday acting class. I noticed that Scott was in early too. I gave him a brief wave through the glass and opened my computer screen to my programming schedule. Not unexpectedly, Scott tapped on the glass with his phone and pointed to mine. With a sigh, I picked it up. *I might as well get this over with, whatever it is.*

"Yes, Scott?"

"Did you catch me on the news last night? Your name came up."

"I saw it. 'Thanks for noticing me,'" I said, quoting Eyore of Winnie-the-Pooh fame.

"Good job on all of those. I liked the Family Farm one a lot. I thought you might like to know I'm interviewing another one of your old friends this morning. Doug Sawyer."

"No kidding. Are you going to talk to him about Barney and the old TV series?"

"Not this time. Nope. We're going to talk about movie makeup. He's going to change himself from the lawyer he plays in the modern-day Salem part of the story into the evil old hangin' judge he plays in the witchcraft half. Right on camera." He smiled. "Pretty good, huh?"

"Really good," I told him—meaning it. "I had no idea he did his own makeup. Doug is a man of many talents."

"Yep. He's always had to stay busy to earn that whopping-huge salary they pay him."

"I wonder why he never went to another studio where he wouldn't have to do every little thing they want," I said, "even if it meant less money."

"Can't," Scott said. "I heard that he signed a wicked noncompete clause. He works for Paragon or nobody."

"I'll try to watch your interview," I promised. "It should be interesting. Meanwhile, I need to start earning my own whopping-huge salary. Ha ha. Bye."

First, I called Pyramid Books and ordered a dream book, then got started on my program schedules. *Shopping Salem* was doing Day of the Dead items from all over the city, and Ranger Rob had invited a few kids from the Double R Ranch along with their ponies to do some riding demonstrations. River had some of the very best old Halloween scary movies ready for the week, and the *Saturday Business* guy had a guest lined up to talk about Quickbooks, so that part of my job looked squared away.

My next imaginary hat to don was the one with Executive Director of Documentaries on it. Because the topic Doan had assigned me, along with my fancy new title, had to do with the making of the movie *Night Magic,* virtually every bit of work I'd done during the past week related to that category. I was sure I could borrow some of Scott's work too, including the upcoming interview with Doug. I'd get with Marty and have her do a little splicing and dicing of the various pieces and I'd have something new to show to Mr. Doan.

I kept an eye on the clock, knowing it would take some time to get to the Witch House from the WICH-TV building. Because Pete and I had just done it on foot the previous night, I'd already decided that the surest way to keep this important date was to hoof it again, rather than trust any mode of transportation to the vagaries of Salem's Halloween month traffic. The distance from the WICH-TV building to the corner of Essex Street was a tad longer than the distance from our house to the same spot. No problem. "*Vámanos!*" shouted my inner Dora. "I know that we can do it!"

With everything around me speeding up the way it seemed, doing a mile or so along Essex Street, indulging in a bit more window-shopping felt like a walk in the park. It didn't take long to reach Crow Haven Corner, and I hadn't yet reached the pedestrian mall when I saw a familiar form approaching from the opposite direction.

"River! Where are you going at this time of day?" It was extremely early for anyone who works a midnight TV show to even be awake at this hour, let alone to be walking along at a pretty fast clip. As she drew closer I saw, beneath a Red Sox baseball cap, that her hair was blond and pulled back in a bun. My friend was obviously going to work on the movie.

"Hi, Lee." She gave me a quick, patchouli-scented hug. "They need a reshoot of some of the women in the wagon, heading for the gallows. Paulina was supposed to do it, but she said she had a hot date and she'd pay me double time. You know I'm saving up for a wedding, and that's a good chunk of change."

I'd worked the late-show gig long enough to know that you're permanently jet-lagged, and that loss of sleep catches up with you eventually. "Don't wear yourself out," I warned her. "You want to look good for the wedding."

"I know." The dimpled smile was as wide-awake as ever. "I'll be careful. She doesn't ask me to do it very often." It occurred to me that maybe Paulina's circumstances had changed and that maybe hot dates could become more frequent. I shook the nonobjective thought away.

"Have fun on the gallows ride," I said, "then take a nap." Another brief hug and we went our separate ways, River at the same fast clip, me speeding mine up a little more. I approached the jewelry store window where I'd seen Doug and Paulina's reflections the night before. What had they been admiring? I wondered, and paused to take a look at the display of pricey baubles.

Diamond rings—lots of them. Forcing myself to draw no conclusions, I moved on toward the museum, checking the time on the restored Almy's Clock across the street. I figured I'd arrive at the Witch House early and slowed my pace accordingly. The attraction didn't open until ten anyway, so I was pretty sure there'd be no line. It was fun looking into the many witch shop windows, while at the same time thinking of Aunt Ibby's descriptions of old-time Essex Street, before the advent of *Bewitched*—when witches suddenly became cool.

When the Witch House came into sight I was still thinking about how Samantha and Darrin and Endora and Aunt Clara and the others had affected my city— and probably much of the rest of the TV viewing public. There's even a statue of Elizabeth Montgomery as Samantha just down the street from City Hall, and witchcraft-related shops dominate our retail district. I paused in front of a shop window full of pink witch hats, crossed North Street, and approached the back door of Jonathan Corwin's seventeenth-century house where the whole thing started.

The Witch House director—young, buff, and tanned, with a prematurely white beard—welcomed me into the ticket office, gift shop entrance way, to the house. "Good morning, Ms. Barrett," he said. "I understand from Bruce Doan that Mrs. Doan needs to have a video and perhaps some still photos taken here in our courtroom."

"Yes, sir," I said. "Can you give us a time and date when it will be convenient for you? Mrs. Doan will arrive in costume with our mobile crew. It would take only a short time to produce. WICH-TV will be so appreciative." The free extra publicity on-site programing provides is always happily received by businesses, and an historical tourist attraction is no exception.

"Any morning, like this one, will be fine. The morning light shining through the diamond-pane windows in the courtroom is quite flattering. I'll show you the room."

I followed him to the dark-paneled room. He was right about the windows. Tiny leaded panes gave close-up glimpses of bits of vines, as well as blue sky and a next-door building—like little patchwork glass quilts—and the patterns of light shining through to the dark wood floor was almost hypnotic. Did the doomed women watch the shifting light as they listened to their death sentences?

"Will nine tomorrow work for you?"

"Excuse me?"

He repeated the question, bringing me back to reality. "I'm sure nine will be fine. Thank you." I shook his hand, followed him back to the entrance, and let myself out, back into welcoming, present-day Salem's October merriment. I almost skipped across North Street, smiled at the silly pink hats, and hurried back along Essex Street, happy to return to the comforting glass walls of my little office.

CHAPTER 34

As soon as I got back to WICH-TV, I took Old Clunky up to the second floor so I could tell Mr. Doan that Buffy's appointment for her nine a.m. screen test was secure. Afterward I stopped at Rhonda's desk to check the whiteboard. "Nothing more for you today so far," she said. "Look." She pointed to the monitor above her chair. "Scotty's interview with the creepy makeup guy is on."

Somebody had done some fast editing to get the thing ready to air so soon. I hadn't thought of Doug as creepy, but as I looked at the screen, he applied face putty to his nose, forehead, and chin, rearranging his face from that of a good-looking young guy into a scowling, bloated, jowly old man. He applied makeup swiftly, giving a grayish tone to his skin, and pulled on a wig of wispy, white hair. "Wow. What a difference," I said, "and he hasn't even put the beard and mustache on yet."

"Creepy," Rhonda repeated. "Imagine being able to turn yourself into another person that fast. It takes me half an hour to put on bronzer, eyelashes, mascara, and lipstick and get it right."

"I didn't know those weren't your own lashes."

"Don't tell anybody. Look. There goes the beard. Creepy as hell. I can't watch anymore." She clicked off the monitor. I didn't object.

I took the ramp down to my office. Looking through my glass wall, I saw that Scott was watching himself on his own monitor. I tuned mine on too to catch the end of the segment. There was the 1692 judge, maybe old Jonathan himself, ready to levy punishment on innocent women. I listened as Doug, in a voice much unlike his own, read from a script some questions I recognized from the original trial transcripts I'd seen in a display case at the Witch House.

"How long have you been a witch? Who made you a witch? What did the devil promise to give you?" His voice quivered, then rose to a shout.

Rhonda was right. He was creepy. And besides that, he was a damn good actor. Why had he ever signed that stupid contract?

I turned off the monitor. *They're not paying me to watch TV. They're paying me to create it*, I scolded myself. *I have plenty to keep me busy right here*. I reached for a yellow sticky, a reminder to get tickets for the Tabby's annual student production. I'd heard that they were doing *Beauty and the Beast*. It occurred to me that maybe Doug Sawyer could be convinced to do the beast's makeup. I made a pale blue sticky, *Call Doug re: beast* and stuck it onto the glass. I ordered the tickets online, tore the yellow square in half, and tossed it into the wastebasket.

Had Darla torn the first threatening note into pieces and tossed it into her wastebasket as casually as I had just tossed my sticky, thinking it was just a crank joke? Had the notes come in rapid secession? The fact that several of them were in the one basket suggested that they had.

Again, I reminded myself that I needed to concentrate on WICH-TV business, not on pretending that I was Jennifer Hart, helping my husband solve a murder.

I buzzed Marty's number. She answered on the first ring. "Hey, Moon. What's going on?"

I asked her about helping me turn the bits and pieces of the many aspects of the making of *Night Magic* into something cohesive enough to show to the station manager.

"Sure. I'll be glad to be working with you again," she said. "I've been keeping an eye on you, you know. They never should have taken you off the field reports. You have a gift for the immediacy of it all."

I was flattered. "Thanks, Marty. But I'm married now, and the program director hours are a lot better."

"Yeah. The cute cop. That was a nice wedding. I've always enjoyed the single life myself." Short sigh. "I suppose you're planning a family."

I was searching for an answer when Roney McBiel appeared outside my office door. "Sorry, Marty," I said. "Somebody's at my door. Gotta go."

"Okay, Moon. I 'll get with Jim and Scotty and see what we've got to work with," she promised.

I said goodbye and waved Roney in through the unlocked door. "What's up?" I asked, "I thought you'd be swinging a wrecking ball over at Gallows Hill by now."

"I was," he said. "Well, not exactly a wrecking ball, but I'd put a pretty good dent in the place when I found something maybe you'd want to take a look at." He held out a small, flowered gift bag in my direction. "This was under the magistrate's desk in the replica courtroom."

I reached for it. "What's in it?"

"Chocolates."

I withdrew my hand. Fast. *Don't touch anything.* "What kind?" I asked, knowing perfectly well what the answer would be.

"I sure wasn't about to taste one," he said, "but they sure look like the ones Darla always used to keep stashed around."

"Just put it on the desk." I reached for my phone. "I'll call Pete."

He answered fast. "I'll be right there. Tell McBiel to stick around. I want to talk to him," Pete said. "Don't touch anything."

I knew that.

It didn't take long for Pete to get there. He must have used lights and sirens, I figured, and must have scared poor Chester out of his shoes. It had also alerted my nosy next-door newsroom neighbor, Scott Palmer, that something was going on. He got to my door before Pete did, along with a cameraman.

I pulled the door open, admitting my husband and waving Scott away. Of course glass walls don't keep nosy reporters from filming. Pete turned his back to the camera and motioned Roney to a corner of the room. I followed. "McBiel," he said in cop voice, "your fingerprints are all over everything in that package you say you found in Darla Diamond's California dressing room, including the taped-together note. Now you claim to have found some of her candy here in Salem. I have a few questions."

I wondered if Pete was about to read Roney his rights. I hoped he wasn't and was glad when he just pulled out his old leather notebook. "Did you tape the note together?"

"Sure. I tried to do another one too, but it's darned hard to fit all those ripped edges together. I had to leave for Salem and the new demo job, but I thought the one note was important enough to have a cop look at. Then I found out that my contact here was married to one—so . . ." Big smile. "Here we all are!"

"You didn't mention to Lee or me that you'd handled all of the materials in the package." Serious cop voice. "You touched every single torn piece of notepaper. When we spoke just this morning you could have told me that."

"Nobody asked me. You wanted to know about the movable panels in the dressing room, and about how I packed all the papers and the completed note up in the tissue box because it was right there. Is it important? That I touched everything? I'm always looking for something I can sell. Once I put the note together and saw what it said I knew I didn't want anything else to do with any of it. Good riddance."

"Tell me about the candy." Pete inclined his head toward the flowered bag. "How did you happen to find that? When nobody else had noticed it?"

"Because that's what I do. I demo things, but first I make sure I have the right to keep the pieces." Another smile. "Like they say, one man's trash is another man's treasure. Some guys would just take an axe to the magistrate's desk. I mean, it's not like it's a real antique or anything. It's made out of cheap pressed wood with a coat of dark paint slapped on it. I look things over carefully. You never know what you might find—like three-hundred-dollar face cream or expensive chocolates."

"You realize I'll have to take the chocolates and examine them for dangerous substances," Pete said.

Roney shrugged. "Poison."

"We'll have to—um—open each one."

"I guess I won't be able to sell squished chocolates, then."

"I'm afraid not. Sorry."

Roney grinned and pushed the pretty bag toward Pete. "Easy come, easy go."

Pete's features relaxed. Roney's explanation about finding the chocolates made sense to me. I wondered if it made sense to Pete too. Pete put the notebook back into his breast pocket, took a pair of blue latex gloves from another pocket, and lifted the flowered bag from the bottom. "Thanks, McBiel," he said. "We have your number and I understand you'll be staying just down the street from us. You're not planning on leaving town anytime soon, are you?"

"I'm not planning on it, but in my business, you never know."

So far I'd been trying to ignore Scott's intrusive camera. All three of us in my office had stood with our backs to that wall, so lipreading wasn't possible. I didn't think a long, soundless picture of three people's backsides would rate a breaking news banner or a seat beside Buck Covington. But I was equally sure it would make a curious reporter like Scott Palmer dig for more, and that he wouldn't be shy about the digging.

CHAPTER 35

That day continued at warp speed right up until I opened the sunroom door at a little past six o'clock and was greeted by a yawning, stretching cat and a warm hug from my husband. The world resumed its normal spin. There was a comforting smell of Italian food—ravioli maybe—wafting from the kitchen. Pete had stopped at Bella Verona, and our dinner was already in the warming oven.

What a guy.

"That was quite a session in your office today. How do you feel about McBiel in general?" Pete asked as I put plates and silverware on the table, avoiding stepping on the cat, who'd followed me in from the sunroom.

Back when I was doing field reports, we'd both carefully avoided any talk about Pete's job. Confidential police business and television news stories can't be comfortably combined in one family. Marty's complimentary remark about my affinity for the news had reminded me of that, and I felt a warm rush of pleasure that Pete now felt at ease in sharing some aspects of his job with me.

"He's a piece of work, isn't he?" I mused, not actually sure of how to answer the rather broad question. "On the one hand, he seems to be very straightforward about his own background. I haven't done any actual checking past the Wikipedia write-up about his stunt-man exploits and his résumé on the Paragon site. Frankly, I didn't feel any need to. I'm sure you have access to more information than I do anyway."

"I do," he agreed. "The chief said I should keep going with the death threat aspect of this, and he's agreed on having Ibby and Louisa and Betsy help with assembling the notes; all three of them have impeccable reputations, and the chief's wife is friends with Ibby. I've done some more extensive digging into McBiel's California past. Everything he claims about his football aspirations and about working on construction with his dad and about how he got into stunt work checks out just as he described it." Pete removed an aluminum pan of ravioli and a brown paper bag containing garlic bread from the oven. "I already knew he had no police record there or here. Everybody I've spoken to who's met him since he arrived in Salem has nothing but positive things to say about him."

"But you aren't convinced?"

He answered my question with one of his own. "Did you ever meet somebody who seemed just too darned perfect?"

I thought about that. "Yes," I said. "There was a girl in high school. She was pretty and smart and popular and homecoming queen and a cheerleader and everybody, including everybody's parents, loved her."

"And did she finally turn out to be flawed somehow?" he wanted to know.

"Heck no. She married a great guy. Her wedding was perfect. She's had two beautiful children and her figure is still spectacular and she now has her own catering business. Did I mention that she's a fabulous cook and was once Mrs. Massachusetts?"

"So there are people who are just too darned perfect?"

"Apparently."

"You're perfect for me," he said.

"And you for me," I told him. "But face it, I'm never going to be Mrs. Massachusetts."

"I spent most of my high school football career on the bench," he said, "and it's a good thing Salem PD doesn't require jumping out of burning buildings or rolling cars."

"I'm glad we're regular normal people—well, sort of normal," I said.

"Sort of," he agreed.

We raised our Pepsi cans and clicked them in a toast to our perceived normalcy. O'Ryan looked up through the clear Lucite from under the table where he'd stationed himself practically on top of my feet.

"Tomorrow morning I'm escorting Buffy Doan to the Witch House to film a screen test for Paragon," I told Pete. "She and Bruce are excited about it. Imagine that. Buffy might wind up making movies. She'll be playing a Salem woman being condemned to hang as a witch."

"I suppose Doug Sawyer will play the judge," he said, "after seeing that makeup job he did on the news."

"It makes sense that he would," I said, "He's very convincing in the part. But he might upstage Buffy."

"He doesn't have to knock himself out over a little screen test," Pete observed. "I guess the contract he already has with Paragon is iron-clad."

"So I've heard. They haven't left him any wiggle room to allow him to accept work with other studios. I feel sorry for him," I admitted. "I guess it's true that a big paycheck doesn't buy happiness."

"Chances are we'll never have to deal with that." Pete laughed. And we clicked our Pepsis together again. "To normal people like us," he said. "I brought spumoni for dessert."

What a guy.

After dinner, dessert, and clean-up we adjourned to the living room for a couple of episodes of *Bridgerton*. By the time we climbed the stairs to the bedroom, the sped-up day felt as if it had dropped into reverse and everything was calm, relaxed, and drowsy. We didn't even watch the late news. Sleep came easily with Pete's arm around my shoulders and a warm cat snuggled up to my full tummy, with his silly, yellow feather toy clutched in one paw.

We had another early start in the morning. Pop-Tarts and coffee and on the road at seven. Rhonda had already arranged with Jim to have the VW gassed up and ready to roll by eight, and Doan had promised that Buffy would be dressed, made-up, and ready to leave at the same time, giving us a full hour to keep our appointment. Paragon's casting director had promised that the supporting actor who'd play the role of the judge would be at the Witch House at nine.

Pete dropped me off behind Ariel's bench. I stepped up over the low banking leading to the studio door, tapped in my code, and pushed the heavy door open, almost bumping into Howie Templeton. "Hi, Howie," I greeted him. "How was the class reunion?"

"Good. I just got back last night. I was coming out to tell Jim that Aunt Buffy wants me to go with her for her screen test. We're getting Francine and the new mobile unit." He gave me a condescending pat on the shoulder. "So you and Old Jim won't have to do it."

"Thanks, Howie," I said, hoping that Buffy's choice of escort would work out well for her. Actually, it worked very nicely for me. It meant that I should have time to get together with Marty and, hopefully, make some sort of sense from the bits and pieces and snippets of videos and stills I had gathered into a disorganized folder labeled *Night Magic Movie*. I intended to use some of it for the documentary and some for the proposed walking tour promo. There'd also undoubtedly be enough information within the cache to put together several short pieces that could be run anytime. I wished Howie a good day—meaning it sincerely—and hurried to the second floor to check in with Rhonda, hoping there'd be no note on the whiteboard announcing another new hat for me.

The only notice for me told me to cancel my nine o'clock meet at the Witch House, and I already knew about that. So, with a clear conscience and a clean deck, I headed for my office, let myself in, and sat at my desk prepared to give WICH-TV a good, solid day of promotion manager work, along with the two related movie duties I'd been assigned.

I'd barely touched my laptop when Scott knocked on my door. "It's open," I called, tapping in PetSmart's website. I needed a Western outfit for Paco the Wonder Dog. I smiled at the on-screen illustrations that included a vest with a sheriff's star, a red-and-white neckerchief, and a broad-brimmed hat with appropriately placed ear holes. Paco would look great and Roney would get a kick out of that hat.

Scott sat in the chair facing my desk without being invited to do so. "What do you want, Scott?" I asked.

"Did you see me on the late news last night?" he asked.

"Sorry, no, we turned in early. Why? What did I miss?"

"Mostly we ran the interview I did with Doug Sawyer when he turned himself into the witch trial judge," he said.

"Great piece of work," I told him, anxious to get on with my day. "Sorry I missed the rerun."

"I was interested in what you thought of what I said about the off-camera chat Doug and I had while he was taking off the makeup, but I guess you didn't see it." He leaned forward in the chair. "It's about the bear."

"About Barney?"

"Yeah. I know you've been wondering why he hadn't been over to that petting zoo thing to visit his bear," he said. "He told me he's going to make the visit soon."

Now he had my complete attention. I ordered the outfit for the dog and closed the app. "Tell me about it."

"He says he's been so busy he hasn't had time to

visit his old partner and playmate, and that people have been telling him he should. Then he had a recent heart-to-heart talk with a dear friend, and he realized that Barney must miss him, must be heartbroken, might even think he's dead. So, he and his friend are going together to visit old Barney." Now he leaned back in the chair and made a steeple shape with his hands. He gave me the long stare. "Guess who the dear friend is."

I thought of the reflection in the jewelry store window. Only one name came to my mind, but I didn't speak it. Instead I said, "Most of the Paragon crew has already left town."

Scott spoke the name. "It's Paulina. Paulina Fellows. The look-alike Darla."

I wanted to pretend surprise at Scott's revelation about the friendship between Paulina and Doug, but all I could manage was raised eyebrows. "An odd couple for sure," I said. "What happened to her old boyfriend? The lighting tech who stopped somebody from breaking into their apartment?"

"Left town, like most of the others," he said.

"Did Doug say when they were planning on the visit? That would be newsworthy, wouldn't it?" I asked. "The TV team from everybody's childhood, man and bear, face-to-face once again?"

"You bet. I tried to pin him down, but he was vague about when it would happen."

"I'll bet the guys who run the Family Farm would tip us off if the two show up. They love TV coverage as much as anyone else. Free publicity is always welcome," I suggested. "I'll give them a call." I wrote a note to myself on a hot-pink sticky. *Call F. Farm.* I copied the number from the card one of the overall guys had given me and posted it directly in front of me onto the glass. "Thanks for the update. Now scram; I've got a lot of work to do."

He complied.

Okay, I told myself. *Enough about Doug Sawyer's private life and Barney's broken heart. I have plenty in my own little world to keep me busy.* I buzzed Marty.

"I thought you'd never ask," she said. "When do we start?"

"Wait a sec," I told her. "I have to call a man about a bear." I poked in the number, asked for Gino, and relayed my request that he give me a call if Doug Sawyer showed up to visit Barney.

"Sure will, Ms. Barrett," he told me. "And don't think we don't appreciate the fifty-dollar bills we find in the donation box whenever you visit us."

"My pleasure," I said, "and thank you."

Getting together with Marty was exactly like old times. Rapid-fire conversation while images flashed by on Marty's screen. "This one," she said. "That one. No, that's too flat. Here. Look. This will be perfect." I saw the baby goats. The diamond-pane windows of the Witch House. That narrow first shot of the Gallows Hill setup Jim and I had grabbed with the zoom lens. The twin trailers. The lucky shot from the Aborn Street backyard. Me with leaves in my hair. My first meeting with Doug, when he was security guard at the Gallows Hill Park gate. The footage Roney had captured at the courthouse. The little sailor suit at the warehouse. The sad picture of the medical examiner's van removing poor Darla's body from the replica set.

"You've got all the makings of a classic documentary here, Moon," Marty told me. "I mean, once we get it all sorted out, this is Emmy award stuff." I managed a modest aw-shucks kind of response, but inside I was bursting with pride at her words.

Working with Marty has always been a pleasure. Sometimes we even finish each other's sentences. Marty did some magic with her computer and we seemed to be walking up a grassy hill toward the Gallows Hill Park entrance. I smiled when the filming came to a sudden halt when the security guard came into view. "We cut and ran as soon as we saw the guard. We didn't know it was Doug Sawyer then," I explained. Somehow, she'd made the little sailor suit, some of the adult uniforms, and Buffy's lavender dress appear to be floating, unencumbered by coat hangers, with soft music playing in the background. Then in a neat segue, we approached the Witch House, where I appeared in the green jacket, opening the back door, and suddenly we were inside the courtroom. The music turned dark and foreboding as a group of women wearing drab, long dresses came into view, their hands outstretched to where a bearded, black-robed judge sat at a long table—almost smiling.

"Good job," I said, then one of the floating articles of clothing in particular caught my eye. "Can you back up to where we saw the security guard coming?"

"Sure. Here you go. This shot?"

I moved closer to the screen. "Exactly. Now, can you

float that security guard jacket over next to it? I think it's the same one."

"Looks like it," she said. "But why not? It's not as if Sawyer is a *real* security guard. He's an actor."

"I know." My mind raced—and I looked back at the other uniforms—the short bomber jacket of the messenger service—the doctor's scrubs—the priest's vestments—how many of the Paragon costumes had the actor worn? "Please bring up the video of the medical examiner's van outside of the replica set."

Within seconds she'd found it. "The priest," I said. "The elderly priest with the very sorrowful face. He's wearing the same suit. Even the cross is the same."

River's tarot reading. The Page of Swords. An imposter.

Marty caught on fast. "A makeup genius with a warehouse full of costumes. Oh my God, Moon. We've got to tell somebody."

CHAPTER 36

While I waited for Pete to answer my call, I tried to
be objective about what Marty and I had just
observed on a big screen in real time—my makeup-
genius childhood idol had access to hundreds—maybe
thousands of costumes—and the ability to play hundreds—maybe thousands—of parts. But what did it all
mean?

"Pete, I've learned something important." I tried to
keep the chilling fear of what the sudden realization
could mean out of my voice. "It's Doug Sawyer." I
spoke slowly. "He's been hiding in plain sight. He does
it with makeup and costumes. Nobody knows it's him.
It all has something to do with Darla. Marty and I have
found some of it on video. There's probably more."

"Take it easy now, love." Calming cop voice. "Can
you be more specific? Exactly what is it that you have?
And what do you think Sawyer has done?"

"I don't know what he's done." I took a deep breath.
"It looks like he's been a security guard more than

once. He's been a priest too, and I don't have pictures, but if Mary Catherine Mahoney has footage of the courier who delivered the invitation for Lamont Faraday, I'll bet he's wearing a short bomber jacket that says *City Messenger Service* on it. Maybe he's the scar-faced pirate who scared Paulina. Maybe he's . . . oh, I don't know, Pete."

Calming cop voice again. "We've got a good handle on this, sweetheart. Listen. Your aunt and her friends have pieced together a couple of the notes. One was: *Slash your wrists*, the other was: *Why not jump?* Our handwriting team is on it. We'll get this guy." Confident cop voice. "Don't forget, Lee, it's Salem, and it's Halloween. Everybody is in costume and there are bound to be duplicates. Remember when Chris King ordered a gross of *assorted* costumes and the shipper sent forty-eight *astronaut* costumes and every other trick-or-treater that came to the door had a bubble-head mask?" He laughed, then paused. "You say you have video?"

"We do."

"You could be right about the courier and the jacket. We have Mahoney's tape. The man's face was indistin-guishable. That may be a coincidence. Can you send over what you have?"

"Of course. Are you going to look for Doug? I'm pretty sure he's going to be at the Witch House at nine for Buffy's screen test."

"Buffy's getting a screen test?"

"Yes. She's playing an accused witch."

"We'll handle it. Don't walk home this afternoon. I'll send an officer for you."

"Marty just sent you what we have so far. I'll see you at home."

I told Marty about the two new notes. It wasn't easy for me to put aside the discovery she and I had made. I was sure Marty was still thinking about it too, but we needed to get back to work on the initial projects—the documentary about the making of the movie and my prep work for the proposed Witch House tour. After all, as Pete had pointed out, with all the usual Halloween commotion going on, and most of the town in costume, it could all be one big fat coincidence.

I don't think so.

We're both professionals. We do what we have to do—especially if Marty is right about the documentary having Emmy potential! We let the little floating garments drift away over Gallows Hill and concentrated once again on the story about moviemaking. I'd recorded a couple of off-screen interviews with the director of *Night Magic* and we had a half hour of one of Scott's conversations with the casting director, so those gave us some nuts-and-bolts information about who does what, and Marty had even found a short, Paragon-produced piece about lighting techniques that featured Paulina's old boyfriend. We had some news department footage about Darla's death and the police chief's clipped announcement of that event.

"Let's put some of the reactions of Darla's coworkers together in a montage," Marty suggested, "and try to keep it as positive as possible, going easy on the negative stuff. After all, the poor woman is dead."

"I know. And she loved animals."

"She did? Who told you that?"

"Roney McBiel told me. I recorded a phone call with him before he came here from California. I didn't use much of it. A lot of the conversation was about how he became a stuntman. I had his permission to record, though, and he told me that Darla loved animals. That she took in rescue cats and dogs. He thinks she may have been the one who turned Paragon in to PETA for the way they were treating Barney."

"Do you still have it?"

"Sure." I searched. Found it—no problem. I played the whole conversation for Marty.

"Great stuff, Moon," she said. "This is a whole new, softer aspect of Darla. I like it."

"I do too," I said. "It will be nice for people to know that she wasn't always a mean, crabby bitch." As soon as the word escaped my lips, I thought of the pieced-together blue note. "Die bitch," it had said. "You know something, Marty? Paulina told Pete that when Darla was in California, someone wanted her to jump off the Golden Gate Bridge. I wonder if that and the 'Die Bitch' note are connected. I wonder if someone wanted her to take her own life."

"I wouldn't be one bit surprised," she said. "And I'll bet the reason she tore the notes into tiny pieces was because they made her furious. Not suicidal."

"So someone figured out another way to make her kill herself. With chocolates, with something she loved," I said. "What a dirty trick."

"I'll bet the killer doesn't feel guilty at all." Marty's eyes sparkled. I could tell that she was getting into the subject—brainstorming it. "After all, she didn't *have* to eat the poisoned candy."

I piggybacked on her idea. I love brainstorming. "So Darla, in the killer's mind, took her own life. He—or she—had hardly anything to do with it."

"Sick, huh? Imagine it." Disgust was in her voice now. "Preparing the poison. Injecting it into the candy. Putting it where she'd be sure to pick it up, then sitting back, all innocentlike, and waiting, waiting for it to actually happen."

"I wonder what the killer felt when she died," I said. "Satisfaction? Regret?"

"If the killer is the same person who's been running around town in various faces and costumes—not that I'm saying that person is guilty of anything—that person felt grief." She sounded surprised when she said it—but repeated the word. "He felt grief. His creation—his story was over. The play has ended. The final act has occurred." She extended both hands and lowered them slowly. It would mean *curtain* if we were playing charades. "Curtain," she said. "Finis."

A terrible thought occurred to me. "What if he doesn't want it to end? What if he decides to write a second act?"

"You mean he might kill again?" Eyes wide.

"He doesn't think he's a killer. You said so," I remined her. "He thinks he's an innocent observer of somebody else's misfortune."

"If you're right about a second act," she said, "he's lurking around somewhere near the next victim, figuring out what his—or her—weaknesses are. Maybe he's the one who was peeking in Paulina's window. She hasn't got her boyfriend around to protect her anymore. We should warn her somehow."

"Or maybe," I thought, "he's the one who was barely hiding behind my maple tree. Maybe he's the one who kicked a poor, innocent cat who now thinks it's her job, along with O'Ryan's, to protect me. From what?"

I hardly had time to wonder about it. My phone buzzed. "Hi, Ms. Barrett? It's Gino from the Family Farm. You called me about Mr. Sawyer coming over to visit Barney."

"Yes. That's right."

"Well, he called. Right after you did. He's coming over at around noontime. Bringing a friend with him."

"Okay. Thanks, Gino. I'll be there with a camera, and another reporter." It was, after all, Scott Palmer's story. He deserved to be in on the reunion.

"I used to watch that show every Saturday when I was a kid," Gino said.

"Me too—and hundreds of other kids," I told him. "What a great reunion it will be. I can hardly wait to see it myself."

I put down my phone and looked at Marty. I had that feeling of everything speeding up again. "Things are moving fast," I said. "Doug is finally going to visit Barney. I'll get in touch with Scott. Want to grab a camera and come with us to record some TV history?"

"Not me. I'm used to the big, rolling studio camera—not those little shoulder jobs. Grab Old Jim and get over there and get us that Emmy—and Lee, be careful. We're just guessing about the faces and costumes and all that, and there's no proof of you-know-who doing anything wrong at all—but Lee, be careful."

"I'm always careful."

I checked in with Rhonda, reminding her that I was still on the clock. "I'll be at the Family Farm if you need me. How did Buffy do with the screen test?"

"She's happy as a clam at high water. She's still prancing around the office in the lavender dress," Rhonda reported. "She says the guy who plays the judge was so good, they did it in one take."

Next I called Scott. "Where are you? Doug and Paulina will be visiting Barney at noon."

"I'm home having my breakfast, I'm not due in for another hour—on account of doing the late show again."

"Okay. Rub it in. Anyway, I'll get Old Jim and we'll meet you in Topsfield."

"On my way. And thanks, Lee."

"It's your story. See you there."

CHAPTER 37

It took a while to get the VW out of Salem's near-gridlocked traffic—but once we got onto Route 97 it wasn't too bad. We drove onto the Family Farm property at eleven thirty and were greeted by Gino—or maybe it was Greg. *They should wear name tags.* I recognized Scott's new Ford Explorer in the parking area. Jim pulled in beside it as Scott stepped out of the driver's seat.

"Why not stash the VW over behind those bushes?" Scott suggested, pointing, "so that we don't draw a crowd with the TV station logo. Let's keep this as exclusive as we can."

"Good idea," I agreed, still thinking of that Emmy. "Are they here yet?"

Our overall-suited greeter answered. "Mr. Sawyer and his friend are running a bit late. Gino and I were thinking it might be nice if you all could put your camera and equipment a little distance away from Barney's cage so things will be more natural-like when they meet up, so they won't feel like they're being watched. Know what I mean?"

He was right. It would be better. For everyone.

"No problem at all, Greg," I answered. "Just show us where you'd like us to be and we'll be as quiet as three little mice." Scott didn't object, and with Jim carrying the camera and an extendable boom mic with its furry wind muff, me with the stick mic, and Scott already wearing his usual collar mic, we obediently followed Greg single file past the goat enclosure and the llama pen to a small stand of young ash trees, still clinging to fall leaves, close enough to the bear's cage, so that we'd be able to catch the action but dense enough so that we wouldn't be in plain sight. I'd grabbed a couple of powdered sugar doughnuts from the break room and stuffed them into my hobo just in case we got to visit Barney ourselves.

Barney noticed our little parade and gave a friendly woof in greeting. I waved and Scott whistled in reply, and we settled ourselves into our autumnal enclosure. Waiting.

The wait seemed longer than it probably was, what with low branches tangling themselves in my hair, trying not to slap too loudly at buzzing and nonbuzzing insects crawling and bumping themselves on any exposed skin they could find, and hoping against hope that the pretty green vine around our feet wasn't poison oak or ivy.

Scott's tap on my shoulder alerted me that someone was coming. False alarm. Just a small group of excited kindergarten kids having a wonderful adventure. So darned cute. It would have made good footage to go along with our other shots of the Family Farm, but we don't take pictures of kids without permission—unlike the rules for public figures. Politicians, movie, and TV stars are fair game.

The next shoulder tap had a feeling of urgency about it.

I heard Paulina's giggle before the couple came into sight. I recognized the outfit too, one of Darla's Diors for sure, and the three-inch-heel Manolos making her legs look fabulous—even though they were not appropriate for walking through grass, mulch, and maybe occasional doggy doo-doo. Doug Sawyer held her arm, guiding her carefully—almost tenderly—toward the bear habitat. Jim had already begun filming when Barney spotted the couple and began chattering excitedly. He made joyous jumps like he used to do on those long-ago Saturday mornings.

"Jim," I whispered, "get the boom mic as close as you can to the people." I watched as he positioned the boom in an overhanging pine branch as close to the cage as he could without it appearing in the frame of the planned shot. (The furry wind muffler is also known in the business by the unfortunate name of dead cat, a term I would never, ever use.)

"Look, Barney," Doug called, his voice oddly tremulous. "Look. I've brought Darla with me."

Pauline stopped short. "What?"

He pulled her closer to the cage, not gently now. "Look, Barney. See Darla? She's fine. See how pretty she is? How sweet she smells? She's not dead at all! It was a joke. Look at her, Barney. It's Darla."

Paulina, clearly puzzled, tried to pull her arm away.

Doug held her fast by the wrist. A delicate gold brace-let that had undoubtedly belonged to Darla fell to the ground. "Don't worry about it, my darling," Doug said. "I'll fix it. I have a special jewelry glue gun."

Barney continued his happy leaping, chattering his delighted "chuff-chuff" sounds as Doug maneuvered Paulina nearer to the cage. Barney stood tall, leaning to-ward the couple, extending arms, paws reaching for the bars of the cage. "Chuff-chuff-chuff." By then the chimp had joined in the merriment, jumping and chattering along with the bear.

"What the hell is going on?" Scott murmured. "Why is he calling her Darla?"

"He's trying to convince Barney that Darla is alive," I told him.

Scott's brow furrowed. "Convince Barney?"

"Shh. Listen."

"Look, Barney. Look, Bodie. I've brought Darla to see you." Doug pushed the woman ever closer to the barred cage. "Darla loves you, don't you, Darla?" He pulled up her arm behind her back and she winced. "Don't you, Darla?" he said again. "Tell Barney you love him."

"I love you," Paulina croaked. "I love you, Barney."

The bear dropped to all fours and pressed his nose against the bars. I could hear his audible sniffing, snuf-fling. Suddenly he rose to his full height again. He roared. He roared the terrible roar he'd been trained to do for movies that required an enraged bear.

He's truly enraged right now.

He shook the bars, roaring, groaning.

He knows Paulina is not Darla.

I remembered what Doug had said—that Barney could read his mind.

Barney knows that Darla is dead. And he knows why.

Doug raised his voice. "It's okay, Darla. He just wants a treat. Here." He pulled a flowered bag from inside his jacket. I'd recently seen a bag exactly like it. "Here. Toss him a chocolate. You know how he loves your chocolates." He forced the bag into her hand. "Toss him a handful of them. Do it!"

The terrified woman did as she was told. A handful of chocolates scattered onto the ground inside the cage. The bear, distracted, dropped to all fours again. The chimp picked up one of the chocolates, squeezed it, licked it, and spat out a black substance. Barney growled a deep, low, moaning growl.

I broke from the stand of trees, running, stumbling, screaming—"No, Barney! They're poisoned! Somebody help!" I ran toward the cage. "Call 911!"

Greg and Gino both came running. So did Scott. Doug backed away from the cage, holding both hands in the air. Pauline, free from his grip, ran toward me.

"You saw what she did, didn't you?" Doug pleaded. "She tried to kill the poor bear. I tried to stop her. You must have seen me trying to hold her back!"

"He hurt me." Paulina rubbed her arm. "The man is crazy."

"No. The bear is crazy. Look at him, moaning and carrying on!" Doug shook his fist at Barney. "Why don't you die, crazy bear? The drunk, Faraday—got himself arrested because I bet him a measly thousand bucks! He even fell for the same old note Darla sent to me all those years ago." He laughed then. "I sent her a few notes too." Another laugh. "I even gave her a gift of special chocolates."

The Six of Cups. River said it could mean a childhood acquaintance who offers a gift.

Doug glared at Paulina and took a step toward her. "Don't ever call me crazy!"

Scott put a protective arm around her shoulders. "The police are on the way, Paulina," he said. "Lee, are you all right?"

Doug wheeled around and faced me, his face contorted with rage. "Oh sure. Everybody worry about dear little Lee! She's the one I should have picked to do it," he said. "The damned bear would have let you kill him. He trusts you. It would have been you. Should have been you!"

He pointed a finger at me, exactly the way the old judge in my vison had. "What did the devil promise to give you?" he yelled. Then, surprisingly, he lay on the ground and began to cry, great wrenching sobs. Nearby, blue and red lights flashed and police sirens wailed. Little goats bleated and dogs barked and howled.

Within seconds Doug, still on the ground, was handcuffed, while Pete read him his rights. I thought of what Marty had said about how the killer would feel at the end of his story. She'd said he'd feel grief. I looked at the man on the ground, his tears flowing, his body heaving. I extended my hands, palms down and lowered them.

"Curtain," I sighed, relieved.

Greg and Gino together corralled the distraught bear with a catchpole and a snare. The on-call veterinarian arrived within minutes and administered a tranquilizer to Barney and took Bodie with him, along with the chocolates the chimp had spat out, to be checked for poisoning. Pete seized the discarded, flower-sprigged bag as evidence.

Jim, who'd stayed in the tree grove, emerged, camera still on his shoulder, and calmly handed me my hobo bag. "I've got it all right here, Officer," he said. "This guy made the lady throw chocolates to the bear, twisted her arm—then he threatened Mrs. Mondello."

Wordlessly, Pete took me in his arms. "Come on. Let's go home."

"Oh sure," Doug, arms cuffed behind him, face still tearstained, complained loudly, his voice whiny. "Everybody gathers around Lee. I watched her day after day, night after night. Too many people care about her. Her husband, her aunt, her neighbor, coworkers, even the disgusting cats. Why couldn't she ever be alone, like Paulina? She would have killed the damned mind-reading bear easily. He trusted her. I could have made her do it."

I felt Pete's muscles tense. I sensed his anger, raw and explosive, all objectivity gone.

"Come on," I whispered. "Let's go home." By this time two more police cars had arrived at the farm. Gino and Greg had cleared curious visitors from the area, and yellow police tape festooned the property. Scott Palmer had lost no time in doing a stand-up field report in front of Jim's camera, and the two had jumped into the VW and left in a hurry for the station, where Marty was undoubtedly already at work editing the breaking news piece for daytime viewers.

"I'm taking Mrs. Mondello home now," Pete, holding tightly to my hand, told the driver of an SPD cruiser, where Pauline sat in the back seat beside a female cop. "After that I'll come directly to headquarters to make my report." We climbed into Pete's car and joined hands again across the console. Pete faced me, his jaw tight, his eyes moist. "I wanted to kill him," he said.

"I know." I squeezed his hand. "It's over."

CHAPTER 38

Once back on Route 97, I pulled the phone from my hobo, ignoring piled-up text and voice messages, and called my aunt, hoping she hadn't yet seen the TV news reports. Her cheerful "Hello, Maralee" told me she hadn't. I gave her the briefest rundown possible, assuring her that no matter how sensational the forthcoming news reports might sound, I was absolutely fine and that I'd see her soon.

Nibbling absently on one of the doughnuts I'd been saving for Barney, I told Pete about the vision I'd had of the old judge pointing at me, and how Doug's recreation of the scene had finally made sense of the vision for me. "That doesn't happen very often. Sometimes I never figure out what they're trying to tell me. I even ordered a dream book to help me understand."

"I recognized the scene too," he said. Cop voice. "The old judge is trying to make a woman confess. When you told me about the conversation you and

Marty had—how you suspected Sawyer because of the costumes and the makeup and all—I actually went to the Witch House to watch Buffy's screen test."

That surprised me. "You did?"

"Sure did. You sounded, well—you sounded frightened, so I went to see if there was anything to worry about. And like they taught us at the academy, I looked at the facts. Objectively. Unemotionally."

"And?"

"And I didn't find anything solid there. I mean, he was a professional actor. A costume and makeup expert. Everything he did was in his job description. I couldn't see anything beyond my built-in, automatic rejection of guesswork and things that can't be proven. I'm so sorry. I wish now I'd put a tail on him. My God, Lee, the man was following you—spying on you. And on poor Paulina too."

Once again, I said, "It's over."

When Pete pulled into our driveway and backed into his space, a delicious feeling of relief washed over me. We were home—and all of the wonderful, amazing things that the word *home* means became very real. I looked at our little half a house, where a large, yellow cat sat waiting for us on the doorstep, knowing that inside there was warmth and love and safety. There was enough food and a comfortable bed and some worn but good furniture. There were books and pictures and memories and future plans. I got out of the car and looked around our yard. The maple tree was young and strong—and so were we.

Will I ever get an Emmy? Will Buffy Doan ever get a movie contract?

Who knows? Who really cares? Things were almost back to normal.

Normal meant that Pete kissed me goodbye at the sunroom door and left for headquarters to file his report. *Normal* meant that I called Rhonda and told her that as soon as I'd taken a shower and changed my clothes I'd walk across the common and get to work on the documentary. She informed me that I'd ordered the wrong-size legal pads for the *Saturday Business Hour* host and he was none too pleased about it, and also that Paco the Wonder Dog's ears didn't fit into the new hat, and that Mr. Doan wanted to know what date I'd booked for the first Witch House tour.

I took the promised shower, made it a nice long, hot one, towel-dried my hair, and selected my favorite comfortable-but-well-fitting jeans, an almost new pink sweater, my best name brand sneakers, and a gorgeous, tan Brahmin cross-body handbag Betsy gave me last Christmas. Feeling good about myself in general, I decided to stop at Aunt Ibby's house to reassure her that all was well with me, that I was proud of the Angels for piecing the blue notes together. Besides, I hadn't had a meal since breakfast. I was greeted with a big, relieved hug, loving words, and a grilled cheese sandwich and a bowl of tomato soup—the ultimate comfort food. Thus fortified, I set out across the common toward Derby Street and normalcy.

When I stopped at Rhonda's desk to check in I was surprised when Wanda and Phil and Mr. Doan all crowded into the reception area to welcome me. Wanda, in her "Cooking with Wanda" very short smock and towering chef's hat told me that she'd been praying for me. Phil

Archer pumped my hand and offered a gruff, "I was worried about you, kid. Glad it all turned out okay." Bruce Doan announced to all that he'd named me employee of the week and wondered—since Paragon had announced that filming of *Night Magic* was complete—when the documentary would be ready to air.

"I'll get with Marty today and wind it up," I promised. That Paragon announcement was news to me— good news. I was more than ready to close the final curtain on that particular project.

Marty welcomed me back too, not wasting time with a long speech, and we got down to the business of chasing that Emmy. She had Jim's unedited film ready to show me. "This stuff is TV gold," she enthused. I realized that Scott had joined us and had quietly taken a seat next to me. "I hope you don't mind," he said.

I didn't mind. "It's your story too."

We three watched as Paulina's terror grew, as Doug's demeanor changed from solicitous—almost playful— to aggressive, to demanding, to cruel. I watched Barney— the sweet, dear, smart bear I'd learned to love on those long-gone Saturday mornings. I saw his joy at recognizing his two best friends—and heard his agonized roar when his mind met that of his master and he understood at last the terrible deception. His pain brought tears to my eyes and I vowed to visit him at the farm often—with doughnuts.

I had to close my eyes when the judge raised his arm to point. I was relieved when the showing was over. Marty explained some of the mechanics involved in production. There'd be time and date captions, split screen adaptations, credits for network material used.

She'd acquired permission to use relevant statements from Paragon's director and Lamont Faraday. "I understand that they used some AI voice and image technology to finish the movie and that the finished version is flawless."

"Did anybody get a picture of Paulina's new look?" Scott asked. "As soon as that flick was in the can, she got her hair dyed black. She'll never be mistaken for Darla Diamond again."

"She dyed her hair black? Now she'll look like River."

"I know." Big smile. "That's exactly the look she wants. She's going to hook up with her old boyfriend again as soon as she's through testifying against Sawyer."

By five o'clock we'd put together a preliminary tape with enough information on it to prove to Doan that we knew what we were doing—that we'd not only covered the nuts and bolts of making a movie in Salem but we'd managed to tell a story within a story, which might be a lot more interesting than *Night Magic* was in the first place.

I didn't have to walk home after all. Once again there was a police escort waiting for me behind Ariel's bench. This time it was my husband. "It gets dark earlier at this time of year," he explained. "I worry."

"I'm fine," I told him as I slid into the car beside him. "The danger is over. Soon October will be over too, and everything will be okay—even the traffic. No worries."

"You're right," he admitted. "It's over. Sawyer has lawyered up. But this time he has to pay the bill himself. You know, the whole point of causing the accidents, wrecking sets, disrupting production—it was all in an attempt to drive Paragon out of business. Even killing Darla was part of it. He thought without their biggest-earning star, they'd fold—and his contract would end."

"He was that desperate." It was hard for me to understand.

"He was. But in the end he violated the one clause in that big, fat contract that makes it null and void."

"What's that?"

"He can't be involved in any criminal complaint or action that could bring negative publicity to Paragon."

"That must be why he had to blame others for everything he did. Like making Paulina throw the chocolates and making sure he was nowhere around when Darla ate a poisoned one."

"Funny, isn't it?" Pete asked. "The one thing that would get him out of the contract—that would make it possible for him to work for the other big studios—means there's a good chance he won't be working for anybody. He could be trading that fancy hotel room for a prison bunk. I don't think any lawyer at any price is going to save him."

"I guess the trailers are getting towed to another movie site in a day or so, and Paulina is planning to leave Salem as soon as she can. What's going to become of Darla's dog? Toby?"

"I suppose they'll turn Toby over to animal control. They'll try to find a home for him." Sad face. He repeated some words I'd heard him use before. "A rescue dog. One that's older and trained and needs a home."

"We have a home," I said. "Do you think maybe we need a dog?"

* * *

We arrived home to *two* cats on our back step. Frankie had shed the Elizabethan collar and the pink sock—with or without permission—and looked quite pleased about it. "Hi guys," I greeted them as Pete unlocked the door. The two dashed inside ahead of us, and once again, as they'd done before, arranged themselves in a protective stance in front of me, while Pete moved toward the living room.

"It's all right, cats," Pete told them. "You can relax. She's not in danger anymore." He gave each one a pat on the head and motioned for me to follow him. O'Ryan stepped over the sill into the living room, looked from left to right, then sat. Frankie did the same. "They're still in protective mode for some reason."

"It's weird," I said. "They didn't want me near Darla's wastebasket remains. Now they want to know where I am every second. O'Ryan's never behaved this way. You had cats when you were a kid. Did any of them ever act goofy like this?"

"Nope." Then he nodded and smiled. "Except for Donnie and Marie's old cat, Gloria. She used to get all purry and lovey and cuddly with Marie whenever she was expecting."

I sat down on the couch. So did Pete.

"Whenever she was expecting," I repeated.

"With both boys," he said. "Gloria got lovey and Marie craved dill pickles. The vet said Gloria could sense changes in Marie's hormonal levels."

"I'm not crazy about pickles," I said.

"But you're awfully fond of powdered sugar doughnuts lately."

One fast trip to the nearest drugstore and another to the bathroom answered our question.

The cats were right. We were definitely pregnant and over-the-moon excited. After much hugging and kissing and happy tears I called Aunt Ibby. Pete called his mother. I called River. Pete called Marie. I called Rhonda. Pete called Chief Whaley. I called Marty. Rhonda had already called her. Pete called Donnie. Marie had already called him. Wanda called me. Betsy called me, but Louisa had already called her. Scott called me because he'd heard about it from Pascal at the tavern. I had an email from Amazon with an advertisement for a stroller.

I'd been only halfway serious about needing a dog. I knew that Pete had talked about getting a puppy and I'd pretty much shot that idea down. Anyway, acquiring an animal isn't a spur-of-the-moment decision. It's a lifetime commitment—for the lifetime of the animal. We'd have to come to an agreement about it for sure, and we weren't the only ones concerned.

"We're going to have a baby, but that doesn't mean Toby has to go to the dog pound," I said. "On the other hand O'Ryan needs to have a say in this too," I said. "We already know he wants to protect the baby. Let's invite Toby over for a home visit and see how that works out."

My doctor's appointment came before the scheduled dog visit and Paulina was leaving for California, so Toby had to spend a couple of days at animal control before we arranged for him to meet O'Ryan. He was a little skittish at first. O'Ryan has a way of puffing himself up, fur on end, and arching his back so that he looks twice as big as he really is. After a moment Toby seemed to enjoy the spectacle. Pete and I watched from the couch. The lab lay on the carpet, hind end up, tail wagging, his head with big, soft ears between his front paws. He gave a soft "woof." O'Ryan relaxed the arch and inched forward until they were almost nose to nose.

With a quick, approving lick to the dog's nose, O'Ryan joined us on the couch. He wedged himself between us, one possessive paw stretched over my still-flat tummy, thereby establishing, as far as we could tell, that he was still top cat but that the dog could stay.

The doctor prescribed a healthy diet, suggested some light exercises, determined that I could continue with my job at WICH-TV for as long as I felt good. And boy, did I feel good!

I'm at the very beginning of my happily ever after!

Aunt Ibby's Dark as Night Devil's Food Cake

(Aunt Ibby attributes this recipe to her cousin, Jane Davis)

- 1 15-oz. box devil's food cake mix
- 1 cup cold black coffee
- 1 cup regular mayonnaise (not light or no-fat)
- 3 medium eggs (or as directed on cake mix package)
- 2 16-oz. containers of dark chocolate frosting
- ½ 12-oz. jar seedless raspberry preserves

Preheat oven to 350 degrees, Spray two 9" round pans with nonstick spray. With hand electric mixer, beat cake mix, coffee, mayonnaise, and eggs in a large bowl on low speed for about 30 seconds. Move to medium speed for about 2 minutes. Pour evenly into the prepared pans. Tap the pans on counter, then bake about 25 minutes or until a toothpick in the center comes out clean. Cool in pans for 10 to 15 minutes, then carefully remove cakes to wire racks to complete cooling. When cool place bottom layer on stand or platter.

In a small bowl stir about one half of a container of frosting until smooth, then add the raspberry preserves and blend. Use this as the filling between layers. Top with second layer. Stir the remaining frosting with the second container of frosting until spreadable to cover top layer and sides of cake. (Save leftover frosting for cupcakes or cookies.)

Coffee Gelatin

Place one envelope of unflavored gelatin (1 tbsp.) in a mixing bowl and soften it with ¼ cup of cold water. Stir in 1¾ cups of hot, strong coffee. Stir in ⅓ of a cup of sugar. Pour into six individual Jell-O molds or six small custard cups. Chill until set. Unmold and serve with whipped cream.

Aunt Ibby's Real Whipped Cream

For light-as-air whipped cream like Aunt Ibby's, start with a chilled bowl and chilled beaters. Then, beat 1 cup of cold heavy cream until just thickened, about 1 minute. Add 2 tbsp. confectioners' sugar and beat until soft peaks form. (For a kick, add a kiss of bourbon!)

Aunt Ibby's Half-Hour Chicken Marsala

4 chicken breasts sliced horizontally
8 oz. white button mushrooms, sliced
   ½-in. thick
8 oz. cremini mushrooms, sliced
½ tsp. salt
2 tbsp. minced onion
¼ tsp. pepper
2 cloves minced garlic
⅓ cup + 1 tbsp. flour
⅔ cup dry marsala wine
5 tbsp. olive oil
⅔ cup beef stock
3 tbsp. butter
Minced parsley for garnish

Heat 2 tbsp. olive oil and 1 tbsp. butter over high heat in a large skillet. Sprinkle the chicken slices with salt and pepper on both sides and dredge lightly in the ⅓ cup of flour. Shake off excess flour and put them in the pan. Cook about 3 or 4 minutes on each side until golden, then set them aside in a plate. Put 2 tbsp. olive oil and a tbsp. of butter in the pan and add the mushrooms. Sauté the mushrooms for about 6 minutes, seasoning with salt and pepper to taste about halfway through, then put the mushrooms on the plate with the chicken. Add the remaining olive oil, then the onions and garlic, and sauté about a minute until soft. Sprinkle in the remaining tbsp.

of flour and cook for a minute to get the flour taste out. Pour in the wine and beef stock and stir until the sauce is slightly thickened. Then slide the chicken and mushrooms into the pan. Add a tbsp. of butter and cover the pan and cook it for a couple of minutes. Spoon the sauce over the chicken, garnish with parsley, and serve.

Aunt Ibby likes to serve this over pasta or rice or mashed potatoes. Betsy likes it over quinoa.

Aunt Ibby's Grandmother Russell's Fish Chowder

¼ lb. salt pork
Dash of cayenne*
4 medium-sized onions, peeled and thinly
    sliced
Pinch of rosemary**
4 medium-sized potatoes, peeled and cubed
¼ cup butter
4 lbs. haddock, cod, or grouper
½ cup flour
1½ tsps. salt
1 qt. rich milk
¼ tsp. pepper
1 large can evaporated milk
¼ tsp. sugar
⅛ tsp. thyme

Cut salt pork into small pieces and fry until crisp. Remove from pan and add onion slices. Cook onions slowly until tender—about 10 minutes. Add potatoes to onions and barely cover with water. Cover tightly. Cook until the potatoes are tender but not mushy. Save water.

Cut fish into 3 or 4 pieces. Place in saucepan. Add enough water to cover the bottom of the pan.

*A dash is about ¹⁄₁₆ of a teaspoon.
**A pinch is what you can hold between thumb and forefinger.

Cover tightly and simmer for about 15 minutes or until fish is tender. Cool. If there is liquid left, strain and add to onions and potatoes. Remove any skin and bones from fish, keeping the fish in as large pieces as possible. Combine with onions, potatoes, and the onion-potato liquid.

Make white sauce as follows:

2–3 tbsps. butter
2 tbsps. flour
1/4 tsp. salt
1/8 tsp. pepper
1 cup milk

Melt butter and blend in flour and seasonings. Reduce heat and cook 3 minutes, stirring constantly. Remove from heat and stir in about 2 tbsps. milk. Blend away from heat. When paste is smooth add more milk and blend again; when perfectly smooth add the rest of the milk and return to low heat. Cook slowly for 5 minutes, stirring constantly.

Now add the fish with the onions, potatoes, and liquid to the white sauce. Add the evaporated milk. Simmer very gently 15 minutes. Chill in the refrigerator overnight. Before serving, simmer to serving temperature. Drop in a big lump of butter and sprinkle with paprika.

ACKNOWLEDGMENTS

Before I became a mystery writer, I wrote several novels and a couple of biographies for middle-grade readers. I remember my then-editor, Tanya Dean, telling me, "Those of us who write for children have the ability to touch lives." That's why, on this page of acknowledgments for my fourteenth Witch City Mystery, I want to thank and acknowledge those children's writers who touched *my* life.

Of course, like most woman mystery writers, the adventures I shared with Nancy Drew and Judy Bolton shaped my taste for the mystery genre early on. My Christmas lists in those days consisted largely of Carolyn Keene and Margaret Sutton titles. My day-to-day reading was usually made up of the material I could afford on my meager allowance—comic books. My favorites were Captain Marvel and Wonder Woman. (Comic books were only a dime back then!)

But the actual life-changing, mind-altering, honest-to-God-affecting-my-life-forever-more book experience took place when I was in the seventh grade at the Pickering Grammar School in my home city of Salem, Massachusetts. There was a small branch library almost across the street from the school that included a slim section of shelves devoted to kids. By chance, or maybe by divine providence, I read two books from one of those shelves, back-to-back. When I'd finished them my mind was made up. I would have a career in advertising.

The books were *A Star for Ginny* by Phyllis Whitney

and *Nathalie Enters Advertising* by Dorothy Dwight Hutchinson. In the Whitney book, heroine Ginny is a budding artist who, through luck and talent, gets a job in the advertising department of a large Chicago department store. *A Star for Ginny* was the yet-to-be-famous writer's second book. Dorothy Hutchinson's heroine, Nathalie, in *Nathalie Enters Advertising,* gets a job as a copywriter. What an inspiration Nathalie turned out to be! The book, written in 1939, showed Nathalie as a strong, determined young woman—probably quite ahead of her time—with plenty of nuts-and-bolts material on advertising—like mechanics, copy, and layouts, along with a good story and a little romance. I did indeed grow up to work in advertising and, coincidentally—or maybe as fate decreed—I worked for many years as advertising manager for a major department store as Ginny had, using both art and writing skills every day—and, like Nathalie, wrote freelance copy for several Boston ad agencies—some of it award winning!

For years I searched for those childhood books—wanting to read again the inspirational words two long-ago writers for children had given to me. This year I found them both. The Whitney book was expensive because it was one of her earliest—but well worth the money. The other had eluded me for decades because I'd been looking for *Natalie*, not *Nathalie*. St. Petersburg writer Holly Hargett discovered the elusive *h* in the heroine's name and emailed me about it, and within a week I had the second missing piece of my childhood.

Thank you to the writers who touched my life—and big thanks to today's writers of children's books—who touch new lives every day. I love you all.